THE
CHARLESTOWN CONNECTION

THE
CHARLESTOWN CONNECTION

A Novel

Tom MacDonald

Oceanview Publishing

LONGBOAT KEY, FLORIDA

ISBN: 978-1-60809-024-2

Published in the United States of America by Oceanview Publishing,
Longboat Key, Florida
www.oceanviewpub.com

2 4 6 8 10 9 7 5 3

PRINTED IN THE UNITED STATES OF AMERICA

To my wife, Maribeth,
and to my parents, Patricia and Thomas MacDonald Sr.

ACKNOWLEDGMENTS

I wish to thank several people whose input made the final version of this book far better than my initial rendering. Dick Murphy who used his Charlestown upbringing to evaluate the accuracy of the setting and personality of the characters. His input led to many subtle improvements. Chris Hobin for pointing out where I wandered off course and helped tighten the plot. Scott Wolven, a Stonecoast MFA faculty member, who read the story through a number of iterations and told when he thought it was ready for publication. Professor Eve Spangler, of Boston College, and Doug Roberts, both of whom stimulated and encouraged my storytelling voice.

And finally, my wife, Maribeth McKenzie MacDonald, my major supporter and my second reader. William Faulkner's advice to writers was, "Kill your darlings." Maribeth is an expert at ferreting out my darlings that need killing. She trims a page faster than a yachtsman trims a sail.

THE
CHARLESTOWN CONNECTION

CHAPTER 1

I drove my corroded Plymouth Acclaim down Bunker Hill Street and parked at a curb in Hayes Square. The car is too old to be worth any money, but not old enough for antique plates—a double indignity. The summer sun faded to dusk, giving the Tobin Bridge its twilight complexion. Like a tipsy lady in a dimly lit bar, the Tobin looks better at night than in the morning. A wino came out of the package store carrying a flat brown bag. He unscrewed the bottle cap, swigged, and walked into the projects.

Winos are discriminating people. Spanish winos favor Reunite, blacks prefer Boones Farm, whites go for Wild Irish Rose. It's all the same stuff, cherry juice with a punched-up proof.

Me, I wasn't so discriminating. I chose whiskey, the cheapest brand on the bottommost shelf—until twenty-nine days ago. Twenty-nine days without a drink is a month of blue-moon Sundays for a drunk. If I keep the jug plugged until midnight, I get a thirty-day chip tomorrow, by the grace of God and nothing else. The chips are AA awards for different lengths of sobriety. The first ten days don't really count, since I was strapped in a bed after suffering a rum fit. My sponsor said count 'em anyway. Alcoholics need every edge they can get.

On the other side of the street from the package store, nestled into the Bunker Hill housing development, is Saint Jude Thaddeus church, the little parish that could. I run the food pantry there, thanks to a Jesuit priest who recommended me for the job. He took pity on me when I mangled my knee playing football, ending any hopes for the pros. He knew I grew up in Charlestown and figured I'd be a good match. Saint Jude's pastor, Father Dominic, kept me on the payroll after the detox let me out. He said something about his brother being a recovering alcoholic. I think he was just trying to make me feel better.

I locked the Plymouth and crossed the street.

I love to work after sundown, the nighttime solitude suits me. I ambled toward the food pantry in no particular rush, walking between the church and the projects, where the two overlap. In daylight I find used syringes in the church hedges. On home visits I find unread parish bulletins in the tenement hallways. A shriek blurted from an open window, a man told her to shut up, an infant cried. I didn't hear a slap.

I fished out the keys.

A police cruiser sped down Cory Street with no siren. There's something ominous about a speeding cruiser with no siren, more ominous than one with its siren blaring. At the far end of the projects an ambulance wailed on Medford Street. The wailing raised my spirits. It meant they were headed to the emergency room instead of the morgue. An ambulance siren here might as well be an ice-cream truck bell. The kids run out, to see who gets wheeled out, and the numbness to death gets passed to the next generation.

I fit the key into the food pantry door.

To say death doesn't bother me isn't quite right. Better to say I expect death; that death comes as no surprise. Shrinks have a word for my aloofness. They called it desensitization or some big word like that. I learned about it in college. Death rates that would make an actuary blink don't faze me. It's not that I'm indifferent to death, I don't think. And it's not that I don't care, because I'm pretty sure I do.

I unlocked the door and stepped inside.

I've been blessed. I've only been shot at twice, and neither bullet found flesh. One of the shooters, a hophead hooked on hillbilly heroin, got himself killed a week after he fired my way. The bells of Saint Jude Thaddeus ushered him into the church. Father Dominic draped his casket in a white pall, sprinkled the pall with holy water, recited a few prayers, and sent him to the cemetery for a proper Catholic burial, complete with a bagpipe sayonara.

The projects savor an ugly death.

I never realized this stuff until I went away to college and came home again. I had to come home again, the way a sailor goes to sea again. Anybody can move to a cul-de-sac in the suburbs. The suburbs sound nice in theory. In practice, it doesn't always work out for guys like us. When a project guy moves to a gated community, it's run by the state, the fences are trimmed in razor wire, and the neighbors wear orange jumpsuits with black serial numbers stenciled on the back.

I sliced open a case of canned corn, Jolly Green Giant, a treat. We usually get generic.

I was stocking shelves and heard a bang on the door. I ignored it. The banging grew louder. I ignored it again. The door burst open, and in reeled my godfather, Jeepster Hennessey, a man who'd spent most of his post-Vietnam life in prison. Jeepster was my father's best friend. Both were marines, both fought together in the Battle of Hill 881, the Quang Tri Province.

He didn't look drunk and he didn't look dope sick, but he didn't look right, either. Jeepster careened across the floor, slanting my way, picking up speed with each step. He slammed into my shoulder to stop his momentum. His eyes twitched as if they had shampoo in them. His complexion was pallid, his breathing labored. I asked him what was wrong.

"Dermot," he said to me. "Take it."

"Take what?"

He handed me a brass key. The name McSweeney was written on white tape affixed to the key's head. He choked. Drool bubbled at the corners of his mouth. He tried to speak. His Adam's apple clogged the esophagus, suffocating his words. Jeepster hacked, sprayed blood in my face, and pointed at the key.

"Important, the key opens—"

"Opens what?" I held him up.

The door opened and closed, the same door Jeepster reeled through. Whoever closed it had done so noiselessly. Jeepster pushed me back a step.

"The key." He collapsed in my arms.

"What about it?" I asked, easing him to the floor.

I knelt beside him and that's when I noticed the knife in his back. No blade showing it was plunged so deep. I reached for the hilt to pull it out then balked, thinking about fingerprints. His eyes rolled up, his lids flickered, his nostrils stopped flaring. I opened my cell phone to dial 911. Jeepster grabbed my arm and pulled me toward him, coughed blood, and uttered one word.

"Oswego."

CHAPTER 2

The night dragged on as Jeepster lay dead on the floor. I wanted to cry. I tried to cry. My tear ducts refused to oblige. Just another death in brick city. The police took over the pantry, detectives and crime scene personnel. One uniformed cop was present, a young Hispanic woman who radioed information back to the precinct. The plainclothesmen, all three were men, asked me too many questions for too many hours. I thought about Oswego and the Mc-Sweeney key, as they peppered me with inquiring jabs. They probed for openings, poked my defenses, searched for secret truths. I parried their verbal barrage and wondered if they noticed my caginess.

The medics zipped Jeepster Hennessey into a bag and wheeled him away on a gurney. The crime-scene crew left. The cops continued to peck away at me, repeating the same questions then repeating them again. I answered everything, though not with full disclosure. I never mentioned the word Oswego to them. I never told them about the McSweeney key. I figured Jeepster had given me the key for a reason, and it was my job to find that reason. The cops left the food pantry, grumbling. I knew I'd be seeing them again.

The next morning I walked to the food-pantry office and logged onto the computer, did a Yahoo search on Oswego, and got twenty-one million hits. I narrowed the search to Oswego, New York, since it was closer to Boston than Oswego, Illinois, Montana, Kansas, and Oregon, and got ten million hits. I was closing in. If I knocked off a hundred hits a day, I'd be done in 274 years. The Oswego in New York sat on Lake Ontario, a six-hour drive from Boston. I glanced outside at my rusting Plymouth in the lot and decided to stick with the computer.

My luck with McSweeney wasn't much better. I stumbled onto a website for Clan Sween, whose people lived in Castle Sween, which was located on Loch Sween in Argyll, Scotland. The Mac-Sweeneys were forced to leave Scotland at the sword of Robert the Bruce, migrated to Ireland, changed the Mac to a Mc, and became McSweeney. This happened in the twelfth century. I was better off with the twenty-one million Oswego hits.

I searched for Jeepster, got a mere three million hits, and learned about a vehicle introduced in 1949 under the Jeep marque. Jeep marketed the Jeepster to farmers and foresters, predicting a postwar demand for military-type vehicles. They predicted wrong and Jeepster sales fizzled. In the sixties, the Jeepster Commando was unveiled, and in the seventies the Hurst Jeepster. All flopped.

I found a YouTube video of T. Rex singing *Jeepster*, a pretty good song. Then I clicked on *Bang a Gong*, a great song. The online maze can lead to nothingness. Hours of nothingness become days of nothingness resulting in a life of nothingness.

I turned up the speakers and clicked *Bang a Gong* again, tapping my feet to the rhythm. A knock on the door interrupted my progress. I logged off in the middle of "You're built like a car; you've got a hub cap diamond star halo. You're built like a car, oh yeah." I'd get back to the computer later. I opened the door and saw George Meeks standing on the stoop, a man my father knew and a character of note in Charlestown.

I should've listened to the rest of the song.

I invited him into the office. George was in his sixties and kept himself in pretty good shape, but then George had time to keep himself in pretty good shape, locked in prison most of his adult life. This didn't make George a bad guy, not at all, in fact most Townies liked him. I know my father liked him, and my father, a full-blooded Canadian Micmac Indian, could sniff out a fake. George sat down and said yes to coffee. The kettle boiled and I poured each of us a cup of instant.

He then commenced to play with a pack of Dutch Masters cigars, and with the deft fingers of a button accordionist, he peeled the wrapper, popped the cardboard top, and tapped out a stogie. George held out the pack to me. I shook my head no. He shrugged, smelled the leafy rope, and gave it a lick.

"My father smoked Dutch Masters, so I smoke 'em, too. Most guys today prefer handmade Cubans. Not me. I like drugstore cigars." He rubbed his gray buzz cut and lit the blunt without my permission. "Okay I light up in here?"

"Sure, George." His smoking didn't bother me any, nor did his lighting up without asking my okay. He probably noticed the tobacco burns on my desktop and my overflowing beanbag ashtray. "How long you been out?"

"Five weeks, two days." He read his watch. "Eight hours and ten minutes." He half laughed. "Feels good to be back in Charlestown. It ain't like the old days, real Townies can't afford to live here no more."

"Been that way a long time, George."

"Yeah, I know, and there ain't nothing we can do about it." He blew a smoke ring to the stained ceiling. "Federal time is nasty, man. It's the pressure. Feds crawling up your ass, asking questions, pressuring you to rat out friends."

"Sounds nasty."

"Yeah, nasty shit." George snorted two columns of smoke from his nostrils. "Charlestown keeps changing, man. The Navy Yard's gone, the elevated train's gone, Revere Sugar and the Blue Mirror, they're all gone. Even Shorty Foley's joint."

"Everything keeps changing."

"Yeah." He took another haul. "Well, almost everything. Nothing changes in the projects. Like that thing last night, a damn shame, ain't it? Jeepster Hennessey getting himself stabbed like that. It ain't right, man. He didn't deserve to die that way."

"No, he didn't." I fingered the dead cigars in the ashtray. "What are you getting at?"

"Nothin', Dermot, I'm just saying he didn't deserve to die that way. In his own neighborhood like that, it ain't right."

"True enough."

Maybe George had softened since he got out of the can. Maybe he was feeling Jeepster's loss, and if he *was* feeling it, I envied him. George was right about one thing, Jeepster didn't deserve to die that way. He never sold drugs, never touched little kids. He made his money on stand-up crime: forgery, sports fixing, cons, street hustles, the occasional heist. He had a sharp mind and a knack for spotting opportunity, always with an eye for the big payoff. I joined George in his blaze session, lighting a cigar of my own. George smiled when he saw me stoke it up. He blew a plume my way.

"Who'd a thought you'd be working for the church?" he said. "It's gotta be a downer after college. Every scout in the nation picks Dermot Sparhawk for the pros, a first-rounder, and Dermot goes and blows out his knee. Instead of making millions, Dermot's back where he started, back in the bricks schlepping food. It's gotta be a letdown."

Fuck you too, George.

"Most of life is a letdown," I said, pitching my pat answer to a question I field too often. "I've accepted it. I'm grateful to have a job."

"Sure, keep telling yourself that and someday you'll believe it." He doused the half-smoked cigar in the rabble of his coffee. "Hey, I shouldn't a said that. I can think of worse things in life than missing out on millions of dollars and having to work for a living."

"I get health insurance."

"Boy, that's a cure-all. That makes everything better." He rocked back in his chair. "Seriously, insurance is good. A man can never tell when he's gonna need insurance, especially a man that works in the projects. Fuckin' place is a jungle, everyone's armed back there with machetes and guns, clubs and knives. Cars too, they'll run a guy down with a car or van. Those people love vans, especially if the muffler drags."

"It's not that bad."

"The country's crazy, ain't it? You get rushed to the hospital and the first thing they wanna see is an insurance card. Your head's cut off, they want an insurance card before they sew it back on." George shifted in his chair. Unfortunately, it didn't tip over. "I heard some talk around the neighborhood, the rumor mill about last night. People're saying Jeepster walked into the food pantry and died at your feet."

"That's right."

"That's right? Well, yeah, that's what I heard out there," he said. "So, Jeepster died at your feet?"

"Correct."

"He dropped dead, just like that."

"Yup, just like that," I said. What was George getting at? "Knifed. He never stood a chance."

"He never called for an appointment, never said why he wanted to see you?"

"I didn't even know he was out. Besides, most guys don't call for an appointment with a blade stuck in their back."

"He just wandered into the food pantry?" He tilted the chair forward and propped his feet on the desk. "Makes you wonder, don't it? Why did Jeepster go to a church food pantry for help? Why not go across the street to the police station?"

"Since when does a Townie go to the police for anything?"

"Fair point," he said.

"Maybe Jeepster wanted last rites." I inspected my petering cigar and puffed it a few times to get it burning. "Maybe he came to the pantry because we're in the projects. He got stabbed in the bricks, saw the lights on, and came in for help. The pantry was the closest building to him, that's all. The guy had a knife in his back. It's not like he could walk to Mass General."

"Seems strange, dying on church grounds."

"Not when your church is in the projects."

"Yeah, I guess so. Maybe you're right."

"Yeah, maybe."

We quieted down and listened to the drone of the morning rush hour. Cars and SUVs jousted for position on the Tobin Bridge. An eighteen-wheeler crossed and shook the stanchions, which in turn shook the building we sat in. George leaned forward in his chair.

"I did time with Jeepster out there in New York, FCI Otisville. I took a pinch for passing bad paper. Jeepster got nabbed for bribing a jockey. Imagine that? He bribed a four-foot-ten Fed, fuckin' FBI. He wasn't really FBI, just a short guy hired by the FBI to wear a wire. Rotten luck, boy."

"Rotten luck, all right."

"Anyway, he got federal time. We both did."

"I heard about it."

"I guess everyone did."

"Everyone in Charlestown," I said.

"We were ace-deuce on the inside. Jeepster and me, covered each other's backs, just like in Nam. I remember your father in Nam. Hell of a marine, your father, a natural soldier. Musta been that Indian blood." George spit a fleck of tobacco to the floor. "I don't know which was worse, Vietnam or prison. All them years behind bars, and I never got used to it. Jeepster was different. He read books and solved arithmetic, stuff like that. Me, I mostly did pushups. Not Jeepster, Jeepster was smart."

"Smart as hell."

"He belonged to a book club or something." He rocked back again. "Mighta been the smartest guy in Otisville."

"Including the guards?"

"Huh?"

"Tell me about the book club."

"Don't know much about it, except you had to be sharp to get in."

"And Jeepster got in."

"Talented guy, Jeepster. Could forge anything. Checks, papers, documents—it didn't matter—the guy was a genius. I'm gonna miss him." George Meeks stood and walked to the door. "I gotta run. Maybe I'll see you at Mass some Sunday."

"Sure George, see you around." I joined him at the door. "I'm planning a vacation later this summer, going up to Lake Ontario for a little fishing."

"It's good to get away. Where to exactly?"

"New York, a town called Oswego."

"Be glad it's Oswego and not Otisville." He laughed. "I'm more of a saltwater man myself. Gimme the ocean any day. I hunt big game, Dermot, not freshwater shrimp. You can't catch bluefin tuna in a freshwater lake, not even a Great Lake."`

George left the building. Either he knew nothing about Oswego or he didn't nibble the bait.

CHAPTER 3

Scores of addicts and alcoholics jammed the Saint Jude Thaddeus hall for the noontime AA meeting. The meeting catered to low-bottom burnouts of every stripe—whiskey drunks, crack heads, muscatel winos, heroin addicts—and our stories reflected the nuts that filled the room.

I walked out after the meeting, flipping my thirty-day chip. and bumped into Captain Pruitt of Boston Homicide in the parking lot. I figured I'd be seeing him soon, he's a homicide cop and Jeepster Hennessey died at my feet. I'd helped Pruitt a few months back, in the twilight of my drinking days, and an unlikely respect budded between us. Pruitt reached out his big black hand and snagged the chip out of the air, examined it, and tossed it back to me.

"Thirty days sober and still practically a kid," he said. "Your whole life is ahead of you, Sparhawk."

"Thanks, Captain," I said. "It's been a spell."

"But not long enough?"

"That's not what I meant." I pocketed the chip. "It's Jeepster Hennessey, that's why you're here."

"You should've been a detective."

AA members flowed out of the meeting and when they noticed Pruitt, veered wide. Half of them probably had outstanding warrants. No sense finding trouble with a cop.

"We're ruling Hennessey's death a homicide," Pruitt said.

No shit, Captain. Was the knife in his back your first clue?

"We believe the killing was drug related. Hennessey flunked his last urine test." Pruitt's ebony brow glistened in the summer sun. "I need your help on this. Keep your ears open, listen for the chitchat in the projects."

"Be glad to, Captain, but I won't hear anything," I said. "Nobody gets involved in the projects."

"Tell me about it." He looked down from the sun. "What happened, Sparhawk? Why do you think Henessey got killed?"

"I told the homicide cops everything last night."

"Tell me again, and go nice and slow. Give me all the details."

"Aye, aye, Captain."

I told him what happened, sans Oswego and McSweeney. He listened, wrote a few notes, and walked back to the unmarked Crown Victoria.

CHAPTER 4

The Oswego-McSweeney thing frustrated me. I didn't know where to start. I'd tried dozens of Internet search combinations using variations of Oswego and McSweeney, Jeepster and Charlestown, Hennessey and Otisville, Meeks and Otisville, Meeks and Hennessey. I tried every pairing I could think of and found nothing. Despite what everyone says, there's only so much a computer can accomplish. At the AA meeting I talked to three ex-cons who did time with Jeepster, and all three claimed to know nothing.

I thought about giving up. I thought about chucking the McSweeney key down a sewer grate and forgetting the whole thing, but Jeepster had given me the key. He tracked me down that night. Half dead, he tracked me down. I owed him some kind of effort on this thing, he was my godfather. Where to begin? An idea came to me. It wasn't much of an idea, but it was something.

Before I got sober I had stopped for a pint at a taproom on Utica Street in the Leather District, a place called the Cazenovia Club. I remembered the club's owner, a woman named Aunt Bea. She told me she came from central New York State, not far from Syracuse, and that she'd been a big Syracuse Orangemen fan since she was a kid. Oswego wasn't far from Syracuse. Maybe Aunt Bea could help me with Oswego.

I rode the train to South Station and walked to the Cazenovia Club, a converted basement with casement windows. My eyes dilated in the darkness when I stepped inside. Large black-and-white tiles checkered the tavern floor, making me feel like a chess piece slanting to the bar. I hoped I didn't get checkmated by a jug of whiskey. Aunt Bea, a chubby woman with rosy cheeks and a bib apron, was tending to business at the other end. She came to me when I took a stool.

"Goodness gracious me, the return of the prodigal son, and you're still alive," she said. "You look much better than last time."

"I had nowhere to go but up."

"And still very funny, praise to God." She dried her hands on a towel. "How's about a frosted stein of Genesee cream ale? You lapped the keg dry last time. Put a pretty good dent in the Old Thompson, too."

"How's about a coffee?"

"Gotcha." She poured me a cup of coffee and put out cream and sugar. "On the water wagon, are we?"

"For today."

The coffee tasted fresh, better than the sludge I usually drank. I studied a row of liquor bottles in front of the bar mirror. Bacardi rum, eighty proof, established 1862. Hemingway drank it, or maybe it was Santiago. Canadian Club whiskey, bottled in bond, survived Prohibition. My shoulders began to unknot, in spite of facing the deadly enemy. Aunt Bea waddled to the far end of the bar, refilled a patron's drink, wiped down the already spotless countertop, and came back my way.

"So, my big Indian friend, you stepped into the Cazenovia Club for a cup of coffee?"

"Not exactly," I said. "The last time I was here you said you were originally from central New York State."

"You remember that day? I'm amazed," she said. "Correct, I moved here from Cazenovia."

"I never heard of Cazenovia before, except for the name of this place."

"Most folks haven't heard of it. Caz is a cozy little village outside Syracuse. We have a beautiful lake, resort hotels, a college."

"Why leave such a cozy town?"

"It was time for a change." She opened the dishwasher and

rolled out a rack of steaming glasses. "My husband and I owned a tavern up there on Albany Street. When he died a few years back, I sold the place, too many memories, too painful for me to stay."

"Sorry to hear that."

"I moved to Boston hoping to open a tavern down here on Albany Street, to honor my late husband. Nothing was available on Albany. Then I found this building on Utica Street and opened here instead."

I took in the tavern interior. The walls were encased in oak wainscoting halfway up and horsehair plaster up to the molding of the stamped metal ceilings. On one wall hung a framed print titled *The Procuress,* by an artist named Van Baburen, and next to that a coat of arms with the name DeBeers. Aunt Bea DeBeers, it had a ring to it. Similar paintings hung on the other walls.

I had nearly forgotten I was in a taproom when a boozer raised his shaggy gray head and wobbled my way. He draped his noodle of an arm around my shoulder and sprayed words into my face.

"Hey, big guy," he said. "Brother, you're a big bastard, how're ya doing?"

"Never better."

"How'd ya like to buy me a special coffee? My top-shelf coffee, only the very best for old Skinny." His head jerked up. "Fuck man, you're bigger'n I thought, a fuckin' moose. Don't hit me, I got a soft skull."

"Don't worry."

"Don't worry, be happy. Remember Bobby McFerrin?" he said. "Where you from?"

"Charlestown," I said. "How about you? Southie? Dorchester?"

"Fuck Southie and Dorchester." He caught his breath. "For that matter, fuck Charlestown too. I'm from the New York streets, the best neighborhood of all time. Troy, then we moved to Oneida." He sat back on his stool. "The streets are gone."

His head hit the bar, which made me glad I went to an AA meeting earlier in the day.

"That's Skinny Atlas," Aunt Bea said. "Skinny gets confused sometimes, thinks he's still in New York. I don't worry about him too much. He doesn't drive, and he has an open taxi voucher to get home."

"That's good." My father took cabs when he got too drunk to drive. He was smart like that. "Skinny said he was from Troy and Oneida."

"He sure did," she said. "Skinny talks about Troy and Oneida, usually when he's had a few sips over his allotment."

"I hear that area of New York is beautiful, Oneida, the Finger Lakes, Oswego."

"Don't forget Cazenovia, Cazenovia is beautiful, too." She refilled my cup. "You mentioned Oswego. My husband loved Oswego. He fished there on weekends with my father, not every weekend, three or four times a year."

"They say it's a good fishing town."

"One of the best, it's on Lake Ontario, a beautiful spot. They have summer festivals, fun stuff like that. My husband would take me along for the Fourth of July. Every summer he'd take me for the Fourth, we never missed it."

"Sounds romantic." This was a stupid idea. Why was I asking Aunt Bea about Oswego? What could she possibly tell me? I pushed the cup away. "Thanks."

"What's the hurry? A big guy like you must be famished. Today's special is a hot beef sandwich with salt potatoes, cooked it myself this morning. Stay put and I'll wrestle you up a plate, okay?"

"Sure, I'll take an order." I threw a twenty on the bar. "Give Skinny Atlas a drink, too."

"He'll appreciate it." She poured dark liqueur into a white mug and mixed in coffee. "Skinny likes his sugar sweet. Vandermint and coffee, he drinks it all day long."

CHAPTER 5

Later that afternoon I answered a knock on the office door. Standing on the stoop was a short man holding a thick walking stick. A tweed scully cap topped his large head. A pink birthmark stained the right side of his face. The man didn't smile. His eyes twinkled, or maybe they glowered.

"Liam McGrew," he said, with a Northern Irish brogue. He must've noticed me staring at the walking stick. "My blackthorn shillelagh, hand-carved from the Isle of Innisfree. That's where they filmed *The Quiet Man*. President Kennedy owned one, said it helped his ailing back."

"I'm sure it did."

"Might'ya spare a moment of your precious time, lad?"

I introduced myself, told him I had plenty of time to spare, and invited him into my office. McGrew limped past me, leaning heavily on the walking stick.

"That's quite a limp," I said. "No offense, I can relate to it myself on wet days."

"The Irish climate," he said. "It's murder on the joints."

"My mother told me about it, damp and rainy."

"I was referring to the political climate. It rains bullets in Belfast, used to anyway. My knee's got more lead in it than a fisherman has sinkers." He hobbled a couple more steps. "I'm told you suffered quite a knee injury in your own right. American football, as I understand it. Violence takes its toll, does it not?"

"We're just a couple of gimpy guys," I said. "Coffee?"

"Tea suits me better," he said, saying he preferred it hot and black.

"Tea, it is." I steeped a teabag while I poured my coffee. We both sat at my desk. "Your tea, I hope I made it right."

"Thank you, Mr. Sparhawk." Liam blew away the steam and sipped. "The tea is grand."

"How can I help?"

"You don't waste time with small talk. And that's fine with me. I deal with far too many mealymouthed men these days, men who blather on and on about this and that." He set the teacup on my desk. "A reliable source told me that a lad named Jeepster Hennessey fell dead at your feet quite recently. Murdered, I'm told, stabbed in the back. Is this information correct?"

"What's your interest?"

"I am friendly with his kin back home, most notably his uncle, a Belfast man named James Hennessey. We ran together back in the day, if you know what I mean."

"I think I know what you mean," I said. "Okay, good enough."

I told McGrew his source was correct, that Jeepster Hennessey had in fact dropped dead at my feet with a knife in his back. And then I beat McGrew to the next question, telling him the basics of what happened the night of the killing. I stretched the telling of it, eating up minutes to make it sound thorough.

"A fascinating story indeed," he said. "Did Mister Hennessey say anything before he passed on to his great reward?"

"Why?"

"I'm curious." He smiled like the leprechaun on a Lucky Charms box. "I want to tell his uncle in Belfast, that's all. The more information I have to tell him, the better he'll feel about his nephew's passing."

Another guy asking about Jeepster's death. George Meeks asked about it, and now Liam McGrew was asking about it. Usually when a Townie gets killed nobody asks a thing, not if they're smart. George was a smart guy, despite his unpolished talk. McGrew was no dummy, either. Something was up.

"He didn't say anything to me."

"Nothing at all? That's most difficult for me to believe." McGrew sat up on the chair. "He must have said something."

"Not a thing. You have to understand something, McGrew. Jeepster barely had the strength to walk into the pantry," I said. "He fell into my arms and died immediately. What's so hard to believe about that?"

"I'm told you're a relative of Mr. Hennessy's."

"He was my godfather, my father's friend." I picked a crushed cigar butt from the ashtray and whiffed it, buying time to think. "I don't know what else to say. By the time the medics got to the scene, Jeepster was cold. They didn't bother to put the pads to him he was so dead. What I'm saying is Hennessey was nearly gone when he walked in."

"Dead man walking, is that it?" He tapped the stick. "What if I said I don't believe you?"

"I'd say there's the door, little man." I stood. "Have a swell day."

"Excuse me?" He whacked my desk with the shillelagh. "What was that?"

"Get the hell outta here. And if you swing that blackthorn thing again, I'll stick it up your ass and you can pogo back to Belfast."

He raised the stick, stopping mid windup.

"You're making a grave mistake, lad." McGrew limped to the door. "A grave, grave mistake."

"I've made them before, pinky," I said. "Now get out of here. Screw."

"A grave mistake." He stood at the door. "In my youth, I'd have lathered your ass."

McGrew left the building. It's funny how things work out. I'd made no progress on the Internet and even less at the Cazenovia Club, but when I sat idly in my office, things came to me. First George Meeks, now Liam McGrew.

McGrew's bullshit about Jeepster's Belfast uncle was less believable than my bullshit about Jeepster's saying nothing before he died. The McSweeney key must open something important.

CHAPTER 6

"You were kinda rough on the little guy. He ain't exactly a spring chicken, you know, and he came all the way from Ireland."

"Northern Ireland," I said. "The guy's an asshole. He whacked my desk with a stick, got real pushy."

"I understand, the man got pushy. You got a little pushy yourself, tossing him out of the office like that. And calling him pinky, McGrew took offense to that crack. He's sensitive about that blotch on his face, his size, too. He's probably got that Napoleonic complex, short as he is."

"I lost my cool, Jackie, I went a little overboard."

"He's dangerous as a bastard, Dermot. McGrew still thinks it's Bloody Sunday back there in Belfast, thinks the Black and Tans are out to get him."

I was talking to Jackie Tracy, a parishioner, a union boss, and a high-ranking Townie reputed to have underworld ties. To achieve such a status, Jackie had to be an all-around guy, a guy who could pass the basket on Sundays and hand out envelopes on Fridays. We got along okay, because of my days at the Boys' Club when Jackie instructed us in boxing. Man, he made the heavy bag jump.

We were standing outside Saint Jude Thaddeus after the eight o'clock Mass as congregants emptied onto the sidewalks in Hayes Square. It was one of those hot, windless days when the flags droop limp. Jackie moved closer and talked into my ear.

"Liam McGrew has important friends in Boston, friends that share important interests with him." He finger combed his thick gray hair, bulling his neck when he did. "The man rates a little respect."

"Fine, he's got my respect."

"Show a little patience here," Jackie said. "I'll admit that Mc-Grew went out of order. He shouldn't a gone directly to you like he did, he shoulda come to us first. McGrew's not from these parts. He didn't know better."

"Just keep him away from me."

"It's not that simple." Jackie unpeeled a Sky Bar and broke off a piece. "I'm tryna quit smoking. The candy helps the craving. Can't get Sky Bars in Charlestown, I have to drive up to Tewksbury to get 'em. Here, take the fudge section. I don't like fudge much."

"Thanks."

"Hear me on this thing, Dermot. There are people in Boston, they have dealings with McGrew, and these dealings need to be handled carefully. We can't have no loose cannons rocking the boat, understand?"

"I'm not sure I do."

"McGrew needs information. Nobody's saying you have to talk to him directly. We can work around talking to him face-to-face, so you don't gotta worry about that."

"What are you getting at?"

"McGrew needs to know things about Hennessey's death."

"Tell him to buy a newspaper, it's all in there."

"Listen to me, Dermot." Jackie chewed the caramel. "We don't care two fucks about a newspaper article a cub reporter copied outta the police blotter. We need specific details, understand? We need to know exactly what happened the night Hennessey died. Everything he said, every goddamned syllable."

"We?"

"That's why they sent me. We know each other, we go way back. They figured the two of us could hash this thing out and be done with it. Another thing, there's money in it, maybe a grand or two, maybe I can get three if I talk to them. Yeah, I can probably get you three." Jackie stuffed the Sky Bar wrapper into his pocket. "We figured Jeepster came to you because he's your uncle. We figured he said things that didn't get in the police report."

"He was my godfather, not uncle."

"Whatever." Jackie held his temper. "Tell me everything he said, everything he did. I can smooth things out with the higher-ups if I know what happened."

"No problem." I gave Jackie Tracy the G-rated version, leaving out Oswego and McSweeney. "Then I called 911."

"There's gotta be more to it. He musta said something else, he's your fuckin' godfather. I'm tryna work with you here. How 'bout a little cooperation?" He shuffled his feet and planted, a boxer prepping to launch. "Did he say anything else?"

"Like what?"

"Whadda ya mean, like what? Anything. Any fuckin' thing at all," he said. "Did he hand you anything, any, ah, items?"

"That's all that happened."

"Jesus, Mary, and Joseph, you don't get it."

"Sorry I can't help."

We stood on the sidewalk in the morning sun. The orange ball had risen to the Tobin Bridge and shined between the upper and lower decks. The parishioners were now gone, the ushers had locked the doors. Jackie looked east toward the Navy Yard, shading his eyes with his right palm.

"Think about what I said. Call me if you remember anything." He lowered his hand. "I'd hate to see bad things happen."

"I can take care of myself."

"I know, I know, you were always a tough kid and I respect that. But sometimes you gotta use your head, sometimes you gotta think things through. It ain't all about tough, Dermot," he said. "Make a smart decision."

"My self-esteem soars whenever I talk to you, same as when I talked to my old man," I said. "He used to say, 'Dermot, you're not as stupid as you look. You're stupider.'"

Jackie pitched forward laughing.

"I always liked Chief, God be good to him." He waited for the 93 bus to pass. "Think about what I said. Call me."

"There's nothing to tell."

"Sure, sure." He opened another Sky Bar. "You're making a mistake here."

Jackie got into his black Lincoln Navigator and drove up Bunker Hill Street. He was telling me something every project man knows. There's only one unpardonable sin, the sin of stupidity. Jackie Tracy said it plain: don't be stupid, kid.

CHAPTER 7

The next morning I answered a phone call from my uncle, Glooscap, a Canadian Micmac Indian from Nova Scotia and my father's brother. He wanted to talk to me. We agreed to meet at his auto-body shop in Andrew Square in an hour. The air was cool and the sky was bright, so I decided to set out on foot. I got to his shop an hour and a half later. Harraseeket Kid, my cousin and Glooscap's son, was flailing a rubber mallet at a fender. I couldn't tell if he was banging out an old dent or banging in a new one.

Kid had moved into the basement of my two-family house last year, transformed the musty dugout into a subterranean palace, and barters the rent by maintaining the property. The arrangement has worked for both of us. Kid needed a place to live, and I don't know a claw hammer from a clodhopper.

"Glooscap's waiting in the office," said Kid, who wore his shiny black hair in a ponytail. "He's kind of antsy. Is everything okay?"

"I'll find out in a minute."

I walked to Glooscap's office and stopped for a deep breath before entering. I don't know whether it's a Micmac thing or something else, but whenever I dealt with Glooscap, I had to slow myself down—way down. Listening to Glooscap is like listening to a seventy-eight vinyl on thirty-three. Each word elongates. Each pause has three commas. He enunciates syllables with a grammarian's intent. Every sentence ends with an abrupt halt, as if the period were a shot put thudding to earth. He never swears, never uses slang, never speaks a contraction. Contractions are for the lazy, uttered only by sluggards. He rarely varies his monotone drone, which rolls out like a tired Tibetan chant.

I knocked on the door and went inside.

Glooscap was sitting in a swivel chair behind his oaken desk. We said hello. He told me to pour myself a cup of coffee and take a seat. Like Harraseeket Kid, Glooscap's hair was wound into a ponytail, his gray. With a prominent brow, a bull nose, and a jutting jaw, his profile could have been on a buffalo nickel. The heads side. He twirled his chair to face me.

"I have heard disturbing things. Perhaps they are rumors, perhaps more," he said. "I am concerned for your welfare."

"My welfare?"

"A trusted friend told me you stepped on dangerous toes. Whose toes, I am not sure. People are angry." Glooscap leaned forward on his desk. "I want to give you something that once belonged to your father." He took a White Owl cigar box from his desk drawer, placed it on the desk, and opened the lid. The box contained a large handgun, a spare magazine, and a stack of newspaper clippings. "Chief smuggled the gun from Vietnam, a military-issue .45. He took it off a dead second lieutenant after the Battle of Hill 881. Now the gun is yours. Read the newspaper clippings, too."

"Why the clippings?"

"Because of the toes you stepped on, that is why. If my information is correct, you offended a group of IRA men, men who are members of a criminal element of their cause. Their interest is not in politics any longer, but rather in profits. After the Good Friday Accord was signed, these men turned to crime, mostly heists I am told."

"I ruffled a Belfast mick named Liam McGrew. He came to my office the other day," I said. "Is McGrew one of the guys I offended?"

"I cannot say for sure. It sounds quite possible. The timing of McGrew's visit seems to fit with the information I received." He inhaled slowly through his hawk-bill nose. "The IRA men must be handled with the utmost caution, Dermot."

"It might be too late. I told McGrew to shove a shillelagh up his ass."

"You did not." He laughed. His shoulders shook. "Be careful as you move forward."

Glooscap told me that my father admired my mother's Northern Irish heritage, particularly the role of the Irish Republican Army. My father viewed the IRA in tribal terms, a clan fighting to reclaim rights and lands stolen from them. My mother, who died of cirrhosis of the liver when I was seven, told me all about Bloody Sunday and the British paratroopers opening fire on unarmed civilians during a peace march. She said Belfast turned into a hellhole in the aftermath of Bloody Sunday, a hell that prompted my grandmother to move the family to Dorchester in the mid-1970s. They struggled to survive. Some Irish never get out of steerage.

"I do not know whether or not your father did jobs for the Irish Republican Army. I know he kept company with a number of connected Irishmen in Boston. Let us call them reputed men. Your father has been dead for a long time now, so there is probably no connection between him and Liam McGrew." He paused. "Chief loved your mother very much. Do you know what he loved most about her?"

"I remember he loved her."

"Your mother undertook a near impossible vow. She vowed not to drink while she was pregnant with you, an arduous undertaking for an alcoholic, and yet she fulfilled it. And for that, your father admired her. In his youth, he saw the damage alcohol did to Indian children. To show his support for her, he did not take a drink either, not until your birth."

"And then he never stopped."

"True, he never stopped after that," he said. "Your parents were a thirsty couple, drinking partners more than husband and wife."

"I know."

"They loved you dearly, more than they loved whiskey."

"I know they did."

"Because your mother fulfilled her vow of abstinence, you did not suffer fetal alcohol syndrome, a horrible malady. I have seen many cases of it on the reservations of our people. You were spared." Glooscap closed the cigar box and slid it to me. "Have you ever fired a gun?"

"A BB gun."

"Talk to Harraseeket Kid, he belongs to a gun club. Kid will teach you how to shoot." Glooscap tapped his fingers on the cigar box. "Be careful. You do not have a carry permit. However, I would sooner see you arrested for a gun violation than killed unarmed."

"That makes two of us."

CHAPTER 8

I knocked on the door of my first-floor tenant, Buck Louis, a black paraplegic who played football with me at Boston College. His playing days ended when a linebacker paralyzed him in an Oklahoma drill during summer sessions. Buck never played in a game. We reunited a year ago at a chance meeting in Thompson Square. That's when Buck moved into the apartment. When my aunt died she left me the house, and I had plenty of room.

"That you, Dermot?" He opened the door and backed up his wheelchair. "Just made a pot of fresh joe, want a cup?"

"Sounds good." I closed the door behind me and sat in an upholstered chair in the parlor. "Been keeping busy?"

"Pretty busy, doing my usual thing on the computer, Facebook, e-mails, chat rooms, blogging, things like that. It breaks up the day." He wheeled over and handed me a cup. "Anything new on Jeepster's murder?"

"He tested positive for drugs."

"Are you surprised?"

"His parole officer told the police he flunked his last urine test." I sipped coffee. "He probably got killed in a drug deal."

"Makes sense."

I listened to the sounds of the housing project across the street. Everything was quiet for the moment. The smell of Spanish cooking wafted from open widows. On the rooftop across the street, a white kid painted graffiti on a chimney, a shamrock or something green.

"If you're bored I might have something to keep you busy," I said.

"I'm bored as a bastard, fill me in."

"Jeepster Hennessey did time in a federal prison."

"Which one?" he said. "My cousin did federal time in New Jersey."

"Otisville, New York," I said. "An ex-con named George Meeks visited me at my office. He told me he did time with Jeepster at Otisville. George said that Jeepster belonged to a prison book club."

"And?"

"You're an expert on the computer," I said. "Is there any way to find out about the prison book club using the Internet?"

"I can try. Prison firewalls are tough to crack, especially federal prisons, 'cause of those terrorist assholes." He rolled back and forth. "It's tough to get clearance, too. I tried e-mailing my cousin in prison. It wasn't easy."

I wanted to learn more about Oswego and the McSweeney key and thought Jeepster's book club might provide a clue. I hesitated to tell Buck about Oswego and McSweeney, not because I didn't trust him, not at all, but I didn't want to put him in any danger. Between George Meeks and Liam McGrew and Jackie Tracy and a murdered Jeepster Hennessey, the whole matter was taking on a menacing feel.

"On second thought, never mind," I said. "It's not that important."

"Bullshit, I can tell it's important. And I can tell you're holding something back, because I know that face." He wheeled up to me. "Tell me about it."

Why did I bring Buck into this?

"Things might get rough."

"The rougher the better. Come on, Dermot. I'm dying on the vine here, gimme a shot, or pretty soon I'm gonna roll myself off a pier."

I sat down on the couch and held up my hands, signaling Buck to give me a minute to think. Jackie Tracy was no one to screw around with, and Liam McGrew was probably hooked into the

IRA, but Buck Louis was hooked to a wheelchair, wanting something to do. How would I feel if I were stuck in a wheelchair? Would I want people pushing me off to the side to protect me? Or would I want them to throw me into the mix?

"Okay Buck, you're in on one condition. I'm pulling you out if things get too dangerous," I said. "Do we have a deal? Will you back off if I say so?"

"Hell yeah, we have a deal." He reached out to shake my hand. "Now tell me what's up, give it to me, gimme all of it."

He asked for all of it, I told him all of it.

"This is pissa, Dermot, and I mean A-plus pissa. Oswego, McSweeney, a secret key, a prison book club, the threats. Shit, even the IRA. It doesn't get any better."

"I'm glad you think so."

I went upstairs and read the newspaper clippings inside my father's White Owl box. The clippings detailed the Irish Republican Army's role in policing Catholic Belfast, a task forced on them by their own kind, because the Royal Ulster Constabulary refused to patrol papist strongholds. The articles showed how a subculture of Catholics punishing Catholics arose.

Believing a baseball bat got better results than a gavel, the IRA structured a hierarchy of punishments to discourage criminals from pursuing a lawbreaking life. The IRA were not unreasonable men. They first issued the wrongdoer a scolding, a good talking-to as they like to say, and if that failed to deter his villainous ways, punitive measures were taken as follows:

Kneecapping: the lowest rung on the IRA punishment ladder, reserved for petty criminals. The procedure is simple. The accused is placed facedown on the pavement and shot behind the knee. The bullet typically rips through the front of the leg, taking with it bone and cartilage. Some complications have arisen with kneecappings. In one case a bullet ricocheted into an artery, causing a man to bleed to death. This led to the power-drill solution. Drilling a knee with a steel shank eliminates the risk of bouncing bullets, and though a slower process, the IRA deems power drilling a viable alternative and recommends it for advanced kneecappers.

The Cadillac of kneecapping, however, is shotgunning, where both barrels of a shotgun are fired into the knee, blowing off the bottom half of the leg. Some argue that shotgunning deserves its own rung nearer the top.

Six-pack: The outlaw is shot six times, two apiece in the ankles, knees, and elbows, leaving him a virtual cripple. Six-packs are recommended for the more serious criminal: rapists, armed robbers, informers. Six-packs are also used when kneecaps don't bring reform. It's not unusual for a stubborn Belfast Catholic to get kneecapped and six-packed before he learns his lesson.

Fifty-fifty: a shotgun blast to the spine, rendering an O'Hobson's choice: a 50 percent chance of death, a 50 percent chance of paralyses: tough odds for the street thug. Fifty-fifties occupy the top rung on the punishment ladder. Gun squads consider it effective, particularly in difficult cases. One recidivist scoffed at a kneecap, sneered at a six-pack, but yielded to a fifty-fifty. Today he robs no more. He walks no more, either.

One thought came to me after reading the clippings. Be wary of Liam McGrew.

CHAPTER 9

Captain Pruitt dropped by the food-pantry office the next day accompanied by a slim white woman. She wore a navy blue blazer and matching skirt, pressed white shirt, and black leather shoes. If the outfit had a chevron on the shoulder, it'd be a uniform. Her shiny silver hair stood coiled atop her head. The premature silver belied her age. She was no more than thirty-five.

"Come in," I said to them.

They stepped into the office and sat around my desk in metal folding chairs. Pruitt wasted no time.

"Sparhawk, this is Special Agent Hague, FBI. She's up here on assignment from New York, as part of the Joint Terrorism Task Force." Pruitt wiped sweat from his ebony brow. "Miss Hague is following up on Jeepster Hennessey's murder. The FBI, or more specifically the JTTF, has taken an interest in the case. Ms. Hague will be the bureau's point person on it. The Boston Police Department has agreed to cooperate with her."

"It's a pleasure to meet you, Mr. Sparhawk."

"Dermot," I said.

"Call me Emma. Everything Captain Pruitt said is right on the mark. I am part of the FBI Counterterrorism Division, supporting the Joint Terrorism Task Force in Boston. No doubt you're wondering why the JTTF cares about a killing in Charlestown." She leaned back in the metal folding chair. "We have several reasons, really. For one, Mr. Hennessey was stabbed on federally funded property. The Bunker Hill housing development is subsidized by the federal government."

"You must be kidding," I said. "After decades of killings in the projects, you're suddenly interested in Jeepster Hennessey's killing?"

"Federal housing has become a hotbed for the drug trade, not just in Boston but elsewhere. Charlestown is the worst section in the country for heroin overdoses, percentage-wise. Did you know that?"

"I heard."

"Guess where those poppy fields are located?" She didn't wait for an answer. "Afghanistan. Last year the Afghanis harvested a record crop of poppies. Those profits bankroll terrorism. So you can see why the FBI is interested in a drug-related death in Charlestown. The drug trade must be stopped."

"Wait a goddamn second. Jeepster might've had a drug problem, but he wasn't a drug dealer, and he sure as hell wasn't a terrorist." I planted my feet on the floor. "He served in Vietnam with my father. He had an American flag tattooed on his arm. Jeepster had nothing to do with poppy fields and terrorism. This is bullshit."

"I cannot divulge certain aspects of my work because of their delicate nature," she said. "I'll relate as much as I can."

"I'm listening." *Listening to a bunch of crap.* "Go on."

"We are not interested in Mr. Hennessey's death, per se. We are interested in his apartment, the building he lived in."

"What?"

"The JTTF is monitoring Somali insurgents, led by a group called al-Shabab. Al-Shabab is known to have ties to al-Qaeda. Their goal is to recruit and radicalize young Somalis."

"I still don't see where Jeepster comes in."

"It's not complicated, Dermot." She paused a few seconds. "Numerous Somali immigrants are living in Mr. Hennessey's building, Islamic Somalis, possible terrorists."

"I know they live there," I said. "The women come to the food pantry wearing berkas. They're not hiding, you can't miss them."

"I am well aware of that," Emma Hague said. "The JTTF is concerned about a growing terrorist pipeline coming into the U.S., an underground railroad transporting jihadists into the country. That's why I am here. That's why I need your help. I am moving into Mr. Hennessey's apartment and setting up surveillance to track Somali movements."

"Surveillance in the bricks?" I said. "It'll never work."

"I will enroll in your food pantry, wait in line with the other clients, get the feel of the neighborhood, and learn about the Somalis."

"They'll peg you immediately, Emma. You won't learn a thing back there."

"Why won't I?"

"The projects are balkanized."

"Balkanized?" Pruitt laughed. "Jesus, Sparhawk, did you read a book or something?"

"The Chinese stick with the Chinese, the Spanish with the Spanish, the Irish with the Irish, and the Somalis with the Somalis. Even within ethnic groups there are subgroups, and they close ranks if they suspect an outsider in their midst. You're on an impossible mission."

"Perhaps you are correct, Dermot, perhaps it is an impossible mission. The point is I've been assigned the mission, and in my line of work agents don't pick and choose their assignments. Agents follow orders." She waited a second. "Will you help me?"

"The Somalis are penniless," I said. "They have nothing. No cars, no money, no material possessions."

"Penniless Somalis make the best terrorists."

"What do you mean?"

"The terrorist network is quite sophisticated. The JTTF has been observing Somali advancements in the United States, and we are gravely concerned with what we've seen. Look at the problems in Minnesota, the activity in Lewiston, Maine." Emma leaned forward. "I have a question for you, Dermot."

"I'm listening."

"How many LNG tankers unload in Boston each month?"

"Do you have an easier question?"

"Count them. They chug by your office on their way to Everett, floating right in front of the projects. They might as well have a bull's-eye on them. All it takes is one terrorist with one handheld rocket launcher to fire at an LNG, and ka-boom, goodbye Charlestown."

"Coastguard cutters escort the tankers through the harbor," I said. "Helicopters accompany them into port."

"That's true, but we must take every possible precaution, and rooting out Somali terrorists is an essential precaution."

"What am I missing? The Somalis like living here. They want to be Americans. Why blow up a ship?"

"Most Somali immigrants will become great Americans, I agree. However, a number of Somalis are true believers, extremely easy to coerce. Many young Somali men feel disenfranchised."

"If they feel disenfranchised, why don't they go home?"

"Money, why else? They have nothing back in Africa." She took a folder from her tote bag and read from it. "Al-Shabab has the resources, i.e., the money, to entice future terrorists and foster future terrorism." She put down the folder. "For example, they pay the families of suicide bombers with promissory notes."

"With what?"

"Promissory notes. Al-Qaeda doesn't pay the bomber directly—that would be akin to tossing a check into a closing coffin—they pay his family. Not only does the bomber get seventy-two virgins in heaven, his family gets money here on earth."

"That's insane," I said.

"Promissory notes wreak havoc," Emma said. "The money paid to the families is never paid directly. The payments get back channeled through offshore accounts, impossible to trace."

Emma's information came at me too fast. It sounded like a sales pitch.

"I respect what you're trying to do, futile as it is," I said. "You won't learn a thing back there. A white person won't learn a thing from the Somalis in the projects."

"I have to try," she said. "I ask again, will you help me?"

"What do you want me to do?"

"Be my eyes and ears in the projects. The people here trust you. Perhaps they'll confide in you if they hear whisperings about terrorist activities. Keep your eyes peeled, your ears open. That's what I'm asking."

"I don't know. Maybe. If I do help, I don't want to hear any more garbage about Jeepster Hennessey and terrorism, understood? Jeepster would never betray his country."

"I understand," she said. "I didn't mean to offend anyone."

On warm June evenings, just before darkness swallows up the Boston skyline, when the traffic ebbs on the Tobin Bridge and the gulls drift to their nesting spots underneath it, the projects take on the air of a bygone era. Tenants congregate around concrete stoops, listening to radios and playing cards. The women listen to ethnic music and the men listen to the Red Sox, announced in either English or Spanish, depending on the block. To outsiders the neighborhood might seem heartwarming, even idyllic, a nice place to live. Except for the fear, gloom, and poverty, the scene could be a Norman Rockwell painting.

I pulled over on Corey Street near Starr King Court and found the building where Jeepster Hennessey once lived, a corner apartment on the first floor, soon to be occupied by Special Agent Emma Hague. The FBI was right about one thing: the Somali population was growing in public housing. Tall black women dressed in bright silk scarves walked in and out of the brick buildings that comprised the neighborhood. One of them noticed me and nodded. She was a member of the food pantry and her name was Naddi. I nodded back.

They seemed anything but terrorists. Then I thought about it for a moment and realized I had no gut feeling for terrorism, no inkling at all. It was foreign to me. What do I really know about terrorism, except for two towers getting knocked down in Lower Manhattan, a Boston College teammate of mine trapped inside one of them when it collapsed, his widow and three children left behind to suffer the loss?

CHAPTER 10

The next day I sat in my office reading a book about urban renewal in Boston. The book detailed how developers profited from a land grab by twisting the Fifth Amendment clause of eminent domain. They uprooted Charlestown families, buying their properties for a pittance. They bulldozed the West End. They razed the Albany Street area near Aunt Bea's Cazenovia Club to make room for the turnpike extension. Block after block of residential housing fell to eminent domain. Homes were demolished and streets were renamed, as if the places never existed.

I bookmarked the page when someone banged the door, probably kids from Saint Jude Thaddeus elementary hoping to make a buck sweeping the lot. I answered it. Two men wearing tan caps and black tee shirts stood on the stoop. They were pretty big guys, pretty solid, too—six feet tall and two hundred pounds. They made no eye contact, they didn't smile, they reeked of tension.

"Are you guys here to sign up for the food pantry?" I said.

The spokesman stepped forward.

"Get in the car and take a ride with us, Sparhawk." He spoke with a Belfast brogue, barely moving his lips. A green shamrock was tattooed on his forearm with the name Saint Pat under it. "Our friend needs to talk to you."

"Tell McGrew I don't take rides."

The other man, who sported bushy red sideburns, sauntered forward, shuffled his feet while gazing at the ground, and booted a fifty-yard field goal with my groin. Down I crashed. They kicked my ribs as I tumbled down the stairs to the parking lot, crabbing like a lobster for the chain-link fence. The fence shielded their shod-laden onslaught. I gasped for air as the two threw boots.

Welcome to the IRA.

I shinnied up a fencepost as their Irish step dance picked up speed. Getting to my feet was a good start. I backhanded Sideburns in the ear then swiped at Saint Pat. The two men stepped back and snapped long their telescoping batons. What is it with these Irish guys and sticks?

They stalked me like wolves and sprang in tandem, flailing their clubs and kicking their feet. I lunged low at Sideburns's legs, tasted his kneecap, and tackled him to the pavement. We wrestled on the tar. All the while Saint Pat hammered my back with the club. I spun Sideburns over just as Saint Pat let fly an arcing cut. The club thudded Sideburns's scalp, splitting his head open. Sideburns went unconscious.

His deadweight draped across my torso. I rolled him aside and scrambled to my feet. Saint Pat uncorked a homerun swing at my head. I parried the pipe past my face, stepped inside, and ripped a shovel hook into his ribs, digging into his solar plexus. He grunted and doubled over. I grabbed with both hands, got a handful of his hair, and jerked him. Saint Pat lost his footing and spun to the asphalt, rolling when he hit the tar.

My groin throbbed, my rage flared, and I went canine. Diving atop him, I chomped onto his nose and shook my head, growling like a son of a bitch. His screams echoed off the brick façades of the church and school, a Ping-Pong echo of agony. The thrill of victory filled my chest. I had him beat. A nun dashed out of the school, shrieking that she'd called the police. We continued to fight, while the faint howls of sirens grew louder.

I rose to my feet to stomp on his face and my head swooned, allowing Saint Pat a moment to escape. He scurried into the projects, deserting his clansman, who lay motionless on the blacktop. Beaten to shit, I spit a chunk of nose to the bloody tar. None of my teeth came out in the spew.

• • •

The emergency room doctor told me I had no broken ribs and no fractured bones in my forearm, both of which ached from the clubbing. Despite the clean bill of health, my body felt like a piñata after Big Papi's birthday party. Captain Pruitt walked into the hospital room and watched as I pulled on my bloodstained shirt. He wiped his mirror sunglasses with a tissue and put them in his shirt pocket.

"The tie-dyed style looks good on you, Sparhawk. Let's grab a coffee in the cafeteria," he said. "We need to talk."

"About what?"

"One of the guys you fought in the parking lot got his skull fractured." Pruitt waited for me to jump down from the examination table. "The blow ruptured his brain, he's dead. He died on the ambulance ride, never made it to the hospital."

"Ah, shit." I rubbed my swollen forearm with a scraped hand. "He's dead? Who was he?"

"He had no wallet, no ID. For now, he's John Doe," Pruitt said. "Let's get that cup of coffee and talk."

"Yeah, let's."

The Irishman's death troubled me some. I felt bad about his killing. Maybe my desensitization condition was beginning to fade. Maybe I could grow into a full human being someday, with feelings and emotions, instead of the numbed-out half-breed son of two immigrant drunks.

We ordered coffee and sat at a round table. Pruitt asked me what happened in the parking lot. I told him the story. He listened, occasionally nodded, and then spoke.

"Sister Bernadine Maria witnessed the end of the melee. She said you chewed the guy's nose half off. You came up for air looking like a vampire, blood all over your face. Sister told me the surviving attacker ran into the projects when he finally tore loose from the bite, which pretty much matches your story."

"Did you expect a nun to lie?"

"No, I expected you to lie."

"Thanks."

We drank coffee and watched hospital workers hustling into the cafeteria for afternoon snacks. A hefty man purchased two jelly rolls and two chocolate milks. He was smiling before he even took a bite. I used to smile the same way before I uncapped a jug.

"Two men killed inside of a week, both on church grounds. The killings have to be connected," Pruitt said.

"I don't think so. The guy today was killed by accident. His accomplice was aiming for *my* head, not his buddy's. Jeepster Hennessey was probably killed by accident, too. He got stabbed, sure, but things like that happen in the drug life."

"Two men dead on *your* church grounds? I don't like coincidences, Sparhawk, don't like them a bit." He pushed the coffee aside. "What did they want? They must have attacked you for a reason. What did they say?"

"They wanted me to take a ride with them. They said a friend of theirs wanted to talk to me. I told them I don't take rides with strangers."

"Who wanted to talk to you?"

"They didn't say."

"Come on, Sparhawk. Who do you think it was? If they didn't say, they probably figured you knew. Who was it?"

"I don't know."

"Take a wild guess." His cell phone rang. "Wait here. Don't move." Pruitt walked to an alcove on the side of the cafeteria. After a brief conversation, he clicked the phone shut and came back to the table. "Does the name Edmund O'Gorman mean anything to you?"

"No. Should it?"

"He's the man who got killed, the guy in the ambulance. We found his fingerprints on Interpol. O'Gorman was an IRA operative. Turns out he's wanted for bombing a municipal building in London. He's been underground for a decade. O'Gorman comes from Belfast. This info about O'Gorman, does it shed any light on who wanted to talk to you?"

"Sorry, Captain, it's no help."

"You forgot to mention they were Irish. When the attackers told you to take a ride with them, you must have heard the brogue."

"I forgot about the brogue."

"You're lying."

"The brogue didn't seem important at the time."

"Bullshit, Sparhawk. Sooner or later you're gonna tell me what's going on. I prefer sooner. I'd rather hear it from you before I waste hours figuring it out for myself—and I will figure it out." He got to his feet. "For now, I'll give you a wide berth. Keep me in the loop."

"Sure thing." I rubbed my head and mumbled, "Loop, my ass."

My AA sponsor, Mickey Pappas, another Vietnam veteran from Charlestown, was standing on the stoop when I got back to the office. His reddish-gray hair framed his smiling sober face. Mickey was proud of his Greek-Irish heritage. Before sobering up, he honored his legacy by drinking shots of Metaxa with Guinness chasers. I joined him on the stoop. Mickey rubbed his mouth and winced.

"What's with the mouth?" I said.

"My girlfriend, Brenda. She's forty-seven years old and she goes and gets braces on her teeth. Didn't bother me her teeth were crooked. Now it's like French kissing a chainsaw. She cut my gums to ribbons." Mickey ran his tongue under his lips. "I heard about the brawl in the parking lot. You doing okay?"

"Yeah, I'm fine," I said. "No big deal."

"No big deal? It doesn't look like it was no big deal. Your mug's bruised to shit." We went inside my office. "A man got killed, too. So don't say it was no big deal, because it was a big deal. Tell me what happened."

I laid it out sequentially. I told him about the two Irishmen knocking on the door, the boot in the balls, the ensuing fight, the telescoping batons, the clubbing death of the attacker, the nose chewing, the nun's chiding. I didn't mention Liam McGrew.

"You're lucky to be alive."

"Yeah, I guess."

"Two guys attack you for no apparent reason and it's no big deal?" He got in front of me. "What the hell's going on?"

"It was nothing, Mick. Stay out of it," I said. "I don't want to talk about it right now."

"What do you mean you don't want to talk about it?" He stepped closer. "Knock off the tough-guy act and quit pretending nothing happened. Two men attacked you with clubs."

"I came out of it okay."

"By the grace of God you're okay. I'm grilling you 'cause I don't want to see you pick up a drink. I've seen guys drink over broken shoelaces, let alone a billy club beating. Do you see what I'm getting at?"

"No."

"Alcoholics need to talk about their feelings. To stay sober, you gotta talk. Bottle it up, and pretty soon it's bottoms up."

"I'm not thinking of drinking."

"That ain't the point. If something's troubling you, get it out. That's how we deal with things in AA, we talk about them. If you're not comfortable talking to me, talk to someone else. I won't be offended. It's the way the program works."

"I'm comfortable with you, Mick. It's just I don't want to put you in any danger."

"What the hell are you talking about, danger?" Mickey puffed his chest. "I'll decide if I'm in danger. Tell me what happened."

"It was nothing, let's just forget—"

"Tell me, Dermot. I won't leave until you tell me the whole story." He waited a second. "I ain't got all day, spill it. I'm here to help."

"Okay." I told Mickey the story. "Keep it between us."

"Don't insult me, Dermot. What do I look like, a suburbanite? Obviously, it's between us," he said. "I won't say nothin' to nobody."

"Thanks, Mick."

"I want you to promise me something, I want you to stay close to the program. The Big Book tells us alcohol is cunning, baffling, insidious. It sneaks up on you. It snuck up on me." He stopped. "You know something, Dermot, I never once went to a bar and ordered a shot of anger and a bottle of I'll-show-her, but that's how it always turned out. It was always trouble. In my prime I weighed two hundred and twenty-two pounds of root-tootin' twos, all muscle, no fat. Thought I could whip anybody, and most times I did. Then I met my master, Mister John Barleycorn. Mister Barleycorn turned me into a sniveler, a whimpering sissy."

CHAPTER 11

Later that evening I cleaned myself up and attended Jeepster Hennessey's wake at Clancy's. I arrived at the funeral parlor early and offered my condolences to Jeepster's mother, Mrs. Hennessey. She was alone in life now, her husband long dead, her only child murdered. The loss showed in her Irish face, which was gray and drawn.

Well-wishers crowded into the viewing room. One clown answered his cell phone while kneeling at the casket, carried on a loud conversation, and got up without blessing himself. The large crowd reminded me of something my father once told me: "If you want a big funeral, die young." Jeepster died young.

A washed-out blonde with a serviceable body cried in the corner of the room. She seemed genuinely upset. No doubt her cell phone was turned off. Jackie Tracy sat next to me on the divan. He gestured to a few longshoremen near the coffin, who were doing their best to look mournful, and then he turned his attention to me.

"Jesus, you look like dog shit, Dermot. I heard what happened at Saint Jude's. I find it ugly, very ugly, you getting attacked like that." He waved to someone. "At least you took one of 'em out. That musta felt good, taking one of 'em out. You gonna be all right?"

"I'm fine, Jackie."

"I tried to warn you, but you refused to listen. Now look what happened," he said. "A man dead, another man minus a nose, and it's just beginning." Jackie peeled open a Sky Bar and bit a piece off. "It's been three weeks since my last cigarette."

"Sounds like a confession," I said.

"I didn't want this to happen. I was hoping to avoid this mess." He took another bite. "You gotta understand something, Dermot. I had nothing to do with that parking lot business. It's important you know that. Personally, I think you fucked up. I think you shoulda talked to Liam McGrew." He handed me the fudge section. "Not Dermot Sparhawk, no sir, Dermot's a tough guy."

"What's your point, Jackie? Or are you just busting balls."

"No point, no ball busting," he said. "As long as you know I had nothing to do with the parking lot attack."

"I figured McGrew was behind it."

"Whoa, I didn't say McGrew was behind it. I don't know who was behind it, and I usually hear stuff like that. I *did* hear they were Irish. Think about it. What better way to point a finger at McGrew than hire a couple of micks for the job?"

"They weren't just Irish, Jackie, they were Belfast Irish," I said. "They were soldiers, IRA men. They had to be with McGrew."

"Hey, whatever." He took another bite. "What the fuck do I know?"

Jackie got up and joined the men at the casket. They blessed themselves and stepped outside for a smoke or Sky Bar or whatever. They didn't appear to be crestfallen. I remained seated. Jeepster was my godfather, and I'd be hanging around till the end of the wake.

The night ticked by, the crowd dwindled down, and the undertaker corralled the lingerers to the exit as the clock neared nine. The washed-out blonde walked to the door, still dabbing her tears with a Kleenex. George Meeks approached me on his way out of the parlor.

"What happened to your face?"

"I walked into a door."

"Musta been a big fuckin' door." He ran his tattooed hand through his gray buzz cut. "You hear any more about Jeepster?"

"What do you mean?"

"I thought you mighta heard something, that's all." He patted his coat and took out his pack of cigars. "I guess you didn't hear nothin'."

"I didn't expect to hear anything. Jeepster tested positive for drugs. Bad things happen in the projects when drugs are involved." I snagged one of his Dutch Masters. "The prison book club that you mentioned, tell me more about it."

"Why?"

"Humor me, George. Tell me about it."

"There's not much to tell. See, I wasn't sharp enough to get in." He sniffed the corona. "I know this much, Jeepster was still a member after he got out of Otisville."

"Can anyone tell me about it? Do you know of any other book club members?"

"Can't help on that front, I didn't know any members except Jeepster." He twirled the unlit cigar in his mouth. "Sounds crazy, doesn't it, a literary society in prison? I'll ask around, see what I hear."

"Thanks."

I knelt at the casket to say one last prayer and to take in Jeepster's face one last time. The items inside the box reflected his life: a Townie pillow at his side, a shamrock necktie held in place with a claddagh tiepin, a Battle of Bunker Hill flag folded into a triangle at his elbow, a similarly folded American flag at his head, rosary beads wrapped in his hands. I went over to Mrs. Hennessey after blessing myself.

"I want to walk you home, it's late," I said.

"You're such a dear, Dermot."

We said goodbye to Clancy and walked down Bunker Hill Street toward the projects, where Mrs. Hennessey had an apartment on O'Reilly Way. We passed two teenagers who were speaking in hushed tones. They nodded to us when Mrs. Hennessey said hello. We interlocked arms, crossed Concord Street, turned left on Monument Street to O'Reilly Way. Purple dusk had yielded to darkness. The sodium streetlights brightened the sidewalks. Mrs. Hennessey began to talk.

"Jeepster had this awful fear. He feared he'd live the same life as his father. My husband worked lonely jobs, hated to be around people. Nightshifts, graveyard shifts, he wanted to be alone. One time he took a security guard job at the *Herald,* because it was down in the basement garage, away from everyone. Another time he got hired to work the overnight shift in a museum. Imagine, sitting alone all night in a museum."

"I can't remember ever having a conversation with Mister Hennessey, not once."

"Me either." She laughed. "My husband's life wasn't a bad life, not at all. But it wasn't the life for Jeepster."

"What do you mean?"

"My husband loved predictability and solitude," she said. "Jeepster loved taking chances, mixing with people."

"He sure did."

For Jeepster, a jail cell beat a guard shack. The threat of prison wouldn't faze Jeepster. The thought of sitting through a nine-to-five job would terrify him. Mrs. Hennessey dug out her keys.

"I guess they both got what they wanted in the end."

The outside tenement door swung open. When we reached her apartment on the third floor, I noticed the metal door was bent back at the lock. I pushed into the apartment ahead of her. The place had been ransacked. The kitchen drawers were tossed on the floor. Cushions were sliced open, the mattress and box spring torn up. Ceiling tiles were yanked down. Picture frames were smashed to shards. I checked all the rooms, the place was empty. *What the hell happened?* I came back to the doorway and found Mrs. Hennessey gawking at the remains of her apartment.

"Mother of Saint Patrick." Her knees wobbled. "What a mess."

I eased her onto the shredded couch and dialed 911, reported the crime, gave them the address, gave them my phone number, and sat next to Mrs. Hennessey. It was a warm summer night, yet she had a shawl wrapped around her shoulders.

"Are you okay?" I said.

"I've never been broken into before. What's happened to this neighborhood?" She adjusted the wrap. "I've lived here my whole life."

"Is there anyone you can call?"

"No one's left, Dermot. With Jeepster gone, there's no one left to call."

"You can't stay here tonight," I said. "Let me make a call."

I called a friend who owned a bed-and-breakfast on Monument Square, a converted brownstone that's worth a small fortune today. It used to be a rooming house for drunks and transients, a place where my father crashed when he was too hammered to make it home. My friend remembered Mrs. Hennessey from the neighborhood. He told me he had a spare bedroom. She could bunk there until I got her apartment straightened out. He remembered Jeepster too, and before he hung up, he said no charge.

Minutes later, two uniformed policemen shuffled into the front room of Mrs. Hennessey's apartment. Cops are never in a rush. It's part of their shtick. They lull people into a comfortable space. They come across as sleepy, not too sharp, all the while setting the hurdles. One of the cops, the white one, took out a small spiral notebook and licked his thumb and forefinger. He flipped the pages back and forth then stopped to read a notation. He fished through his pockets for a pen, first his pants then his shirt. He patted his pants again then took a pencil from behind his ear. His eyelids crept aloft.

"Are you Dermot Sparhawk?" he said, "the man who called in the B and E."

I told him he was correct on both counts. He touched the tip of the pencil on his tongue and scratched something into the notebook.

"Is this your place?"

He knew it wasn't my place.

"The apartment belongs to Mrs. Hennessey," I said.

"Right, right, Mrs. Hennessey's apartment." He studied the notebook. "Why didn't Mrs. Hennessey report the break-in?"

"She was too shaken by what happened."

"I bet she was," he said. "Why are you here?"

"I walked her home."

"You walked Mrs. Hennessey home." Another mark in the notebook. "From where?"

"From her son's wake at Clancy's."

"From her son's wake?" He looked up "What's her son's name?"

"Jeepster Hennessey."

"Hennessey?" For the first time his response was unrehearsed. "Hennessey, the guy that got killed?"

"Yes, sir, *that* Jeepster Hennessey."

"I've seen you around, Mr. Sparhawk." His arms dropped to his side. "You work in the neighborhood, yes?"

"I run Saint Jude Thaddeus food pantry."

"The pantry where Hennessey got murdered," he said. "You reported the murder that night and now you're reporting the B and E tonight." He put away the notebook. "What's your tie to the Hennesseys?"

"Jeepster was my godfather," I said.

"Godfather, huh?" He turned to make sure Mrs. Hennessey was out of earshot. "Hennessey spent more time on the inside than the outside, not what I'd call a great role model."

"He was great to me and my father," I said. "After the wake, I walked Mrs. Hennessey home."

The black cop came out of the bedroom on the move.

"We gotta wrap it up here. There's been another break-in, this time with an assault. A lady got knocked out."

"Where?"

"Starr King Court, come on, let's go."

"Another break-in in the projects, must be a full moon." The white cop turned to me. "I'll be in touch, Mister Sparhawk."

CHAPTER 12

The next morning I ate a late breakfast while watching a rerun of *The Dick Van Dyke Show*. Maury Amsterdam asked Mel how it felt to be a member of the FBI: fat, bald, and ignorant. I turned off the TV when the doorbell rang. Captain Pruitt was on the front porch. We went up to my apartment. He sat back on the couch, rested his feet on the hassock, stretched his arms overhead.

"Make yourself at home, Captain."

"I understand you walked Mrs. Hennessey home last night."

"I did. I walked her home after the wake," I said. "You heard about the break-in."

"The break-in got me thinking. Maybe Hennessey's killing was more complicated than I first thought. Maybe it wasn't a drug deal gone awry. Maybe there's more to it."

"Based on a break-in at his mother's? Come on, Captain. Apartments get broken into all the time in the projects," I said. "The bricks are overrun with second-story men. Some scumbag probably saw Jeepster's death notice in the paper and pulled the robbery during the wake."

"I don't think so." Pruitt got up and walked across the parlor. He drew a glass of water from the kitchen faucet, took a long drink, rinsed the glass, and placed it on the counter. "The burglars weren't burglars, not in the usual sense of the word. They were searching for something specific."

"They weren't burglars?"

"You catch on fast."

"The apartment was trashed. How can you say they weren't burglars?"

"Nothing was stolen." He filled the glass again and took another drink. "They didn't take the TV or DVD player, items an addict can sell for a quick fix. They didn't take the jewelry."

"Costume paste, it's worthless."

"Junkies'll take anything to sell. Fuckin' crackheads will filch the gum out of your mouth and try to sell it. No, Sparhawk, they didn't break in to steal something. They broke in to find something, and they didn't find it."

"How do you know all this?" I said. "How do you know they were looking for something specific and didn't find it? And why do you keep saying they? It was probably one guy, a junkie."

"The cabinets and drawers were turned inside out. The furniture was cut open. The ceiling was torn down, the carpeting ripped up. They were looking for something, I'm positive of that. And if they found what they were looking for, theyda stopped looking. They didn't stop. They kept at it until nothing was left to search."

"You keep saying 'they.' Why?"

"Speed, Sparhawk, speed. Two or three guys can rip through an apartment fast."

"I still don't get it."

"Hennessey had something they wanted, and they assumed he hid it at his mother's place. Hennessey was involved in something."

"Jeepster didn't live on O'Reilly Way, his mother did. Jeepster lived in Starr King Court. Why didn't they break into *that* apartment?"

"They did."

"What?"

"They broke into Hennessey's old apartment and did the same thing there. They trashed the place."

"Emma Hague lives there," I said.

"Emma's in the hospital." He laid the empty glass on the kitchen counter. "She's recovering from a whack on the head."

"Is she okay?"

"She'll be fine," he said. "Want to know something? I'm wondering if the whack on her head came from a telescoping baton. See what I'm getting at? See how things link together?"

"Not really."

I walked to the parlor window. The streets and sidewalks were quiet, no traffic or pedestrians in sight. At the top of the hill, a bus pulled over at Saint Francis de Sales. A few passengers got off. Pruitt stood next to me.

"We had two break-ins, one at Hennessey's old apartment, one at his mother's. We had two attacks, one against you, one against Emma Hague. I believe the crimes are connected." He moved the curtains and looked toward Hayes Square. "I no longer think Hennessey was killed in a drug deal gone bad. I think he was killed for something bigger."

"He tested positive for drugs," I said. "No disrespect, Captain. At first you said it was a drug killing, and now you're saying he was killed for something bigger. It sounds like a lot of speculating."

"Let me speculate further." He sat in the parlor chair and rested his feet on the hassock again. "I think Hennessey handed you something or told you something before he died. I think that's why the Irishmen attacked you. They wanted whatever it was he gave you or told you."

Or both.

"Jeepster didn't give me anything and didn't say anything," I said. "You're off track."

"No need to get defensive, Sparhawk. I'm just speculating."

"Speculate somewhere else if you don't mind. I have to go to work."

"Fine, I'll speculate somewhere else." Pruitt walked to the door and nodded. "Nice place, I'd hate to see somebody break in and destroy it."

I sat in the parlor after Pruitt left. I hated to lie.

CHAPTER 13

We had just finished saying the Lord's Prayer at the Saint Jude Thaddeus noontime AA meeting when my cell phone rang. I stepped outside to the archway and answered it. A man on the line cleared his throat.

"You wanna know about Hennessey's prison book club?" He coughed. "I don't got all day. You wanna know 'bout it? Yes or no?"

"Yes."

"You in Charlestown?"

I told him I was in Charlestown.

"Go to the Navy Yard, Gate 4. Go to the end of Terry Ring Way. There's a small building with bathrooms and pay phones. The phone facing the Tobin, answer it on the third ring." He coughed again. "You got fifteen minutes."

"How'd you get my number?"

"The clock's ticking, Sparhawk."

He hung up.

I played his game, following his directions exactly, ending up at the pay phone that faced the Tobin Bridge. I kept waiting for Alan Funt to jump out from behind the small building. The phone rang. Feeling like a fool I answered on the third ring. The same man as before told me to get into the cab when it arrived.

Sure enough, a cab made its way down Terry Ring Way and pulled over in front of me. I balked, not sure whether to get in. The cabbie powered down the rear window.

"You have two seconds to decide."

I climbed into the backseat and looked at the cabdriver's face in the rearview mirror. He wore a natural straw Optimo hat tugged low on his forehead. A black beard obscured his face. Oversized opaque sunglasses masked his eyes. He could have been ZZ Top's uncle. The cabbie drove down Terry Ring Way and turned right on Third Avenue to the north end of the Navy Yard and parked near Dock 8.

"I was friends with Jeepster Hennessey." He lowered the other rear window, letting the harbor air breeze pass through. "We were in a literary society inside Otisville."

"A literary society in prison?"

"I talk, you listen. On the outside, after Otisville, we kept it alive. We're known as the Oulipo Boys."

"The Oulipo Boys?"

"Yes."

I waited for him to say more. He didn't. He adjusted his sunglasses and smoothed the beard. The way he smoothed it, I wondered if it was fake. With a Plexiglas shield between us, I couldn't reach over and yank it. The front doors were locked. No way to get to him that way, either. Uncle ZZ was prepared.

"Are you one of the Oulipo Boys?"

He didn't answer.

"How'd you get my cell phone number?"

He passed a piece of paper through the money slot. The word Oulipo was written on it in pencil. Then he pointed to the door, his hand shaking. I opened the door and barely had my feet on the ground when he sped away, kicking dust into my face. First Pruitt, now this, the Ghost of Charlestown Future.

CHAPTER 14

The cabdriver had said something that nagged me. What was it? I stopped at the Boston Public Library in Copley Square and browsed a book on Oulipo. I learned that Oulipo was a French literary movement that began in Paris in 1960. I read more. The flipping pages affected my eyes like a hypnotist's swinging watch, dazing me into a stupor. I returned the book to the shelf and left the library more confused than when I arrived, a condition I got used to in college.

Out on Boylston Street I took out my cell phone and called my downstairs tenant Buck Louis and told him about the conversation with the cabbie. The Oulipo idea stirred Buck and he wanted to get working on it.

"Drink a double espresso and go for it," I said.

I walked east on Boylston Street. The mild sunny day contrasted with my mood, which grew stark and edgy. I stood on the sidewalk like a troll at a trestle, lousy tempered, pissed at the world. A man bumped into me. I gave him a look. What had gotten into me? I crossed the intersection of Clarendon Street, and the reason bubbled to the surface: booze.

Booze serenaded me with her siren song. Each tavern I passed whispered my name, inviting me in for a taste. The invites became demands, and I entertained those demands. I remembered something my sponsor Mickey said: Think the drink through. I remembered what happens to me when I drink. It was the same thing every time. I'd storm a bar like Rambo and stumble out like Rumbo. Mickey had quoted the Big Book to me last week, reading a passage on acceptance: My serenity is inversely proportional to my expectations. The higher my expectations, the lower my serenity. To an alcoholic newcomer, that meant: hope for a kiss and maybe you'll get laid.

I nearly died from alcoholic poisoning a month ago, so I didn't fool around. I called Mickey Pappas. He listened to my panicked rant, he calmed me down, he told me everything would be all right. We made plans to go to a meeting that evening, and the whiskey itch subsided.

From Boylston Street I cut through Boston Common to Downtown Crossing and walked from there to Glooscap's auto-body shop in Andrew Square. Glooscap wasn't in, which was fine, because I wasn't there to talk to Glooscap. I was there to talk to Harraseeket Kid. Kid shut off the welding torch when he saw me come in.

"I know that face," he said. "What's up?"

"I'm worried about Buck," I said. "I'm worried for his safety."

"His safety? Anyone fucks with Buck, I'll kill the bastard." Kid put down the welding gun. "What's happening?"

"It has to do with Jeepster Hennessey's murder."

"Hennessey's murder?" Kid said. "How does Hennessey's murder put Buck in danger?"

"Got a few minutes to talk?"

"Got all day."

I jumped up and sat on a workbench. Kid leaned against a pickup truck and waited for me to speak.

"There were two break-ins in the projects, both related to Jeepster Hennessey. Hennessey's mother's place got hit, and Jeepster's old apartment got hit."

"I'm with you so far."

"There have been two attacks. As you know, I got attacked at work."

"Yeah, in the parking lot."

"And a woman living in Jeepster's old apartment got attacked. Again, Jeepster is the link."

"I don't see it. What's Hennessey got to do with us?"

"I'm involved, Kid."

"Of course you're involved, he was your godfather."

"My involvement runs deeper," I said. "They might come at me again. The house is vulnerable, which means Buck is vulnerable. I'm afraid our house will get hit."

"Who's coming at you?" he asked, "And why?"

"I don't know who, not yet, but I think I know why. I've been meaning to tell you for a while now."

"Better late than never, let's hear it."

I told Kid the story. He was my cousin, he lived in my house, and he needed to know the truth. I told him about Oswego, the McSweeney key, George Meeks, Liam McGrew, Jackie Tracy, the cabdriver, the Oulipo Boys.

"You've been holding back a lot, Dermot boy." Kid whistled. "Don't worry none about the house. I keep a loaded Winchester under my bed. I'll lean it against the wall so I can get it faster."

"I have a military-issue forty-five."

"A forty-five will rip a hydrant out of the ground. Where'd you get it?"

"Glooscap gave it to me. My father smuggled it back from Vietnam, he took it off a dead second lieutenant. Glooscap gave it to me for protection when all this stuff happened." I thought about the break-ins and attacks. "Maybe I'm handling this the wrong way. Maybe I should surrender the McSweeney key to Jackie Tracy and tell him about Oswego. Then he'll call off the dogs."

"Fuck Jackie Tracy," Kid said. "No one fucks with us."

CHAPTER 15

That night I was watching *The Three Stooges*, a Curly before the dementia. The boys had gotten into yet another predicament and were mulling over their options. Moe concluded the problem wouldn't be easy to solve.

Moe: We're in a tough spot, men.

Larry: Yeah, it's gonna take brains to get out of this one.

Moe: That's why I said we're in a tough spot.

The doorbell punctuated Moe's punch line. Emma Hague was standing on the porch, her silver hair adrift in the breeze, her slinky shoulders slender and bare. I'd never seen her with her hair down. I let her inside. We went up to my apartment, where she said yes to a cup of tea. I lit a burner on the stove and put out a saucer and cup. I served tea. She added milk and sugar before taking a sip.

"Did you hear what happened to me?"

"Pruitt told me," I said. "Are you okay?"

"I'm okay, if a bit embarrassed." She wore white shorts and a navy tank top, showcasing her toned limbs. "I'm an FBI agent, Dermot, trained by the best in the field. Preparation is my mantra. I leave nothing to chance. My getting attacked? That's not supposed to happen to me."

"Stuff like that happens to everybody in the projects, Emma. There's no way to train or prepare your way out of it."

"You do fine back there." She sat next to me on the couch. "Just fine."

"I do fine because I got nothing they want. I'm a leper among cannibals," I said. "Don't forget, I got attacked too—and I grew up here."

"I know you did." She moved closer. "Do you think there's a connection between our attacks?"

"There could be," I said. "I don't know anything for sure."

We sat in the parlor on the couch, almost touching, saying nothing. The wall clocked ticked. My heart beat ten times between ticks. A car alarm sounded below. The 93 bus chuffed up Bunker Hill Street. It didn't stop out front. The faint drone of the Red Sox game drifted through an open window like a lazy fly ball in batting practice.

"I've made almost no progress on the Somali situation," Emma said. "You were right, Dermot, nobody will talk to me. What was the word you used when we first met? Balkanized? You said the Somalis were balkanized, no way I'd learn anything from them."

"Don't feel too bad. I asked around myself and learned nothing. The only person who talked to me was an old white guy, a life-long project man. What could he possibly know about Somalis?"

"What did he say?"

"He said they wore colorful scarves around their black heads, but what the fuck do you expect from a bunch of pontoon pirates."

Emma leaned forward and laughed. Her tank top fell away, baring her taut cleavage. She noticed my gaze and sat up. Our eyes met for a moment, then averted to something on the floor.

"Did Pruitt tell you about the break-in at Mrs. Hennessey's apartment?" I said. "Two apartments were broken into the same night, yours and Mrs. Hennessey's."

"He told me about Mrs. Hennessey's place, yes." Her slate eyes blinked. "Pruitt thinks the break-ins are connected."

"I know he does. Pruitt might be right."

"Do you think I was attacked because of Jeepster Hennessey?" She drew a breath. "Was I attacked because I live in Hennessey's old apartment?"

"Pruitt speculated about that. I don't know, it sounded far-fetched." I tried to think of another hilarious line so she'd lean forward again. I came up empty. "Maybe, he's on to something, maybe not."

"Do you think—No, it can't be."

"What?"

"What if the break-ins weren't random?" Her eyes focused. "What if the thieves were searching for the same thing in both apartments? They didn't find it at Mrs. Hennessy's, so they broke into my apartment next. Is that possible?"

"It's possible."

I was getting uncomfortable with all the questions about the break-ins. What did this have to do with Somali terrorism?

"Is there something you're not telling me?" She moved closer. "Dermot, you said you'd help me. Please talk to me."

"I really don't know shit about it, Emma."

CHAPTER 16

I was sitting in Buck Louis's apartment after a lousy night's sleep. Groggy and confused, my mind rehashed last night's conversation with Emma Hague. Something didn't feel right. It wasn't her words that bothered me, but her body language. She was holding something back. What was she really doing in Charlestown?

Buck rolled up to me.

"I struck out on the prison book club, couldn't crack the federal firewall. It didn't surprise me. The feds are all over online security these days, and they get better at it every year. No go on the book club."

"It was worth a try."

"I've been poking around on the Internet, learning about Oulipo." Buck popped a mini-wheelie, flushing his mahogany skin. Buck's energy counterbalanced my lethargy. "I'm just scratching the surface, D-man."

"Tell me about it."

"You sure you're up for it? You seem kinda tired today."

"I'll snap out of it, tell me what you learned."

"You asked for it," he said. "Oulipians love word games. They're experts at crosswords and Sudoku, things like that. They use codes and puzzles to communicate."

"Perfect for prisoners exchanging messages."

"Exactly," he said. "One guy wrote an entire novel with no Es, a writer name Georges Perec. I never heard of him till today. Imagine that? He actually wrote a book with no Es."

"What does that mean, no Es?"

"He never once used the letter *E* in the book. No *Es* is a re-

striction, what Oulipians call a lipogram. Their writing is con-
strained by lipograms. Perec restricted *E*s from his text. See what
I mean? No letter *E*, that was his lipogram," Buck said. "There's
more to Oulipo than no *E*s, a shitload more. One lipogram is called
the prisoners constraint, I kid you not."

"Where'd you learn all this?"

"The Internet, where else?" he said. "I ordered a book called
the *Oulipo Compendium,* overnighted it so it'll be here tomorrow.
When I get the compendium I'll dig in."

"You're off to a good start, Buck."

"Do you think this Oulipo stuff will help?"

"I don't know enough about it yet." I went to the hall stairs and
stopped. "Play around with the word Oswego using Oulipo codes.
See what you come up with."

"I'm on it."

I was stocking shelves in the food pantry with a Cape Verdean
named Amigo Joao. Joao is in his mid-fifties, fit as a triathlete, and
always helps me out. If I dropped dead today, Amigo Joao could
do my job while he fried linguica and cuttlefish, and still finish the
work faster than I do.

A Somali woman came into the pantry and waved to me. The
woman's name was Naddi, the same woman I'd nodded to a few
days ago in Starr King Court. She was wearing bright yellow silken
wraps that covered all of her head and most of her face. Only her
eyes remained unmasked, eyes that darted between Amigo Joao
and me, assessing the danger we might present.

"I have to talk to this lady, Amigo."

"Go talk to her, go, go, go," he said.

She asked to speak to me in private. We walked to the back of
the pantry where the hum of the refrigerator muffled our conversation. Naddi double-checked the area.

"I scared," she said in broken English. "I come to America to
be good American. No trouble, just good American. Don't want
trouble."

"What kind of trouble? What are you afraid off?" I asked. It didn't seem to register with her. "Are you scared?"

"A bad man is in my building. He say he will hurt my family. We must do what he say or he hurt us."

"Is he Somali?"

"Yes, from my country. He come to America before my family. He is boss man. He tell us what to do. No good. Not American."

"Is he planning to harm anyone?" I asked. Naddi didn't grasp it. "Will he hurt Americans?"

"Yes."

"Who is he, Naddi?"

"I must go. Trouble if seen with you."

Naddi wrapped the scarf higher on her face. Her eyes resumed their surveillance. She walked out of the pantry.

I wanted to tell Emma Hague about Naddi as soon as possible. I allowed twenty minutes for Naddi to clear the area and then walked to Emma's unit in Starr King Court. She answered the door wearing an NYU tee shirt and shorts. I wondered if she checked the peephole before opening the door. Her silver mane fell to her shoulders in a tousled way. She closed the door behind me when I stepped in.

"What's up, Dermot?" She sounded tired. "Sorry I'm a mess, I just woke up."

She looked tremendous as a mess.

"I just spoke to a Somali woman named Naddi. She's a member of the food pantry. Naddi told me that a Somali man plans to hurt Americans. I don't know what she meant by that. I do know she's scared."

"What's the man's name?"

"Naddi refused to tell me," I said. "She was too afraid."

"What is Naddi's address?"

"She lives two doors down the hall." I gave Emma the address. "Please be careful, she's terrified of this man."

"I'll protect her." She walked to the stove. "Coffee?"

"Yes," I said.

After we finished the coffee, I asked Emma if she'd like to get out of the projects for a while, to go out for a bite to eat. She said yes and asked for a minute to get ready. I wanted to ask if I could watch. Like the Oulipo men, I restrained myself.

It had to be tough for Emma, a professional woman with a promising career, living in New England's largest federal housing development, a warren of violence and addiction, and now a possible cell of terrorism. What was the FBI thinking? Why did they assign her here? It made no sense. She came out of her bedroom, casually dressed in jeans and a tee shirt, her hair in a ponytail. I opened the apartment door and we left Starr King Court and headed for my car on Medford Street.

"I know a cozy tavern that serves hot beef sandwiches with salt potatoes," I said. "You won't be disappointed."

CHAPTER 17

We drove downtown and parked in a concrete city garage behind Saint Anthony Shrine. From the garage we went on foot to the Cazenovia Club, walking past the statue of Robert Burns in Winthrop Square with his collie dog and tam-o'-shanter. We took Lincoln Street to Utica Street. Dowdy Aunt Bea was wiping down the bar when we came in, her bib apron spotless and pressed, her beehive hairdo stacked atop her head. She looked up when she heard us enter.

"Goodness gracious me, things keep getting better for you," she said. "Tell me please, what is your beautiful friend's name?"

"I'll assume you're talking to me, not her," I said. "Aunt Bea, this is Emma Hague. Emma, Aunt Bea."

"Emma Hague, a most lovely name. *Gezondheid Nederlands?*" Aunt Bea saluted Emma. "My family tree traces back to The Netherlands, DeBeers is my surname."

"A wonderful name," Emma said. "My father immigrated from Holland."

"Emma and I will take a table, Aunt Bea. We are starved for one of your legendary homemade meals."

"A table, then."

Emma and I ordered hot beef sandwiches and salt potatoes. She drank Genesee cream ale, I drank Coke. Aunt Bea was performing triple duty today, waitress, bartender, and cook. It wasn't too busy and she seemed to enjoy serving us. I turned to Emma.

"You seem to have recovered from that thump on the head," I said. "Are you feeling okay since the break-in?"

"I'm feeling fine. No problems, no headache." She sipped

Genesee from a pewter stein. "I won't let my guard down again. I'll be ready for whatever happens next." She centered the mug on a cardboard coaster. "I won't get caught flatfooted again."

"Flatfooted?"

"I have to be proactive, ready for their next move. I have to anticipate: When will they come back? When will they rob my apartment again? Proactive, see what I mean? People in my line of work have to be ready for everything that comes our way. We have to be prepared."

Pruitt said the intruders were looking for something specific, something they couldn't find. No doubt they were looking for the McSweeney key.

"You don't have to worry, Emma. They won't be back."

"How can you be sure?"

"I . . . ah." I blew it. "It's just a feeling."

"Just a feeling?" She licked Genessee foam from her lips. "Do you know something I don't know? Because I'd never tell someone not to worry based on a feeling. What aren't you telling me? What do you know that I don't know?"

"Not a damn thing." I said. "I just figured they won't break into the same place twice, that's all. I'm talking about the odds, Emma. Lightning never hits the same spot twice. They won't break into Mrs. Hennessy's place again, either."

"How can you be sure?" she said.

"I'm not sure, I'm guessing." I waved to the bar. "Aunt Bea, can we have two more drinks over here?" I turned back to Emma. "There's only one thing I'm sure of, and that's that Aunt Bea makes the best apple strudel in Boston."

We sat quietly inside the Cazenovia Club. Aunt Bea delivered the drinks. A few minutes later she served apple strudel, topped with vanilla ice cream. Aunt Bea must have sensed the tension. She walked away without saying a word. We finished the strudel.

"You must be proud of what you've accomplished," Emma said.

"What are you talking about?"

"The way you clawed your way out of the projects," she said. "I've only lived in the projects a little while, but it's been long enough now to know how difficult it must have been. Getting out the way you did, it's remarkable."

"You got it wrong, Emma. I didn't claw my way out, I lucked out," I said. "My great aunt left me the two-family house on Bunker Hill Street. The house was a gift."

"You have a job, you went to college."

"Yeah, I went to college and majored in hydrology, got straight As." I spread my hands on the table. "I went to college because I played football and Boston College gave me an athletic scholarship. They wanted me because I sacked quarterbacks, not because I aced the SAT. As for the job, a Jesuit priest got it for me, one of my professors at B.C. I'm just a lucky bastard, Emma, nothing more."

"Don't belittle your achievements, Dermot. You own a home—"

"I own a home that my aunt handed me."

"Still, you own a—"

"Sure, I own it. And I have a handicapped tenant who gets Section-8 money and pays me twice the rent I would have charged him, and a cousin living in the basement who takes care of the property. Can't you see it, Emma? The whole thing fell into my lap. Two months ago I was drinking Old Thompson faster than they could distill it. Today I'm sober, thanks to a friend in AA. I didn't earn that either. It was given to me, another unmerited gift."

"Why not take a little credit for your sobriety?"

"I can't."

We finished the drinks. I stacked the plates and put them in a bus bucket and went to the bar to pay Aunt Bea.

"Where's Skinny Atlas?" I said. "I wanted to buy him a Vandermint coffee."

"We won't be seeing Skinny Atlas any time soon. He had an alcoholic seizure. The poor soul fell off the barstool and hit his head on the floor. Happened a few days ago. The medics wheeled him out to an ambulance."

"Sorry to hear that."

"He was unconscious, knocked out or passed out, don't know which. They tell me he's recovering nicely, drying out at a wet-brain hospital in Jamaica Plain." Aunt Bea leaned over the bar and whispered. "Your girlfriend is something special."

"Yeah, she sure is something."

CHAPTER 18

I woke up the next morning thinking about the washed-out blonde I saw at Jeepster's wake. She'd been sitting alone in the corner of the funeral parlor, talking to no one, drying her tears with a Kleenex. She never stood to greet mourners, so she probably wasn't family, though she grieved as if she were. Maybe a girlfriend?

I wanted to talk to her.

Jeepster used to drink at Finbar's Saloon in Hayes Square, so I went there to ask a few questions. I swung open the saloon door and waited for my eyes to adjust to the darkness. Once they adjusted to the darkness, they then adjusted to the clientele, who were old, drunk, and Irish. It's a typical Townie taproom, a quiet place where nobody says a word and where the favorite button on the remote is mute, a place where you might hear a pin drop, but never a dime.

Tall Ed drew a pint of Pabst Blue Ribbon for a patron slumped on a stool at the far end of the bar. Long-limbed and lean, Tall Ed had been a promising lightweight fighter in his day. Townies once called him the white Sandy Saddler. My father told me the nickname had more to do with his build than his punch. I sat and waited for him to come my way, which he finally did. He leaned on the bar in front of me, his eyes averted.

"Sorry, Dermot, no whiskey for you today. You can have beer, but no whiskey. Boss's orders." He wiped down the bar, not looking up. "How 'bout a bottle of Narragansett? Is a bottle of 'gansett okay? No? How 'bout a Pabst draft?"

"I'll have a Coke."

"A Coke?" He stopped wiping. "Come on, Dermot, have a beer. It's summertime. It's hot out there. A beer can't do no harm."

"Coke."

"Jeez, I didn't mean to offend you. It's just, the last time you were here you went kinda, ah, never mind," Tall Ed said. "You ain't on the wagon, are you? We all hit bad streaks, Dermot. You'll get your bearings back."

"I hope so," I said. "I saw you at Jeepster's wake."

"Big crowd, wasn't it? The Townies came out in droves for Jeepster, gave him a right send-off." He flipped the bar towel over his shoulder. "The good die young, don't they? I'll miss Jeepster, he was a good tipper."

"He was always a generous guy."

"Benny the bookie's gonna miss him, too. Benny just left, said he might need to get himself a second job, Jeepster being dead. He was joking, I think." Tall Ed poured me a Coke. Barroom Coke tastes the best. "Yeah, Benny's gonna miss him. Jeepster bet on everything: baseball, hockey, hoops, college or pro, it didn't matter. Fuckin' guy'd wager the number of passengers on the ninety-three bus driving by. He loved betting the Patriots, the Pats were his favorite. Over-unders, birdcages, teases, parlays, he bet 'em all."

"He needed the juice." I drank the Coke. "Do you know his girlfriend, the blonde at the wake?"

"No, not really," he said. "Jeepster and her came in every once in a while, not often. They'd both be stiff when they got here, looking to keep drinking till last call."

"His girlfriend, do you remember her name or where she came from?"

"Don't remember her name. I think she came from Southie." He topped off my Coke. "I remember now, she said she grew up in Southie, don't know if she still lives there." He leaned over the sink and broke up ice cubes with a metal scoop. "Now that I think of it, her name was Sherri. Jeepster came in here one night and sang *Sherri*, real shrilly, just like Frankie Valli. Guy sang up a storm that night. Why you asking?"

"I saw her at the wake and she seemed upset," I said. "I'm just curious who she is."

"Her name's Sherri, that's all I know."

Tall Ed stepped away to answer the phone. I finished the Coke and left.

From Finbar's I walked to Mrs. Hennessey's building on O'Reilly Way. She rang me inside and waited for me at her apartment door.

"I've been meaning to call you." She hugged me, planting her foot on the door to keep it from closing. "Thanks for everything. Getting me the room at the B&B, cleaning up my apartment with the youth group, you are wonderful."

"I didn't do anything. My buddy was glad you stayed at his place, and the kids did the cleanup." We went into her apartment. "Is it okay to ask a few questions about Jeepster? I don't want to be disrespectful, asking so soon after his passing."

"It's good for me to talk about him, that's what Father Dominic told me. And besides, I want to keep Jeepster's memory alive." She walked to the kitchen. "Want a glass of lemonade? I squeezed it fresh today."

"Lemonade sounds good," I said. "I understand Jeepster had a lady friend."

"It seems that he did, a woman named Sherri. She attended the wake and funeral." Mrs. Hennessey handed me a cold glass. Her gaunt face was ashen and dull, looking worse than it did at the wake. "I didn't know Sherri. I met her for the first time at the wake. She seemed nice enough."

"Do you remember her last name or where she lives?"

"I'm sure she told me." She placed the lemonade pitcher on the kitchen table. "She said she lived in South Boston. Yes, that's what she said, South Boston. She works over there, too."

The fresh lemonade puckered my lips. She refilled my glass from the pitcher. I drained it in one gulp. My visit to Finbar's must have triggered the thirst. I thought about the wake again.

"Do you have the register?"

"Excuse me?"

"I think it's called a register," I said. "The book the guests sign when they enter the funeral home."

"Of course, the register," she said. "The undertaker gave it to me just the other day, once the bill was settled. That Clancy is a rascal. I think he was holding it as collateral until he got his money, the pinchfist. Give me a second and I'll get it."

She disappeared into the bedroom. I heard a drawer slide open, a closet door close, and Mrs. Hennessey came out of the room holding the book.

"Here, I have the register." She held it against her bosom. "Father Dominic blessed it for me."

"He's a good man, Father Dominic," I said. "Can I see it?"

"I don't see why not." She held it out. "Take a gander."

It didn't take long to find what I was looking for. Sherri's name was written on the first page: Sherri Anne McGillicuddy, O'Callaghan Way, South Boston. I handed Mrs. Hennessey the register, thanked her, and left for South Boston.

I rode the Red Line to Andrew Square and walked from Andrew to O'Callaghan Way, deep inside the Old Colony housing development. Like Charlestown, the Southie streets are named for war veterans killed in action. I found Sherri's building, found her unit, and knocked on the door. An older man wearing a frayed Bruins sweatshirt answered. I asked to speak to Sherri McGillicuddy.

"Who're you?" he said. "You ain't from the neighborhood."

"My name is Dermot Sparhawk," I said. "Jeepster Hennessey was my godfather."

"So what? We all got godfathers."

"I understand Sherri was seeing Jeepster. I wanted to talk to her about him."

"About what? Sherri can't tell you nothin', she wasn't his wife."

"I'd like to talk to her."

"They weren't married, son, just dating." He reached for the door. "You wanna know about Jeepster Hennessey, go ask his mother."

"I already talked to her." I put my foot in the door and stopped it from closing. "I'm not looking for trouble, Mr. McGillicuddy. Jeepster was an important man in my life and now he's dead. I want to know more about him, that's all."

"Are you some kind of fag or something? Fuck off."

He slammed the door and locked it. I loved project people. They never dither, they're always to the point. I walked out of the tenement onto O'Callaghan Way and headed for Andrew Square. When I got to Dorchester Ave, someone yelled my name. A man trotted toward me. He reached out and shook my hand.

"You're Dermot, right? I heard you speak at the noontime meeting in Charlestown, heard you a coupla times. I'm Sean Dorgan. Whata ya doing over here in Southie?"

"I wanted to talk to Sherri McGillicuddy, but she wasn't home."

"Sherri ain't home 'cause she's working," he said. "She works at Circle Liquors over at the rotary, close to Saint Monica's. I've seen you at Saint Monica's, too."

"I've been to Saint Monica's a couple of times, good meetings."

"If you see Sherri, tell her we're saving her a seat."

"Sure thing," I said. "Thanks, Sean."

I cut through McDonough Way past Saint Monica's to Circle Liquors, where Sherri McGillicuddy was standing at the cash register ringing in a case of Old Milwaukee beer. Her bleached hair was twisted into a pigtail, serving as a nonsurgical facelift, pulling her face tight. I grabbed a bag of peanuts and a bottle of Coke and placed them on the counter. She rang it up and bagged it.

"Jeepster Hennessey was my godfather," I said to her.

"Jeepster." She handed me the change.

"I'd like to talk to you about him." I stepped aside to allow a customer through. "It won't take long."

"Jeepster was your godfather?" She handed the man a receipt to sign. "You must be Dennis. Come back in half an hour, I'm on break then."

"It's Dermot."

I walked to Carson Beach and sat on the seawall. Dorchester Bay had retreated to low tide, giving the gulls plenty of shoreline to peck and claw. A slim woman in a loose tank top jogged on the boardwalk. I thought of Emma Hague. A lifeguard checked his watch and glanced up at the sun. I walked back to the liquor store and found Sherri McGillicuddy on the sidewalk smoking a cigarette.

"I appreciate the time," I said.

"Jeepster talked about you and your father, especially after a few drinks." She flicked the cigarette into rotary traffic. "He reminisced when he drank."

"I know he did," I said. "How long were you seeing him?"

"Not long, he only got out a month ago. That's when we met, a month ago, down at a cookout in Marshfield," she said. "This guy I knew from D Street moved down there, threw a big party. That's where I met Jeepster, at the party."

"You only knew him a month?"

"Yeah, a month. A month is longer than it sounds. Ask anyone who did a month bit at Nashua Street, and they'll tell you, a month's a long time. It ain't really the time that's important, it's the quality of time. We had quality time, me and Jeepster. I liked him and he liked me. A woman can tell these things." Maybe women can tell these things, but she still sounded defensive. "He loved to laugh. He enjoyed a drink or two, sometimes three. Liked to gamble, he always bet the Red Sox. We'd go to different bars and root for the Sox. The West Coast games were the best. They'd run late, take you past last call." A car tooted from the rotary and Sherri waved. "Sometimes he'd play cards on Friday nights, stud poker in barroom booths. Jeepster loved poker, seven card stud was his favorite. He didn't go for that Texas Hold'em bullshit. Straight poker, that was his game."

"Jeepster liked the action."

"He had a positive attitude, upbeat."

"Upbeat?" I'd never heard Jeepster described as upbeat before. Crazy, but not upbeat. "What do you mean by a positive attitude?"

"Jeepster dreamed big. He kept saying, 'We're getting out of the projects, Sherri. We're moving to Florida or Rio de Janeiro.' That's down there in Brazil." She lit another cigarette. "Didn't matter to me where we lived, the projects, Brazil, whatever, it didn't matter."

"You just wanted to be with him."

"Yeah, that's right, just wanted to be with him. Jeepster wanted out of here. He was sick of the snow. That's what he always said, that he hated the snow. He wanted to live somewhere warm."

"Couldn't blame him for wanting that." I sniffed her burning tobacco. "Moving to Florida or Rio takes money. Where was he getting the money?"

"I don't know. I know he didn't have the money yet. He was getting it soon, that's what he said. He kept saying, 'be ready to go Sherri honey,' like we had to get out of here fast when the time came. We'll be flying to a warmer climate, he'd say, basking in the sunshine year-round." She exhaled smoke through a single nostril. The other one must have been busted. "For all I know Rio de Janeiro was nothing more than a fantasy, something to beat the boredom in prison. Didn't matter, I loved listening to him talk, even if it was a pipedream. With his big ideas, Jeepster was an exciting guy to be around. I miss him."

"I miss him, too," I said. "The guy in Marshfield, the one who threw the party, what's his name?"

"Devin," she said. "Jimmy Devin. I know him from D Street, not Marshfield. I'm no high roller on the Irish Riviera."

"I have one more question and I'll be on my way," I said.

"I'm in no rush. It's nice to talk about Jeepster."

"Jeepster tested positive for drugs," I said. "According to his probation officer, he flunked his last urine test. Do you know anything about that?"

"The drug test, what a joke."

"What do you mean?"

"The drug test didn't mean nothin'. Jeepster and me smoked a few bones every once in a while, that's all." She puffed. "That's why he flunked the piss test, 'cause of we smoked pot. Jeepster swore off the hard stuff when he got outta jail, never touched pills or needles, never sniffed nothin' either. We smoked a little weed, that's all. We didn't do drugs."

CHAPTER 19

According to real estate documents filed at town hall last year, Jimmy Devin bought a waterfront house on Ocean Street in the Brant Rock section of Marshfield. The house was built atop creosote timbers, sitting high above the Atlantic whitecaps. I parked my rusty Plymouth Acclaim in front and rapped on his oak door using the brass shamrock knocker. Ten seconds later the oak slab opened.

A bald man with a crimson complexion stood in the doorway. Broken blood vessels mapped his pocked nose. Red eyes added fury to his ruddy face. Dollars to donut holes, his coloring came from a jug, not the sun. Devin was not thrilled to see me.

"What're you selling, Girl Scout cookies?"

"Sorry to intrude, Mr. Devin. My name is Dermot Sparhawk. Jeepster Hennessey was my godfather."

"Congratulations."

"I want to talk to you about him."

"About what?"

"He came to a party here earlier this summer." I was losing Devin, I needed a hook. "Jeepster served in the marines with my father, that's the connection. My father picked Jeepster to be my godfather. They were best friends."

"I knew most of Jeepster's Vietnam friends." He almost stopped scowling. "Your father, was his nickname Chief?"

"Yes."

"I remember him. He came down from Canada."

"Correct."

"Ah, fuck it, come in." He led me inside, while he talked over his shoulder. "I captained a skimmer on the Mekong Delta, part of the Brownwater Navy, got a Silver Star. Jeepster and me got to be friends after the war, met at a veteran's post in Dorchester. He introduced me to your old man. A lot of Nam guys are gone now, either the nuthouse or Agent Orange."

"I know." Agent Orange got my father. Tequila sunrises in the morning, Tango at noon, screwdrivers at night. He didn't lack for Vitamin C. "My father told me the same thing, about the guys ending up in the nuthouse."

We walked to the back of the house and stepped into a large rectangular room. Jalousie windows framed the outside walls. The glass slats were opened at forty-five degree angles, letting in the salt air. The ocean views beat anything a home entertainment system offered.

"Want a drink?"

I told Devin I was fine, that I didn't want a drink. He said he understood and then said something about it not being sundown yet. We sat on padded chairs facing the water.

"I run a food pantry in Charlestown," I said. "Jeepster Hennessey died in the food pantry. He collapsed at my feet, stabbed in the back."

"I heard about it. You work for the church," he said. "I liked Jeepster, liked him a lot. So, why are you here?"

"I was the last person to see Jeepster alive." Soft blue waves glided ashore, white sails sagged on anchored sloops, a bevy of seagulls flocked in the offing. "I heard Jeepster met his girlfriend at your party."

"His girlfriend?" Devin laughed. "You must mean the lush from the liquor store with the nice ass?"

"Yes, Sherri," I said.

"I guess he met her here. I knew her from South Boston. She came to the party with a few Southie people."

"Sherri said Jeepster was into something big. He told her to be ready to move fast. He had serious money coming in."

"Jeepster said that?"

"That's what Sherri told me," I said. "A lot of money, enough to move to Rio."

"Rio de Janeiro, no shit? Boy, that Jeepster was full of surprises. Let me tell you something for a fact. There's no way in hell Jeepster had that kind of money, no fuckin' way."

"That's what Sherri said."

"Well holy shit, I guess that makes it true. Too bad he died before he got down there." Devin stared at me. "I still don't see where I fit in."

"Where would he get that kind of money?"

"How the fuck should I know?"

"I figured you might know, because you came into quite a sum yourself. You moved from D Street to the Irish Riviera," I said. "Where'd you get the cash?"

"The fuck did you say?" His face darkened. "Who do you think you are, sticking your nose into my business?"

"It's just a question."

"Where I got my money ain't none of your fuckin' concern, kid." He stood. "Now get out of here."

"Take it easy, Devin. Slow down."

"Slow down, my ass. Get outta here."

"I apologize, I was out of line."

"Fuckin' right, you were out of line."

"I came here to talk about Jeepster, my godfather. I want to know who killed my godfather. I wasn't sticking my nose into your business." I stood next to him. "I don't care about your business, Devin. I thought there might be a connection, you and Jeepster scoring big sums of cash."

"There's no connection. First off, Jeepster didn't score nothin' that I know of. Second, my windfall ain't no mystery," he said. "I sold my uncle's house in City Point, got a bundle for it, not that it's any of your goddamned business. He died last year and left me the house. Does that answer your question?"

"I'm sorry. With your new oceanfront house, I thought you and Jeepster might've hit it big on a get-rich-quick scheme."

"There's no such thing as a get-rich-quick scheme, kid. You're from Charlestown, you oughta know that."

"I only know one thing, someone killed Jeepster. I want to know who killed him, and I won't stop digging till I find out."

"I can't help with that," he said. "But, ah—"

"But what?"

"Jeepster mentioned a poker game." Devin's face cooled from purple to crimson. "He was scraping together money for a high-stakes poker game. I don't know the when or where of it. I don't even know if he got into the game. He needed fifty grand for an entrance fee."

"Fifty grand?"

"Yup, and he needed it up front. No fifty grand, no seat at the table."

The wind kicked up, the jibs billowed, waves slapped the gunwales.

"Does the name McSweeney mean anything to you?"

"I knew a Father McSweeney in Southie, over at Our Lady of Good Voyage. Why?"

"What about Oswego?"

"Why?" he said. "Oh shit, never mind. I don't want to know."

CHAPTER 20

On the second Saturday of each month at ten in the morning we run the first of our two monthly food-pantry distributions. Today the line was long, extending beyond a basketball court known as Kane's Cage on Corey Street. Naddi was standing at the front of the line with her young daughter, and at the end of the line stood Emma Hague, accompanied by no one. I still found it strange, Emma Hague waiting in a breadline.

With the volunteers stationed and the food organized in rows, I opened the pantry doors and the patrons marched in, filling the hall and signing the log. Ninety-nine percent of the clients expressed thanks, not always in English but always in earnest. Then there's the scant 1 percent: the whiners. Complaints from whiners flow like laments from mourners. Emma came into the pantry last. I handed her the clipboard with the sign-up sheet.

"Naddi's here today. She's up front," I said. "Have you talked to her?"

"Not yet."

Emma told me that she hadn't had the opportunity to get Naddi alone, that she didn't want to place Naddi in any danger by being too conspicuous. I told Emma that she was playing it smart being careful. I nodded toward the front of the line.

"Naddi is wearing the orange wrap. Her daughter is standing next to her."

"What's her daughter's name?"

"Ayanna," I said.

"Ayanna is so young. How old is she, five or six?" Emma said.

"I have to be extra cautious, Dermot. I want no harm to come
to them."

Two hours later and three tons of food lighter, the distribution
ended. I shut off the fluorescents, bolted the doors, and headed for
home. I had just rounded the corner onto Bunker Hill Street when
an unmarked police car stopped next to me. Captain Pruitt got out
and asked if I had learned anything new on Jeepster Hennessey's
murder. I told him I hadn't. He sat on the hood of the black Crown
Vic.

"Come on, Sparhawk, you must've heard something back
there," he said. "The bricks talk, especially to bricklayers like you."

"I haven't heard a thing." Then I remembered my chat with
Sherri McGullicuddy in front of the liquor store. "Jeepster's drug
test, how accurate was it?"

"It was completely accurate. Why?"

"Did the test identify *which* drugs were in his system, the types
of drugs he was using?" I leaned against a lamppost. "I heard Jeepster was only smoking pot, no hard stuff."

"Hennessey was an ex-con, out on probation."

"I know that, Captain."

"If Hennessey got caught doing drugs on probation, any drugs,
he goes back to prison. We're talking narcotics here, Sparhawk.
Your godfather broke the law, end of discussion."

"No argument from me, I'm just wondering what his urine
showed."

"Why?" Pruitt slid off the hood to his feet. "Are you saying it
was okay if Hennessey smoked marijuana?"

"I'm not saying anything," I said. "I'm asking what his urine
showed."

"I ask again, why?"

"It has to do with his murder. If Jeepster got hooked on oxy or
heroin, something addictive, then he probably got back into crime
to support the habit."

"Go ahead, I'm listening."

"If he was hooked on hard stuff, he might have robbed a dealer, which might have got him stabbed." I shouldered away from the lamppost. "But if he was just smoking pot, he wouldn't be in high-risk situations. It's not like buying heroin. There's a difference between pot and heroin."

"Is that your theory, Sparhawk? If Hennessey was smoking dope, he's a choirboy?" Pruitt snorted. "When did you become a social worker?"

"All I'm saying is if Jeepster tested positive for marijuana only, he probably didn't get killed in a drug deal gone bad."

"A little doobie'll do ya, is that it?"

"You know what I'm saying."

"You're saying that potheads are pretty harmless, that they don't turn to violent crime to support their habit." He snorted again, this time harder. "Hell, let's not even call it a habit. Let's call it a hobby, like flying a kite or flicking a yo-yo."

"I get it, it's a lousy theory."

"Not so fast, Sparhawk, I happen to agree with you. Potheads present no threat to society. As a rule they aren't dangerous." He clapped his big black hand on my shoulder. "Tell you what I'll do, I'll call Hennessey's probation officer and see what he says about the piss test."

"It can't hurt to find out."

"How's Special Agent Hague doing? Is she making any progress on the Somali angle?"

"None I can see. I told her about a Somali woman who might be able help. Emma hasn't talked to her yet."

"Emma, is it?" He smiled. "Hague is a fine-looking woman."

"She sure is."

CHAPTER 21

Buck Louis was waiting at the door when I got home. He said he wanted to show me something and invited me into his apartment.

"It has to do with the *Oulipo Compendium*. I've been reading it and I might have found something." He opened the book to a dog-eared page. "It's called homovocalism."

"Homo what?"

"Homovocalism. It works like this." He grabbed a pen and a pad of paper. "You extract the vowels from one word and make another word using the same vowels."

"You better show me."

"Remember you told me to play around with the word Oswego, to decipher it using Oulipo techniques? One way to decipher is with homovocalism. Watch."

He wrote the word Oswego on a piece of paper and applied homovocalism to it.

OSWEGO

O E O

OREGON

"If you isolate the vowels O-E-O, you can build a word like Oregon." He spun his wheelchair to face me. "There's a place called Oswego Lake in Oregon. Of course, you can spell the word Oreo, too."

"You're getting a handle on Oulipo."

"Like I said before, Oulipo uses constraints, restrictions, and patterns on words and letters. They like palindromes and anagrams. You ever try to write a palindrome? Anagrams aren't too hard, for example: latent talent. As for palindromes, forget it. I'm learning the other constraints in the compendium."

"I think I understand homovocalism. The other stuff you said, I can't get my head around it, it's too abstract. Give me something to hang my hat on, something concrete."

"Let's start with a basic Oulipo pattern, the *S* plus seven," he said. "The *S* plus seven is simple to understand."

"I hope so."

"Pay attention. With *S* plus seven, you replace every noun in a text with the noun seven after it in the dictionary." He wrote out an *S* plus seven pattern to show me. "For example: Call me Ishmael. Some years ago becomes, Call me islander. Some yeggs ago."

"*Moby-Dick*," I said, "Translated with *S* plus seven, the story becomes the tale of a Caribbean safecracker."

"I get it, a yegg is a safecracker. There's more, lots more. I can't give it to you all at once." He rolled back a foot. "Any questions?"

I wanted to ask him if he had a large bottle of extra-strength Excedrin.

"I don't know enough yet to have questions," I said. "Keep working on it, Buck. I have a feeling it'll come in handy."

Jackie Tracy lived on the other side of Bunker Hill in a single-family unattached house with a porch and a driveway. It was seven o'clock in the evening when I knocked on his door. He stepped back when he saw me, then led me inside.

"Sit down, Dermot," he said. "What'll it be, beer, a shooter? Both?"

"How about a glass of Charlestown water?"

"I almost forgot, you're on the wagon. Don't matter, I'm not drinking tonight, anyway." He poured me a glass of water and sat in his recliner. "My wife is out to bingo, over there in Somerville. It's just the two of us."

"You could put a bullet in my head and nobody would know."

"You're a real fuckin' hoot. I know you didn't come here to crack me up. What do you want?"

"A chunk of Sky Bar."

"Fuck Sky Bars. I gained twenty pounds," he said. "I'm back

on the butts. My doctor told me my arteries are clogged, probably gotta get a fuckin' bypass. Anyway, what do you want?"

"I asked around about Jeepster Hennessey."

"Who hasn't?"

"I heard he was trying to get into a big poker game, a high-stakes game with a fifty-thousand-dollar entrance fee."

"Who said that?" His eyes widened. "The poker game, who told you that?"

"You seem interested," I said.

"I am interested." He tilted the recliner forward. "This is important, Dermot, where did you hear about the game?"

"Around town," I said. "Probably just a rumor."

"Rumor, my ass," he said, then wiped his face with an open palm. "I don't get it. What's your interest in this alleged poker game?"

"Jeepster was getting ready to leave town, as in adios Charlestown," I said. "He was moving away for good, down to Rio. Supposedly, he had a windfall coming in, enough money to make the break."

Jackie Tracy rested his forearms on his thighs. He took a breath and his face returned to a pinker state. He sat back again.

"This information is serious." He clapped his hands together, they made no sound. "I'm gonna tell you a few things, so listen real good. I know a few people, rich fucks with lots of money." He rubbed his chin. "Hennessey agreed to deliver certain goods to them for a price. He never made the delivery."

"Enough money to set him up in Rio for life?"

"Enough money for two lifetimes of penthouse living down there," Jackie said. "But he never delivered the goods."

"These people you're talking about, did they pay him in advance?"

"No, of course not," he said. "They made a down payment of sorts, you know, a claim on the goods. They held back the real payoff till the delivery of the goods."

"Jeepster got killed and the delivery never happened."

"Exactly right," he said. "We thought you mighta stumbled onto these goods, maybe unknowingly. Now we're not so sure."

"You thought this because I was the last person to see Jeepster alive?"

"That's right," Jackie said. "For now, you're off the hook."

"Is it possible Jeepster sold the goods to someone else for the Rio stake?"

"Not likely." Jackie reclined again. "The goods have a particular value to a particular buyer, a market of one man. The man has associates, people protecting his interests so he don't get screwed."

"Is it possible that these people got angry at Jeepster, *believing* he sold the goods to someone else?" *What was I trying to say?* "Would these associates come after Jeepster if they thought he sold the goods to someone else?"

"It's possible, yes."

"Would they kill him?"

"No," he said. "They needed Hennessey alive."

"They needed him alive to deliver the goods," I said. "Jeepster couldn't deliver the goods if he was dead."

"Something like that, yeah."

"Then these people wouldn't have stabbed Jeepster in the back."

"You catch on fast, college boy." Jackie got off the recliner and walked me to the front door. "By the way, I heard something interesting. Liam McGrew didn't sic the two Irishmen on you."

"How do you know?"

"Just a rumor I heard, probably nothing to it."

CHAPTER 22

I was rotating food in the pantry with Amigo Joao when Mrs. Hennessey called me on my cell phone and asked me to stop by her apartment.

"I hate to be a pain in the neck, Dermot. I need your help with something. I hope you don't mind."

"Of course I don't mind. I'll come by after work," I said. "See you at six."

Amigo Joao and I grabbed a bite to eat at a sub shop on Medford Street, splitting a large pepperoni pizza, a large steak bomb, and a two-liter bottle of Coke.

"Hmm, very good, good, good, good" he said. "Dessert?"

"Dessert sounds good to me. Pie?"

"Pie is good, yes, yes, yes."

We washed down the pizza with Hostess apple pies and coffee. I dropped him off on Decatur Street and drove to Mrs. Hennessey's on O'Reilly Way.

She let me in and poured me a cup of coffee. Her hand shook as she poured. She then picked up a stack of mail from the end table and held it up.

"Mister Rooney at the post office forwards Jeepster's mail to me. He's such a nice man, Mr. Rooney." She blinked and brought herself back to the present. "Anyway, the reason I asked you to drop by is that Jeepster got an overdue notice from Mystic Piers Storage."

"I know the place," I said. "It's on the waterfront out past the Tobin Bridge."

"He owes them two months back rent."

"I'll take care of it."

"That's a generous offer, and I appreciate it." She tapped the overdue notice in her hand. "That's not why I called you. I called you because something strange happened."

"Strange in what way?"

"According to Mister Rooney, Jeepster kept a post office box in Charlestown." She kept tapping the letter. "I was listed as next of kin on the application."

"Makes sense."

"Why would Jeepster keep a post office box when he had a home address? Why two mailing addresses?"

"Lots of people do that."

"The overdue notice came to his post office box, not his Starr King Court address like the rest of his mail." She looked at the notice. "Mister Rooney said he almost forgot about Jeepster's box until the late notice arrived. Another odd thing, the name on the envelope is McEwan, not Hennessey."

"McEwan?"

"That's why I called you, because the whole thing confuses me." She turned her head away and coughed into a hanky. The coughing persisted for a good five seconds. "Like I said—" She coughed again then straightened up.

"Are you okay?" I said.

"Fine. Like I said on the phone, I don't want to be a bother."

"It's no bother, Mrs. Hennessey. I'll take care of it."

"Thanks." She handed me the notice. "I almost forgot. There's another thing you might need. It didn't make sense to me at the time, but it makes sense now. Jeepster gave it to me for safekeeping. I keep it in my purse." She reached into her pocketbook and handed me a key with a piece of white tape on the head. Written on the tape in black ink was the name McEwan. "McEwan, just like the name on the late notice. See it?"

"Yes, I see it."

• • •

They say Indians have a sixth sense, an ability to intuit their sur-roundings, to discern matters of nature, even in the city. Whether that's true or not I don't know, yet I had a feeling someone was watching me. I didn't attribute it to paranoia. Paranoia, I knew from the drinking days. The sensation felt real.

I took a circuitous route to Mystic Piers Storage, just to make sure I wasn't followed. The storage building abutted the back piers, nearest the inner harbor. I parked in front of the office, went inside, and handed the attendant the past due notice. He told me I had to pay the arrears in cash if I wanted to get into the room today, oth-erwise I'd have to wait until the check cleared, which might take three or four days. I paid him cash.

"Wait here a minute," he said. "I'll remove the company lock."

He came back five minutes later and said I was all set. The com-pany lock had been removed. I now had access to the room. I rode the freight elevator to the fourth floor, where Jeepster's storage unit was located, opened the elevator cage, and found the padlocked door. The McEwan key fit into the lock and it clicked open. I nudged the door in and turned on the lights.

The first thing I saw was an oil painting on a bulky wooden easel. The painting depicted a monk or a friar in prayer, his fore-head bright with light, his right hand over his heart. Hanging on the wall behind the praying monk was another oil painting, a por-trait of a man wearing a dark puffy hat with a feather sticking out of it. Like the praying man, only a portion of his face shined with light. The works were of excellent quality.

I heard humming in the corner. The humming came from a hu-midifier. The humidifier was attached by rubber tubing to a fifty-five-gallon barrel, the barrel acting as a makeshift reservoir. Next to the humidifier was a dehumidifier. Both machines were wired to an electronic gadget. The gadget had a dial gauge which must have served as a toggle switch between the two machines, powering one or the other, depending on the reading.

Filtered lamps brightened the room with soft white. The lamps were set at various angles along the edge of the ceiling, illuminating the paintings at indirect angles. Nothing in the room was vivid, yet everything was visible. A large metal desk was pushed up against the outside wall. The desk had a swivel chair. In the middle of the desk sat a large shortwave radio. It had knobs and band dials. A thick cord came out of the back and went up into the ceiling. Standing next to the radio was a microphone, like the ones in old war movies. I'd have to tell Buck about the radio. If Buck got into the radio the way he got into Oulipo, we'd be conversing with Martians by week's end.

I removed the monk painting from the easel and an index card fell to the floor from behind it. The card had four words written on it: Chat, OulipoBoys, Oulipo_Man, Oswego.

I pocketed the index card and then snapped pictures of the two paintings with my cell phone. I sat for a minute to think. I got up, covered the painting of the monk with a green trash bag, and took it with me.

When I got back to my car I called a priest I knew, a professor from Boston College. I told him about the artwork and asked to meet with him. He told me to come ahead.

CHAPTER 23

From the Mystic Piers I drove to Chestnut Hill to meet Father Mullineaux, a Jesuit priest and an authority on the world of art. While an undergraduate at Boston College, I took two of his classes, both titled Introduction to Art *Whatever*. I even passed them. Father Mullineaux had always been good to me, probably because he liked football.

We had agreed to meet in the lobby of Saint Mary's Hall in an hour. Forty-five minutes later I walked into the lobby with the painting under my arm, still covered with the green trash bag. Father Mullineaux was waiting there for me, his hair still dark and parted on the side, his eyes still friendly, his face now more deeply lined.

"Dermot, it's been too many years," he said. He went to hug me. The painting got in the way. I set it aside and we embraced. "You've piqued my interest with stories of found art."

"Thanks for meeting me, Father," I said. "I'm unschooled in this stuff as you well know."

"I know you did well in my courses and equally well on the gridiron. How is your knee?"

"The knee is fine. This painting I found has an expert quality to it. If it's worth anything I'd like to know." I figured Mrs. Hennessey could use the money. "I'd like your opinion on it, your assessment."

"Let's step over to the window and have a look at it. The lighting is quite good over there, even on overcast days."

I uncovered the painting. Father Mullineaux set it on the sill and studied it. He put on his glasses and scrutinized it more intently, tilting the painting to various angles, letting the natural lighting hit it, then tilting it once more.

"The painting is amazing," he said. "Absolutely amazing. This is no cheap knockoff, Dermot. Where did you get it?"

"I found it."

"This could easily pass for an authentic Rembrandt. Its pigmentation, its use of light, this work is breathtaking, absolutely breathtaking. You said you found it. You didn't happen to find it in the Museum of Fine Arts by any chance? Because that's where the original currently hangs." His brown eyes twinkled. "Rembrandt's *Old Man in Prayer,* that's the title of this piece."

"You said Rembrandt?"

"And you said you found it," he said, "I suppose it fell off the back of a turnip truck in Charlestown."

"Something like that."

"The workmanship is expert, the best I've ever seen in a reproduction. It's good enough to fool most people into thinking it was the original. It's more than the workmanship." He studied it again. "I wonder."

"Wonder what? Fill me in."

"Rembrandt taught students. In fifteenth-century Amsterdam the Dutch masters trained promising students, teaching them the craft of art through one-on-one tutoring. The word osmosis comes to mind when I think of the Dutch schools."

"A Dutch student painted this?"

"No, no, it can't be. Still, I wonder, maybe—"

"Maybe what?"

"I suppose it's possible. Maybe this piece *was* painted by one of Rembrandt's students." He nearly hugged it to his chest. "I'm not qualified to render such a judgment, but I can render this much: this work is definitely a historic piece of art."

"I thought it looked pretty good."

"Pretty good?" He stared again at the painting. "May I keep *Old Man* for a few days? I'd like to show it to a friend of mine, a curator. He works independently, always in high demand. He's been employed by many of the area museums, a freelance curator. Can I show him this painting?"

"Show it to him. Hang onto it for a while," I said. "I ask one thing, Father. Please keep my name out of it."

"I understand." His face flushed. "It's not stolen, is it?"

"Not that I know of," I said. "At least we know it's not the original, because the MFA has the original."

"Why the secrecy? Am I being too forward?"

"I have good reasons to keep my name out of it, and it's not because I think the painting is stolen. It's to protect you, the curator, too. Dangerous things have been happening. I don't want anyone to get hurt. I want to play it safe."

"I understand, I'll keep your name to myself," he said. "As far as you know, the painting is not stolen."

"Correct, as far as I know it's not stolen." I thought about Mystic Piers Storage. "There's another painting."

"In addition to this one?"

"It has a similar style to *Old Man in Prayer*." An image of the painting flashed in my mind. "Similar in its use of lighting."

"You learned well in my class," Father Mulineaux said. "I'm impressed with your astuteness, Dermot."

"That's me, Father, an astute kinda guy," I said. "For all I know the other one is nothing more than paint-by-number."

"Based on your appraisal of *Old Man in Prayer*, I doubt it." He looked once more at the painting. "Its quality, its condition, it is a remarkably preserved work. Is the other painting in similar shape?"

"It is," I said. "Both paintings were stored in a room with no windows. The lighting, when on, is muted with filters. The room has a humidifier and a dehumidifier, both hooked to a switching device."

"Fascinating," he said. "The machines probably control the relative humidity. A relative humidity of fifty percent is ideal to conserve artwork. The filtered lighting makes a difference, too.

Somebody knew what they were doing. The other painting, please describe it to me in detail."

"I can do one better," I said. "I took a picture of it with my cell phone."

I fiddled with the phone and showed Father Mullineaux the photo.

"Ah, another Rembrandt, *Self-Portrait, Aged 23*, painted in 1629. *Self-Portrait, Aged 23* is housed in the Dutch Room in the Isabella Stewart Gardner Museum. Thank God it wasn't stolen in the nineteen ninety heist. It's a beauty. Can I get a look at *Self-Portrait*, too?"

"That'd be helpful," I said. "Call me later. Tell me what the curator says about *Old Man in Prayer*. If you think it's worth it, I'll bring the other one over."

"Dermot, do you know what my biggest dream is? I would love to see the Gardner Museum host a Rembrandt show featuring *Self-Portrait, Aged 23* and *Self-Portrait, Aged 63*. The latter resides in London's National Gallery. I'd give anything to see them hanging side by side, a forty-year span of genius, juxtaposed for the public to appreciate."

"I hope your dream comes true," I said. "Thanks, Father. And thanks for keeping my name out of it."

"Your name is safe with me, Dermot," he said, "safe as the seal of confession."

CHAPTER 24

Harraseeket Kid was pacing on the sidewalk in front of my house when I pulled up. I parked the Plymouth and got out.

"What happened?"

"Buck got beat up," he said. "He was over at South Station and a gang of kids attacked him."

"Is he okay?"

"Yeah, he's okay. He's upstairs resting and he's plenty pissed off," Kid said. "The kids said they'd shove him on the third rail next time they saw him."

I pulled out my cell phone.

"Who are you calling?"

"The police."

"Don't," Kid said. "Buck doesn't want the police involved."

"Why not?"

"Ask him."

I knocked on Buck's door and went inside. He was wheeling back and forth, mumbling and cussing. His face was scraped raw, his neck was scratched up. He had a black eye and a fat lip. He stared straight ahead, glowering.

"Jesus, Buck. Are you all right?"

"Yeah, I'm all right, just fuckin' perfect, never better." He stared at the wall. "Never fuckin' better."

"Let me call the police."

"Fuck the police." Buck whipped around, his eyes blazing with rage. "I'll get even myself, on my own terms, understand? I know exactly what the motherfuckers look like. I'll fuck 'em up in my own way." He held up his scraped knuckles. "I landed a few good shots."

"This is awful." His cuts still bled, his scrapes throbbed raw. "I'm calling a doctor."

"No fuckin' doctors, Dermot."

"The cuts will get infected."

"Forget about infections. I'm fine, ya understand?" he said. "I don't want outsiders finding out about this."

"I'm no outsider, Buck." I went to the freezer, bagged a few ice cubes, and handed it to him. "Hold this on your eye. I'll clean those cuts with peroxide."

I dressed the cuts and scrapes, then treated the torn knuckles. I examined his face. He still had his teeth, his nose wasn't broken, no blood dripped from his ears.

"You'll be okay."

"I don't want to dwell on this, Dermot. It bothers me."

"No man likes to take a beating, especially by a gang."

"Let's drop it for a while, okay?" he said. "Let it go."

"Okay, we'll let it go."

"I need a distraction, something to get my mind off it."

"How about we watch the Red Sox," I said. "Beckett is pitching."

"Fuck the Red Sox." He turned the wheelchair to face me. "Anything new on the Oulipo front?"

"As a matter of fact, yes." I held out the index card. "I found this card in a storage room Jeepster kept. It has four words on it."

"Let me see it." He took the index card and read it. "Thanks for cleaning me up, Dermot. I need my space right now, understand?"

"I understand."

"Drop by tomorrow and I'll have this index card figured out."

I left Buck's apartment and went for a walk, hoping to calm down. I took a left on Walford Way, saw Naddi, and nodded to her. She turned the other way. The sight of Naddi triggered the thought of Emma Hague. I went to Emma's tenement building. She let me in and invited me to sit on the couch. She was wearing faded blue jeans and a loose yellow tank top.

"Nice to see you, Dermot."

"Have you talked to Naddi yet?"

"I'm doing fine too, thanks for asking."

"Sorry, I'm having a screwy day," I said. "I just saw Naddi on Corey Street and she walked away from me. That's not like her. She usually stops to talk. Is she okay?"

"I don't know how she's doing," she said. "I haven't found the right opportunity to talk to her. I don't want to place Naddi and her daughter in danger."

"You said the same thing last time, the right-opportunity excuse. Come on, Emma. Nobody knows you're a fed back here. Knock on Naddi's door, pretend to borrow a cup of sugar, and talk to her."

"It's not that simple, Dermot."

"Sure it is."

"No, it's not. I'm required to follow federal regulations. If Naddi gets hurt because I didn't follow departmental procedures, I'll get into serious trouble. It's the nature of law enforcement, Dermot, regulations and procedures."

"Fuckin' government bureaucracies."

"I say the same thing myself most days," she said. "I can't act of my own accord, as much as I'd like to."

"That's a bunch of crap, not having the right opportunity to talk to her. I don't buy it." I stood. "The feds talk to whoever they want to talk to."

"Don't get angry."

"I'm already angry. At least pull Naddi aside and reassure her," I said. "She practically ran away from me."

"My hands are tied."

"That's bullshit," I said.

"The federal regulations say that—"

"I don't give a damn about federal regulations. Naddi is out there on a limb because I put her out there."

"She's not out on a limb, Dermot." She sounded dismissive. "Naddi will be fine, don't worry about her."

"How can you be so sure?"

"I just know, okay?"

"When we first met, you talked about handheld rocket launchers and terrorist plots in the projects. You made it sound like bin Laden himself was gonna parachute into Charlestown. So I asked around, I talked to a few Somalis, I got you a lead. Naddi was the lead. And you've done nothing about it. And now Naddi is terrified."

"Just because she walked away, doesn't mean she's terrified."

"I've got one thing in this neighborhood and that's my word. If my word's no good, I'm no good." I tried to slow down. "I told Naddi I'd be there for her. And then I reached out to you, the antiterrorism FBI agent, and you did nothing. If something goes wrong, if Naddi gets hurt in any way, it's on me. I'm responsible. Don't you see that?"

"You're overreacting."

"Overreacting?" I said. "I told Naddi I was behind her, because you said you were behind me. But you're not behind me."

"These things take time."

"You're full of shit, lady."

I slammed the door on the way out.

CHAPTER 25

My cell phone rang as I was leaving Emma's building. The man's voice on the other end sounded familiar.

"We need to talk, Sparhawk."

"Who is this?"

"The cab driver from the literary society," he said. "Meet me at the halfway point of the ropewalk, the Chelsea Street side."

"The ropewalk?" I said. "It's overgrown on that side."

"Be there in fifteen minutes."

Just inside the Navy Yard's fence on Chelsea Street sits the ropewalk, a long low building constructed of cut granite blocks. Windows like portholes run end to end. The ropewalk once manufactured cordage for naval vessels, notably during the Civil War and the Spanish American War. That's what the nuns told us. A great uncle of mine worked in the ropewalk during the Second World War. He never smoked, but died of lung cancer anyway, probably from breathing in rope fibers. The slate-roofed building, now derelict and obsolete, has been boarded up for decades.

I went to Gate 4, scaled the wrought-iron fence, and trudged in the dusk through a trashy tangle of brush. Crickets chirped and toads croaked. A seagull cawed from the underbelly of the Tobin Bridge. A rat that could have pulled a sled scurried off to my left. I reached the midpoint of the ropewalk and waited in the lowlands for the cabbie to arrive.

Ten minutes later he pulled over on Chelsea Street and got out of the cab, looking much the same as the last time: opaque sunglasses, bushy beard, Optimo hat pulled low on his head. He stood on the sidewalk towering over me, while I wallowed in a drainage ditch below, balancing on clumps of wild grass. From my vantage point, the Navy Yard fence was as high as the Green Monster at Fenway.

"We did what we had to do, Sparhawk." His kneecaps were level with my face. "You must realize that by now."

"What are you talking about?"

"I thought we were pretty clear."

"Clear about what?"

"Your tenant, the colored man."

"Buck?"

"Give us the information we need, Sparhawk," he said. "Or next time it won't end so good for your tenant."

"What?"

"Next time the nigger dies."

I reached for the fence. It was useless, no way to get over it. The cabbie played it smart, putting me in a gully. I searched for a rock to throw and saw one off to my right.

"When I get a hold of you, I will beat you till you beg me to kill you," I said. "That's a promise."

"Right." The cabbie laughed at me. "You ain't beating nobody, half-breed."

Why had Buck lied to me? I inched closer to the rock. It was a smooth rock, the size and shape of a lemon, the perfect rock for a bean ball.

"We'll kill him next time," he said.

"What do you want?"

"You know what I want," he said.

"Promise you'll leave Buck alone."

"I don't make promises."

I lunged for the rock and gunned a fastball at his noggin. The small boulder deflected off a fencepost and plunked the side of his head. I Van Goghed him. He cupped his ear with both hands and grunted as he staggered. I hunted for another stone, feeling more than looking, and found a beauty the size of an egg, perfect to take out an eye. I came up gunning, but I was too late. The cab was speeding down Chelsea Street, the taillights dying in the darkness.

It felt good to land a shot.

I waded through the weeds to Gate 4 and walked under the Tobin Bridge to Bunker Hill Street. Why had Buck lied about the attack? He must have had a good reason, because Buck was a good man. I got home and went down to the basement to talk to Harraseeket Kid. He was listening to Johnny Cash. He saw me walk in.

"Hey, what's wrong?"

"Buck wasn't attacked by a gang of kids," I said. "He was attacked by a cabdriver."

"What do you mean?" His eyes blinked. "The cabbie you told me about, that one?"

"Yeah, him."

"Fuck."

I told Kid about my encounter with the bearded, goggled, hat-wearing hackney.

"Why didn't Buck tell us the truth?" he asked.

"I don't know," I said. "It doesn't make sense."

"There must be a good reason," Kid said.

"I hope so."

We listened to *The Ballad of Ira Hayes*. I thought about my father in Vietnam. He loved that song. He loved *Run Through the Jungle*, too. *Ring of Fire* came on next.

"I can venture a guess why Buck lied," Kid said.

"Go on, Kid."

"He lied because of you."

"Why would he lie because of me?"

"He figured if he told you the truth, you'd yank him off Jeepster's murder." Kid sat back and crossed his long legs. "Buck loves working with you. He loves figuring shit out on the computer."

"I know he does, and he's good at it."

"It's a challenge for Buck. Every guy needs a challenge. Hell, you know that. You almost drank yourself dead because you lost football."

"Yeah, I know."

"I hear Buck typing on that computer all night long."

"I hadn't thought of that." I thought back to an earlier conversation with Buck. "I told Buck that if things got dangerous, I'd pull him off the case."

"There you have it," Kid said. "That's the reason."

"He lied because he was afraid I'd pull him off the case."

"Yup, that explains it."

"He's in danger, Kid. The cabbie said he'd kill him."

"Buck'll be fine. I'll keep an eye on him while I'm here. Hell, I'll take a week's vacation and watch him full time." Kid picked up the Winchester rifle and examined the barrel. "I have an idea, been toying with it for a while now. A friend of mine, another Micmac Indian, breeds giant Alaskan malamutes in northern New Hampshire, up near Canada. The dogs are huge, two hundred pounds of fur, head, and teeth. They're loyal as a bastard, smart as hell, too. I'd like to buy Buck a malamute."

"Good idea. Get the dog," I said. "I guess I shouldn't tell Buck about the cabbie."

"Don't let on, it'll hurt his pride."

I went upstairs to bed.

CHAPTER 26

I woke up with a strange feeling in my gut, a feeling that I had un-earthed a hidden message in my sleep, that my dreams had yielded something concrete. If my dreams yielded something concrete, it was wet concrete, nothing solid. The feeling clawed at the edges of my mind, scratching its way to the surface. Then my conscious mind swatted it down. I went to the kitchen and lit gas under the kettle. The whistle blew a few minutes later and the feelings inside me assembled into a coherent thought.

It had to do with the cabdriver. The cabdriver had said some-thing. He said "literary society" when he referred to Jeepster's prison book club. George Meeks also said "literary society" when I saw him at Jeepster's wake. He didn't say book club, he said lit-erary society. And the day after the wake, the cabbie called my cell phone. George Meeks and the cabbie had to be connected.

I made a couple of phone calls, learned what I needed to learn, gassed up the car, and drove west on the Mass Pike, heading for Federal Correctional Institute Otisville in Mount Hope, New York. Four hours later I pulled into the prison parking lot. After a frisk-ing, a dog sniffing, and a debriefing of the prison rules, they es-corted me to the visitor area, where I waited for for an inmate named Eddie Doyle. Eddie was a Charlestown bank robber serv-ing a twenty-year bit for a botched armored car holdup. He had been good friends with my father.

Eddie came into the room.

"Hey Dermot, thanks for comin' to see me. Seems like every-one in Charlestown forgot I'm in here. Ain't had no visitors 'cept the turnkeys." He gave me a gummy jack-o-lantern smile. "Chief did good raising you, respecting your elders like you do."

"Thanks. Eddie," I said. "Don't get too gushy about my visit, there's a reason I came to see you."

"Shit, I know that. Nobody'd drive all the way from Charlestown just to say hi to me, 'specially in this shit hole. I'm just glad you came, that's all." Eddie forced a laugh that crinkled the corners of his eyes. "It ain't like I'm a short-timer. Got eight more years to go, which sucks like a bastard. Eight more years just 'cause I stuck a gun in a Loomis guard's face."

"Life isn't fair."

"Fuckin' right, it ain't. Ain't like I pulled the trigger, nobody got hurt too bad, and Loomis got their money back. What's the big deal?"

"They made a mountain out of a molehill."

"Fuckin' right, they did." He glimpsed his inked arms. "Anyways, what do ya need?"

"Jeepster Hennessey got killed."

"I heard about it, heard how it happened, too," he said. "The poor prick got stabbed in the back, died in your food pantry. That's the story I heard."

"That's how it happened."

"That's real good work you're doing in the pantry, helping them minorities like that."

Another prisoner came into the visiting area, a black guy with rippling arms and massive shoulders. He sat across from a woman who must have been his mother. The big guy melted into tears.

"I heard that Jeepster started a book club in here, in Otisville. I heard the book club continued on the outside," I said. "Do you know anything about it?"

"Are you shittin' me, Dermot? I never read nothin' in my life."

"I was just wondering—"

"Hold on, let me finish. George and Jeepster asked me to join, probably 'cause I'm a Townie." He laughed. "I haven't touched a book since the nuns beat the catechism into me back at Saint Jude Thaddeus."

"George Meeks was in the book club?"

"Sure, George was in it," he said. "George and Jeepster, it was their club. Both them guys could read like a bastard."

The big black man and his mother prayed together. So George Meeks was a member of the book club. What else was George Holding back? I turned to Eddie.

"Does Oswego mean anything to you?"

"O-what?"

"How about McSweeney?"

"Don't he play for the Bruins?"

On the way out of FCI Otisville, I talked to a corrections officer, who showed me how to credit Eddie's canteen account $25. Then he asked how my visit went. The question surprised me. I told him the visit went fine. He said Eddie Doyle was a model prisoner, never started trouble in the cellblock. I asked the guard if he remembered Jeepster Hennessey or George Meeks. He told me he did. I then asked him if he remembered their book club.

"I remember the book club. They read avant garde books, material way over my head. I'd join them once in a while, invited of course. For some reason they liked me, and I liked hearing what they thought about the readings. Smart guys, both of them. I was saddened when Hennessey died. He wasn't a bad man, not really."

"Forgive me if I'm out of line. You don't strike me as a typical corrections officer," I said.

"I'm thinking of becoming a priest."

By the time I pulled into Charlestown it was dark. After driving eight hours to and from FCI Otisville, I was ready for a cold Coca-Cola, salty chips, and a Red Sox game. I quietly opened the outside door, hoping to get past Buck Louis undetected. I didn't pull it off. He waved me into his apartment as soon as I stepped into the foyer.

"Dermot, get in here. You gotta see this." I followed Buck to his computer. He typed in a few keystrokes. "I figured out the words on the index card. The Oulipo Boys have a chat room. The room's restricted, authorized users only. I logged onto the chat room. The user ID was Oulipo Man, the password Oswego."

"Just so I'm clear," I said, trying to slow things down. "You got into the Oulipo Boys chat room using Oulipo Man and Oswego."

"That's right. Let me show you a couple of things." He clicked the mouse. "This is the dashboard. It controls the chat room messaging. All the messages are time stamped, which makes it easy to track who sent what when."

"When you say who, you don't mean a person's name, you mean the user ID, right?"

"Right. Study these postings. Notice anything unusual?"

"Give me a second," I said. "No, not really."

"Oulipo Man stopped posting messages the day Jeepster Hennessey got killed. That tells me there's a good chance Hennessey was the Oulipo Man."

"That makes sense."

"Yeah, especially since you found the index card in Hennessey's storage room." He waved me closer. "The archived postings are cryptic, which is right in line with Oulipo's wordplay games. One of the users is named The Go Between, another is Main E Ack. The Go Between and Main E Ack, they're the most active chatters, besides Oulipo Man."

"Well done, Buck. This is huge."

"Thanks," Buck said. "Just to see what happens, I posted a message from Oulipo Man tonight. No response so far."

"What did you write?"

"The last thing I wrote was: Oulipo Man will be logging on again tomorrow at nine a.m." Buck turned off the computer. "What do you think?"

"I think we'll be hearing from The Go Between and Main E Ack in the morning." I thought again about Jeepster's storage room, the index card, the shortwave radio, the masterpiece reproductions. "I don't know what to expect from these guys."

• • •

At eight thirty a.m. I showed up at Buck's apartment door, coffee
in hand, nervous of mind. Neither of us knew how to approach
the chat room session, nor did we know what to expect on the
other end. We agreed to team up, figuring that two heads were better than one. Buck logged on at nine o'clock and posted a message.

Oulipo_Man: I'm here.

Within five seconds a reply popped up on the screen.

The_Go_Between: Where have you been?

"What do I say?" Buck said.

"I don't know," I said. "Tell him you were sick."

Oulipo_Man: I was sick.

Main_E_Ack: I thought you disappeared on us.

"Both of them are logged on," Buck said, "The Go Between
and Main E Ack."

"That means we're onto something."

Oulipo_Man: I'm back now.

The_Go_Between: Are McEwan and McSweeney safe?

Buck and I looked at each other. Buck typed part of a message
then stopped. "What do I write?"

"Give me a second." I found myself whispering. "Tell them
McEwan and McSweeney are fine."

Oulipo_Man: McEwan and McSweeney are doing splendidly.

"Splendidly?" I said.

"Oulipians are brainy bastards. Let's try'n sound smart."

The_Go_Between: That's good news about our old friends.

Main_E_Ack: Very good news. When can we make the swap?

"Swap?" Buck said.

"We've bluffed them so far," I said. "Tell them soon."

Oulipo_Man: Soon.

The_Go_Between: Three days. We chat again on Thursday, no
later. Let's get this deal wrapped up.

Main_E_Ack: Don't disappear on us again.

Oulipo_Man: Thursday 9 a.m.

Buck logged off.

"What the hell was that all about?" Buck said. "Swap *what* in three days?"

"I'm not sure, though I can hazard a guess," I said. "The index card wasn't the only thing I found in the storage room. I also found two paintings, both reproductions of masterpieces. I showed one of them to an art expert, and he said the painting was good enough to fool most anybody."

"How many paintings did you say?"

"Two," I said. "Both Rembrandt reproductions."

"And you're sure they're fakes."

"They're both fakes, Buck. The originals are hanging in Boston museums."

"Two fake Rembrandts, what next?" Buck rolled to the middle of the parlor floor. "Main E Ack wrote about a swap. Maybe the fakes are part of a swap."

"I was thinking the same thing." I patted his shoulder. "Good job."

"Is this a pissa or what?"

CHAPTER 27

Timmy O'Hanlon, my cousin on the Irish side of the family, works for the Department of Homeland Security, stationed at the Tip O'Neill Federal Building near the Garden. I called him earlier in the morning, and he agreed to meet me for lunch. The day was sunny and the humidity was low, and we decided to meet at the Moakley Courthouse to enjoy the harbor views.

I rode the Silver Line from South Station to the South Boston waterfront and got off at Courthouse Station, where handsome Timmy O'Hanlon stood waiting on the newly poured sidewalks. We greeted each other and shook hands. Blue skies cheered Seaport Boulevard and a mild breeze wisked inland from the east. On days like today, it's easy to see why the Pilgrims and Puritans settled in Boston. It's also easy to see why the Wampanoag tribe said there goes the neighborhood.

We walked to the courthouse and through its opulent lobby, courtesy of the taxpayers, and went out to the back piazza, which abuts the inner harbor. Neither of us brought anything to eat, neither of us seemed to care. We sat on an iron bench and chatted about family for a few minutes. Timmy made a face that said he was a busy man, so let's get to the point of the meeting.

"I can use your help, Timmy."

His ink-black hair shimmered in the sun, shinier than Superman's in the Sunday comics. His gleaming Irish face showed a hint of a beard line. He probably changed blades halfway through a shave.

"Tell me about it," he said. "If I can help, I will."

I told Timmy about Special Agent Emma Hague and the role

she claimed to have with the Joint Terrorism Task Force. I told him how Emma moved into Jeepster Hennessy's apartment in the projects as an undercover agent, supposedly to ferret out Somali terrorists. I told him about Naddi the Somali, who had talked to me about un-American activities. I told him that I informed Emma Hague of Naddi's allegation. Lastly, I told Timmy about Emma Hague's stalling tactics and her refusal to follow-up with Naddi.

"I'm worried for Naddi's safety," I said. "She's scared shitless."

"Hague's handling of this info sounds iffy."

"What can you tell me about Emma Hague?" I said. "A Boston police captain introduced us, so I assumed she was legit. She must be with the FBI and JTTF. She couldn't have snowed a Boston police captain, right?"

"Probably not."

"Can you clarify what's up with her?" I asked. "I don't like getting played."

"Anything that concerns national security is off limits, Dermot. I have to be careful with that type of thing."

"I'm your cousin."

"Don't get like that. You don't have to." He smiled and his face cracked into a dozen shadowy crevices. You could lose a dime in one of those crevices. I'd bet interrogated suspects lost their composure in those crevices, too. "Some matters I can't discuss, cousin or not."

"Is she even attached to JTTF?"

"JTTF?" He turned his head. A sloop sailed by, tacking inside a channel marker. One of the crewmen cracked a beer, while the other worked the rudder. "This is nice out here, isn't it? It's called Harbor Park. Ever been out here before?"

"No, it's my first time," I said. "You're not going to tell me anything."

"Not directly," he said.

"I was wrong to put you on the spot. I should've handled it myself."

"Hold on now, cousin. Don't leave here half-cocked. I can't

discuss Emma Hague or Homeland Security or ongoing investiga-
tions. That doesn't mean I can't help." He glanced at his watch.
"Naddi the Somali, give me her full name and address and I'll
check her out, see if she's in any real danger."

"Thanks."

"No thanks needed, Dermot. I'm just doing my job. I'll treat
Naddi's information as an anonymous tip, a lead that must be investigated to the fullest extent of our office."

"What do you mean by an anonymous tip?"

"You're going to make an anonymous phone call to my office,"
he said. "That way, I'm protected. If anyone asks who told me
about Naddi, I don't know."

"Because the call was anonymous."

"Yes, because the call was anonymous. The info you give me
might be valid or it might be bogus. Our office must investigate to
find out which. Now give me the details about Naddi."

I gave him the information, which he wrote in a small notebook. Timmy handed me his business card and pointed to a phone
number at the bottom.

"Call this number in twenty minutes," he said. "A reception-
ist will answer. Ask for the Homeland Security hotline. I'll be on the
other end when she forwards the call. The call will be recorded."
He tore out the page that he had just written and handed it to me.
"When I answer the phone, read Naddi's information back to me,
read it off the paper so you don't miss anything. Remember, the call
will be recorded."

"Got it."

"I'll pressure you for your name. Don't give it to me. I'll pressure you for other information. Ignore my coaxing. Coaxing is part
of the interrogation protocol, even over the phone. It's okay to be
spontaneous, in fact it's better. Just make sure you tell me all the information on the page. That way I'm covered. If an FBI honcho
asks how I know Naddi lives in Starr King Court, it'll be right there
on the recording."

"You've done this before."

"Now for Hague. I'll reach out to a friend of mine, a guy I know from college. He represents Homeland Security inside the JTTF. JTTF has weekly conference calls in Boston, and he's at the table. He can tell me about Special Agent Hague."

"I thought you couldn't talk about her."

"I'm not, he is." He smiled again. "Your anonymous tip is my way in, an excuse to poke around, to stick my nose into the tent. Call from a pay phone. Wipe it down afterward. It's an eight hundred number, so you don't need change."

"Now let's do it," he said, "let's do it right." We shook hands and parted.

I rested my feet on the hassock when I got home from the court-house. I'd made the call to Timmy O'Hanlon, using a pay phone just outside the courthouse doors. Everything went as planned. Now the ball was in Timmy's court.

I had barely gotten comfortable when the phone rang. Maybe it was Timmy following up on something. I answered. It was Jimmy Devin, formally of the D Street projects, currently of the Irish Riviera.

"I learned something new about our friend," he said. "We need to talk about it. I'll be in Charlestown in an hour, Finbar's."

"I'll be there."

He hung up.

I walked into Finbar's and saw Jimmy Devin sitting at a table at the far end of the saloon, his back pressed against the wall. I ordered a Coke from Tall Ed and joined Devin at the table.

"Still off the sauce?"

"For today."

"One of them guys, huh?" He took a sip of beer and licked his lips. "Nothing beats a frosty Narragansett on a hot summer after-noon."

"You said something about our friend," I said. "I assume you mean Jeepster Hennessey."

"A titanium trap, nothing gets past you."

"Is that your first drink of the day?"

"Don't be a wiseass, Sparhawk. I don't tolerate wiseasses, not at my age." His words ran together, inching toward slurring. Devin drank more beer. "Any more flap from you and I'll leave this dump, pally boy, and won't tell you nothin'."

"Hey, pally boy, you called me."

"Just don't gimme any shit, that's all I'm saying."

"I thought you were Jeepster's friend," I said. "Will you help me or not?"

"Maybe, maybe not."

"You're like a fickle teenage girl." I finished my Coke and stood. "Call me when you make up your fucking mind."

"Take it easy, I was joking around a little. Jesus, you Townies are touchy bastards. Come on, sit down. I need to tell you something."

"I'm listening."

"Sit down, Sparhawk. Be a regular guy and sit down. I didn't mean nothin'. You took a few shots yourself." He tried to look sincere. "I shouldn't a cracked wise like that, I apologize. Sit down, it's important."

"Just for a minute." I sat down. "What's so important?"

"Remember that high-stakes poker game I talked about, the one Jeepster was tryna get in?" He drank. "Remember?"

"I remember. He needed fifty grand for an entrance fee."

"Yes sir, that's the one. I heard something about the game, the ground rules," he said. "The game was limited to ten players, broken into two groups of five. They had two games going at once. Every player had to have fifty grand to get in."

"That's a lot of cash in one room."

"Fuckin' right it is. After six hours of poker, the top five winners continue to play, the other five are out." He finished the Narragansett and waved the empty mug at Tall Ed. "The five losers, the bottom five, they gotta leave their money behind. Whatever's left of their fifty thousand, they forfeit to the winner. The winner gets *that* money too when the game ends, kinda like a bonus payment. The Wall Street maggots call it a zero-sum game."

"Say that again, about the bottom five."

"The players that don't finish in the top five forfeit what's left of their fifty Gs. The dough goes to the winner at the end of the game. To the victorious goes the spoils, or whatever that fuckin' saying is."

"Who would be crazy enough to play in a game like that?" I thought for a second. "Other than Jeepster Hennessey."

"When the game ends, the winner takes all the money, every friggin' penny. Understand what I'm saying? The winner walks away with five hundred grand, no consolation prizes, no dough for place and show." He slid the empty mug across the table. "I never heard of such a game before. That's how it worked, them's the rules."

"Did they play the game?" I asked.

"Yes."

"Where did they play the game?"

"I don't know, maybe Southie, maybe Dorchester. I'm not sure." Tall Ed poured Jimmy Devin another draught. All beer, no foam, the way it's supposed to be served. "That's five hundred grand, Sparhawk. The winner got himself half a million bucks."

"And Jeepster played in the game."

"That's what I heard."

"Did he win?"

"He didn't win, not by a long shot."

"Did he cheat?"

"He didn't cheat in the usual sense of card cheating, but he cheated." He drank a third of the fresh mug. "And it cost him."

"He didn't cheat in the usual sense?" I said. "What does that mean?"

"He played honest cards, he bet dishonest money. Jeepster showed up with fifty grand, all right, fifty grand in counterfeit bills." Another sip of Narragansett. "The winner wasn't too thrilled when he counted up his cash at the end of the night. Somehow or other he figured out Jeepster used bad money and hunted him down in the projects. That's what I heard."

"How reliable is your source?"

"There's no such thing as a reliable source." A muffled burp. "I'd a never called you if I thought the info was bad."

"Why *did* you call me, Devin?" I stared at his bubbling beer. "We didn't exactly hit it off the last time we met."

"I thought we hit it off okay. Eh, that's beside the point." A generous gulp, a lick of the lips. "This meeting we're having has nothing to do with you. It has to do with my Vietnam comrade, Jeepster Hennessey. I want Jeepster's killer caught."

"And you think the poker player killed him because of the counterfeit money?" I ogled his beer again and salivated.

"Yup, that's the way I figure it."

"What's his name, the card player?"

"They didn't tell me his name. They only said he was from out of town. He flew in for the game, I think maybe from Florida."

"Where in Florida?"

"They didn't say specifically, maybe Miami," he said. "That'd be my guess, Miami."

"Doesn't matter, I can't go to Florida," I said.

"Can't blame you. That's a long way away." A bottoms-up swig, an empty mug on the table. "I wanted to tell you the story anyway, in case you were serious about finding Jeepster's killer."

I sat, thinking. Was Devin's story solid, or was he trying to get me to drop Jeepster's case? Was he betting I wouldn't go to Miami to hunt down the poker player? Was he also betting I'd drop the whole thing, because Jeepster's killer was from out of town and therefore out of reach? Or maybe he was telling the truth. Maybe he was trying to help his Vietnam comrade, just as he said. I didn't know what to believe. On my way out of the saloon, I dropped a five on the bar and told Tall Ed to pour Devin another draught.

CHAPTER 28

That evening Father Mullineaux called and said he wanted to see me, asking if I had the time to drive out to B.C. that night. I told him I had the time and I'd be there in an hour. We agreed to meet at Saint Mary's Hall again. An hour later I was driving up Commonwealth Avenue toward the upper campus. A security guard waved me through the gate.

Father Mullineaux was waiting in the lobby when I came in, and he was pacing like an expectant father in a maternity ward. He slapped me on the shoulder and turned me back to the door I'd just come through, saying, "Its a beautiful night outside. Let's take a relaxing walk around the college grounds and enjoy the out-of-doors." And that's what we did, except it wasn't very relaxing. He got right down to business.

"The *Old Man in Prayer* painting is an extraordinary work," he said. "My curator friend gasped when he saw it, which immediately indicated to me it was something special. At first the curator thought it was the original, God's truth. The pigmentation, the network of craquelure, he found the painting stunning."

"Good news," I said.

"We both agreed that the painting had to have come from one of the Dutch schools of the fifteenth century, probably Rembrandt's school. The curator is convinced of that, as am I. The problem with works produced by students is establishing provenance."

"What's craquelure?"

"Craquelure is the cracking pattern of a painting, the hairline fractures on the surface." Father Mullineaux dipped into a professorial tone. "Each painting cracks in relation to its environment, thus the cracking is particular to a given region."

"Please say it in English."

"I get carried away when I'm excited," he said. "French, Dutch, and Italian masterpieces have cracking patterns that are unique to their climates, unique as DNA or a fingerprint."

"Dutch craquelure is different than French and Italian?"

"Precisely right, Dermot."

"Sounds like your curator friend knows his stuff."

"Oh, he's an expert," Mullineaux said. "The curator did preliminary testing on the painting. Paint-chip tests, x-rays, things like that. All the tests indicate the work was done in the fifteenth century. The news gets better. A generous benefactor of the college, a man who just happens to be a dear friend of mine, said he wants to buy *Old Man in Prayer* for the Jesuit residence here at Saint Mary's Hall."

"Really?"

"If you're willing to sell the painting, the benefactor will pay fifty thousand dollars for it," Father Mullineuax said.

"Fifty grand?" Something felt funny. "That's a lot of money."

"I need to explain a few things first."

"I knew there was a catch. Go ahead, Father." I thought back to the conversation on the Oulipo Boys chat room. They said something about a swap, though they didn't specify what. Maybe this painting? "I'm listening."

"The painting could be worth more," he said. "Here's the dilemma. The painting might be the work of a Rembrandt student from the fifteenth century, or it might be the work of a superbly talented forger, say, who painted it last year. If a Rembrandt student produced *Old Man in Prayer*, the painting is worth far more than fifty thousand. However, if a forger produced it, it is worth far less."

"I see."

"Establishing who painted the reproduction is next to impossible, and frankly I don't care who painted it, because I love it. Fifty thousand is quite high for a recent forgery. However, fifty thousand is an insufficient amount for a reproduction by one of Rembrandt's students. If this painting is the work of a fifteenth-century Dutch student, the benefactor will pay full value, which could run in the millions."

"Millions?"

"No matter what the value of the painting, he wants to buy it." Father Mullineaux kept talking, now waving his hands. He could have been in front of an orchestra. "That's why he's offering fifty thousand. It's an initial offering, a down payment to secure the reproduction. In other words, don't sell it to anyone else."

"Heads I win, tails I win," I said. "It must be nice to have enough money to give away fifty thousand and not feel the pinch." I thought about Mrs. Hennessey with fifty grand thickening her purse. "It's hard to believe the painting's worth that much."

"This was quite a find."

"Sure was," I said. I thought about Mrs. Hennessey again and the way Housing adjusted the rent according to income. "Can your man pay cash?"

"He said he'd pay cash. If you agree to sell the painting, I can have the money here tomorrow."

"I agree."

Father Mullineaux shook my hand.

I drove home and went to bed and dreamt I was trapped in an old house with a single secret passageway out. A mermaid flopped along the floor and led me to the entrance of the passageway, then went away before she suffocated. Floating in a puddle she left behind was a wooden key, which turned to gold when I picked it up. The key unlocked the door to the secret entranceway and I looked inside, afraid to go in because hundreds of mice scurried on the floor. I thought: a mouse can't hurt me and stepped inside. A snake coiled in the corner sprang and bit me. The venom killed me.

The next day I stood beneath a stained glass window within a gleaming gothic recess inside Saint Mary's Hall as Father

Mullineaux handed me fifty thousand in hundred dollar bills. Ben Franklin never had so much company. We shook hands. I left the Jesuit residence, thick in the hip pocket. I drove back to Charlestown, called Mrs. Hennessey, and asked to see her. She told me to drop by any time. I said I'd be there in five minutes.

She buzzed me inside and waited at her apartment door.

"Come in, Dermot." She closed the door behind us. "Coffee or tea?"

"No thanks, Mrs. Hennessey. I only have a few minutes." I tapped the bulky envelope in my hand. "I have something to give you."

I handed her the envelope. She opened the flap, and her mouth dropped.

"What's this?" she said.

"The money belonged to Jeepster," I said. "Now it belongs to you."

She opened the envelope. "I don't understand. Jeepster never had this kind of money." She tossed the envelope on the kitchen table. A few of the hundreds splayed out of the open flap. "Where did the money come from?"

I gave her a sketchy version, leaving out the names involved and the nature of the goods exchanged.

"They paid me fifty thousand for an item that once belonged to Jeepster," I said. "I made the deal for you. The money goes to you because the item I sold was Jeepster's property."

"You're being awfully careful not to say what the item was." Her eyes focused. "It wasn't drugs, was it? I won't take money that came from drugs."

"It had nothing to with drugs," I said. "I have a good reason for keeping the nature of the item to myself."

"I trust you, and I trust your judgment," she said. "I've never seen this much money before."

"Me either."

"It kinda makes me nervous, having this much cash." She opened the envelope again. "I don't know what to do with it."

"Enjoy it, Mrs. Hennessey. Go to the Cape and enjoy the rest of the summer. Take the vacation you never had. Rent a cottage in Chatham on the ocean and watch the whitecaps roll in. Jeepster would've liked that."

The bells of Saint Jude Thaddeus rang. The gongs echoed off the brick tenements. Mrs. Hennessey sighed.

"I'll accept the money on one condition."

"What's that?"

"That you take half of it. I don't want any arguments, and I don't want any excuses. It's fifty-fifty or nothing. Do we have a deal?"

"I don't know, Mrs. Hennessey." It didn't feel right taking twenty-five thousand of her money. "The money belongs to you."

"We split it. End of discussion," she said. "I have my reasons for this decision, just like you had your reasons for keeping things to yourself about the item you sold. Do we have a deal?"

I didn't like it, but it would be impossible to change her mind.

"We have a deal. I'll put it to good use," I said. "I'll use it in memory of Jeepster."

"I'd like that." She slid the envelope to me. "Do the honors and divvy it up."

I counted the money like a bank teller serving a five-o'clock customer and handed her two hundred and fifty one hundred dollar bills, twenty-five grand each in cash. I've never been rich before.

CHAPTER 29

Captain Pruitt came to my office the next morning carrying two cups of coffee in a cardboard tray. He handed me one and sat on a folding chair across from my desk. He opened the lid of his and took a sip.

"Anything new on Hennessey's murder?" He sat back in the seat, his ebony face glistening with beads of sweat. It was only nine in the morning. "Did anyone in the projects say anything about it?"

Should I tell Pruitt the conversations I had with Jeepster's girlfriend Sherri McGillicuddy and his Vietnam pal Jimmy Devin? It might earn me brownie points and throw him off the art angle.

"I heard something around the neighborhood," I said. "Don't know whether to believe what I heard, it sounded farfetched. You hear stuff on the streets and nine times out of ten times it turns out to be bullshit."

"Which means ten percent of the time it's true," he said. "Humor me, Sparhawk. Tell me what you heard."

"I heard that Jeepster was looking to get out of town," I said. "He had plans to hightail it to Rio de Janeiro."

"What do you mean, hightail it?"

"When the time was right, he wanted to get out of Boston fast. He needed a stake to make the move," I said. "Apparently the stake was coming from a big poker game."

"A poker game?" Pruitt said. "How much could Hennessey make in a poker game? Certainly not enough to move to Rio."

"The poker game was high stakes," I said. "To get to the table he needed fifty grand up front, kind of like an entrance fee."

"Fifty grand," he said. "Are you sure about the amount?"

"I'm not sure about anything, Captain. That's what I heard." I picked up a pencil from my desktop, just to have something to fiddle with. "I also heard Jeepster came up with the fifty grand for the game."

Pruitt pushed away his coffee cup and pulled it back. It was the closest he ever came to fidgeting. Something I said had rattled him.

"Who told you this about the fifty grand?"

"Nobody, just stuff I heard."

"Did you hear anything else?"

"Yeah, I heard another thing, but it sounded crazy."

"Let me decide if it's crazy or not."

"I heard Jeepster's money was counterfeit. Jeepster got into the game with fifty thousand in counterfeit bills. I heard that one of the players, probably the winner, because it was a winner-take-all game, figured out what Jeepster had done and killed him for it. Like I said, it's crazy."

Pruitt continued to play with his cup, faster now, side to side, as well as back and forth.

"Anything else?"

"That's it," I said.

"Suppose I told you something in confidence."

"I suppose I could keep it to myself."

"The forensics team found fifty thousand dollars on Hennessey." He studied my face. "Hennessey had fifty grand in counterfeit cash, all hundreds. Does this information trigger any new thoughts, something you forgot to tell me?"

Now I was the one fidgeting.

"I heard the winner of the card game came up from Florida, maybe Miami. He flew in for the game. I know nothing about the other players."

"Someone told you all this, the poker game, the fifty grand, the Florida player?" He was making circles with his cup. "Why tell *you* all this information?"

"Maybe because Jeepster was my godfather and I want to find his killer."

"Who told you?"

"I got bits and pieces from different sources," I said. "It's hard to keep track of them all."

"Bullshit, you know exactly who told you what," he said. "I'll let it go for now. Keep your ears opened, let me know if you hear anything else. And thanks, the information about the poker game is important."

Three days had passed since Buck and I logged into the Oulipo Boys chat room. It was now Thursday morning, time to log on again. At nine o'clock we entered the chat room, neither of us knowing what to expect. Buck typed the first message.

Oulipo_Man: I'm here

The_Go_Between: It's time to get this deal done

Main_E_Ack: I'm sick of waiting

The_Go_Between: We need to move now.

An orange icon flashed at the bottom of the monitor in the taskbar. Buck and I looked at each other.

"What's that flashing?" I said.

"A sidebar," Buck said. "If a chat room member wants to send a private message to a particular user, he sends it with a sidebar, so no one else can see it."

"What should we do?"

"Let's open it."

Buck clicked on the flashing orange icon, which opened to a small window on the screen. The window had a message from another user.

The_Eggman: Who are you?

"Shit, now what? This guy's new." Buck slid the mouse back and forth. "Who the hell is The Eggman?"

"I don't know. Tell him—I don't know what to tell him."

"We might as well answer his question." Buck typed and hit send.

Oulipo_Man: I'm the Oulipo Man.

The_Eggman: The Oulipo Man is dead.

"What do I say?" Buck waited. "Think."

"Tell him we're taking over for the Oulipo Man or something like that."

Oulipo_Man: I'm his replacement

The_Eggman: Replacing who?

"Buck, think of a code, a secret way to tell him we're replacing Jeepster. Try something from the *Oulipo Compendium*."

"Like what?"

"I don't know, try anything."

Oulipo_Man: I'm replacing JH

The_Eggman: We need to meet

Oulipo_Man: Where, when?

The_Eggman: Fields Corner, tomorrow, 10 a.m. Go to a bar called the Roscommon Room. Tell the barman you're Mr. Smith from out of town. Don't drive. Take a cab.

Buck said, "What's with the cab?"

"Just tell him okay."

Oulipo_Man: Friday 10 a.m.

Buck closed the sidebar session and we bounced back to the Oulipo Boys' main window.

The_Go_Between: What took so long to answer?

"Tell them we need a few more days to iron out complications," I said. "Tell them to log on again Sunday morning."

"Got it."

Oulipo_Man: Something came up. I need more time. Log on again Sunday 9 a.m. We'll continue this discussion at that time

Buck logged off before they had a chance to reply.

That night I met my sponsor, Mickey Pappas, at an AA meeting in the North End. We sat in the front row, as is suggested for newcomers to the program. Mickey told me he started sitting in the front row twenty years ago and doesn't plan to stop. A curvy young woman with long black hair walked past us with a confident air. She wore cutoffs and a tight green tank top with the word Brazil written in yellow across the front. Mickey's eyes widened.

"Brazil," he said. "God, I love Mediterranean women. She ain't wearing a bra, that's for sure. I wonder if she's wearing underwear."

"It's tough to say."

"Boy, I hope not," he said. "Even if she is, maybe they're edible."

"Maybe." I laughed.

"If her shorts were any shorter—" He leaned closer to me. "I'm kidding around, Dermot. I ain't into kinky stuff, too old for it. And besides, Brenda already tried it. She told me I wasn't missing a thing."

The meeting started. The first speaker said he thought he couldn't be an alcoholic because he was Italian. His parish priest told him that Italians can't be alcoholics. Two drunken driving arrests later, the man changed his mind, or rather, the courts changed his mind. He celebrated nine years of sobriety last week.

After the meeting I saw a familiar face walking toward me. I couldn't place him at first. As he drew nearer it came to me, Skinny Atlas from Aunt Bea's Cazenovia Club. His face was gray, his hands were shaking.

"Hey," I said to him, "how goes it, Skinny?"

"Fine," he said.

He walked out of the hall with his head down, his eyes focused on the tiles. I knew the feeling. Mickey came up and nudged me with an elbow.

"You know that guy?"

"Not really," I said. "I met him a few weeks ago."

"The poor bastard's mocus from booze. He's got wet brain." Mickey threw his empty cup in the trash can. "He'll be okay if he stays sober. I've seen worse cases clear up."

"Really?"

"Sure, look at you."

CHAPTER 30

I awoke the next morning with butterflies in my stomach, thinking about The Eggman and Fields Corner. I needed no coffee to shift my brain into drive. I called a cab, as instructed. Twenty minutes later it honked out front. A half hour after that, he dropped me in front of the Roscommon Room on Adams Street in Fields Corner, with fifteen minutes to spare. I went inside and approached the bartender. He was a stocky man with short arms, stooped shoulders, and a receding hairline. His nose was runny, his armpits were stained. Other than that, he was an attractive man.

"I'm Mister Smith from out of town," I said.

"Gimme a second, Mister Smith," he said with a husky voice. He served a round of drinks to a table of working men wearing khakis. They must've just got off the night shift. He refilled a drink for another patron, a sad sack with a rum-soaked face at the end of the bar. He came my way. "So, you're Mister Smith."

"That's what I'm told."

He went to the cash register and came back.

"Here you go Mister Smith." He handed me a key and a piece of paper. "Wanna wet your whistle before shoving off? It's a shingled roof, on the house."

"I'm all set." I slid a ten into the bar gutter. "Thanks."

Outside the Roscommon Room, I opened the folded paper and read it. It said the key started the black 1970 Bonneville convertible parked in the tavern's back lot. The note instructed me to drive the Bonneville to an address on North Munroe Terrace and to park it in the garage. The directions were written at the bottom. The note said I had five minutes to get there, or else the drawbridge goes up.

I turned the key, revved the engine, shifted into gear, and pulled out of the parking lot, driving Detroit's version of the *Titanic*. The sheet-metal barge handled as if it had a butter-knife rudder, swimming to and fro with each turn I made. I drove up Train Street, steering the colossus between parked cars. I turned left on North Munroe, a one-way slope running from the top of Popes Hill down to Neponset Avenue. I pulled into the driveway and parked in the garage, got out, and knocked on the back door.

A graying man wearing a paint-spattered sweatshirt with cut-off sleeves answered the door and invited me in. He had a Rollie Fingers handlebar moustache held in place with wax. The house was dark and the windows were cloaked with heavy drapery. The man closed the door behind me.

"The Oulipo Man arrives," he said. "I should say the Oulipo Man's replacement, because Jeepster Hennessey was the Oulipo Man. Who are you?"

"You first," I said.

"My name is Remy Menard, or as you know me, The Eggman."

I looked around the kitchen.

"Nice house, you own it?"

"I do now," he said. "It's a family's house. I'm the only one left."

"I'm Dermot Sparhawk," I said. "Jeepster was my godfather."

"Ah, yes, he talked about you. I served in Vietnam, with the Army, Eighty-second Airborne, did two hitches. I met Jeepster after the war at a veteran's post here in Dorchester. We'd drink a few beers." Remy walked down the hallway, leading me deeper into his dark dwelling. "Jeepster and me, we'd get talking about different things, kicked around ideas, ways to make money. Most all of them went south, harebrained schemes, the stuff of Norton and Kramden. Then we got involved in this thing that was supposed to make us some serious cash."

The doorbell rang and Remy answered it. A delivery man carried in a case of beer and a couple of shopping bags of food. Remy handed the man a tip. Apparently Remy kept a tab at the store, because that's all he gave him.

"I don't get out much these days, so I get my supplies delivered." He pulled a can of beer from the case and ran his index finger along the rim. "Hope you didn't mind what I did at the Roscommon Room. I figured I'd kill two with one, having you deliver the car then meet you at the same time. Musta thought it was weird, driving the Bonneville here."

"Didn't mind," I said.

"I don't drive the Bonneville anymore," he said. "I change the oil and have it detailed every three months. I love that car."

"Not to rush into things, Remy, but how do you fit into the Oulipo Boys?"

"I did things for Jeepster, and as a result, he invited me to join. To answer your question, I don't know how I fit in."

"What are the Oulipo Boys about?"

"Nobody really knows, not even the members. Only one man knew how the Oulipo Boys fit together and that man was Jeepster Hennessey. Jeepster set up the website and assigned the usernames. It was Jeepster's gig, the whole thing."

"Who are The Go Between and Main E Ack?"

"Beats me."

"Come on."

"I don't know who they are. Only Jeepster knew." Remy went back to the kitchen and grabbed another beer. He asked me if I wanted one and I said no thanks. He cracked it open, a tall Budweiser. The foam caressed the top of the can. "I know this much. I was the only member of the Oulipo Boys who knew Jeepster was the Oulipo Man. The others didn't know the Oulipo Man's identity, only I did."

Maybe Liam McGrew and Jackie Tracy figured out that Jeepster was the Oulipo Man. Maybe that's why they confronted me.

And there was George Meeks, who definitely knew more about the Oulipo Boys than he let on, according to Eddie Doyle at FCI Otisville. Or maybe McGrew and Tracy and Meeks had nothing to do with any of this. Remy swallowed a gulp of Budweiser.

"I know this much. Jeepster and the Oulipo Boys were verging on a deal, a deal with lots of moving parts, lots of parties involved. I'd bet anything that each party knew only his own role in the scam. That's how Jeepster would set it up. He'd kept us in the dark. The man played chess, positioning us pawns. Only Jeepster knew the pieces."

"Why did Jeepster tell you so much?" I said, thinking as I was talking. "Why did he confide in you and not the others?"

"What do you mean?"

"Jeepster revealed himself to you as the Oulipo Man. That's huge."

"Yeah, I guess it was huge, him telling me. It was also simple. I was the key to his plan. Without my expertise, there was no money to be made." He rested the empty beer can on an end table. "Come on, follow me."

We walked through the darkness to a stairway leading up.

"I got three full stories, a Philadelphia two-family," he said. "I'm the only one living here, so I took over all the floors."

"The heating bill must suck," I said.

"It's worth it, not dealing with tenants."

We reached the second floor, which was better lit, the visibility improved to two feet. I followed Remy to the third floor, and it was as if someone snapped open the shades. We stepped into bright sunlight. The ceiling panels had been removed, exposing the joists and rafters. Above the rafters, beveled skylights slanted along the roofline to the peak. Floor-to-ceiling windows lined the sidewalls, massive plates of thick glass separated by window studs. Easels covered by sheets dotted the floor like teepees.

Remy Menard removed the sheets, flinging them in the air like Gatsby's shirts, baring the paintings beneath. I saw a painting of a seascape in choppy waters, another of an artist standing at an easel, another of a man sitting at a window beside a spiral staircase. He removed each sheet with an illusionist's flair, revealing a fresh work of genius with each unveiling. I lost my breath.

Soft Dylan music played in the background: *It Takes a Lot to Laugh, It Takes a Train to Cry.* A quote, circa 1533, from Sebastian Franck was tacked to the wall: The world wants to be deceived, and so it is. *The Art Forger's Handbook* by Eric Hebborn sat on a bookshelf. Remy interrupted my trance.

"This ain't armchair forgery, Dermot. Some of my paintings I sell as known reproductions, perfectly legal. I dress them down, so it's obvious to everyone they're reproductions. I hate it. Painting facsimiles makes me feel like a whore. I refuse to keep any of that crap up here."

"None of these looks like a velvet Elvis."

"The loft is reserved for my best works. The legal market bores the hell out of me. It's tedious. I prefer the underground, because forgery is my business." He guided me to a painting. "My real stuff is good and I mean damn good. The best in the world, I guarantee it."

"The paintings are breathtaking."

"Fools dabble with paintbrushes and pretend to be forgers," he said. "That's what they are, pretenders."

"Gondoliers acting like pole-vaulters."

"Hey, I like that." He stepped closer to the seascape painting. "I've been working on this baby for over a month now, Rembrandt's *Storm on the Sea of Galilee,* oil on canvas. Nice, huh?"

"Awesome," I said.

"Check out the corner of this painting. Note the foxing." He pointed at them. "You look confused."

"It's my Greek-to-me expression. You'll get used to it."

He pointed to a section of the painting.

"Foxing is the little rust-colored markings, very tough to replicate. I nailed 'em perfectly," he said. "A light foxing is one of the subtle touches necessary for a convincing forgery. Wanna know the trick?"

"Sure, I guess so."

"Nescafé coffee," he said. "I dampen the canvas and flick a teaspoon of Nescafé in the air. The coffee adheres to the dampness, and presto, fox-marks. I learned the fox-mark technique from Tom Keating, a legendary forger."

"Your works are unbelievable."

"Yeah, I know."

"This is beautiful." I walked to an easel. "*The Storm on the Sea of Galilee*, it's stunning."

"Jeepster hired me to paint it just before he died."

Another quote, this one from Plato, was nailed to a weight-bearing beam: Everything that deceives may be said to enchant. I sensed a theme developing. I looked again at the painting.

"Did he say why?" I said. "Why did Jeepster want it?"

"He never told me anything. He just placed the order," Remy said. "This one over here is *Pilate Washing His Hands*, another Rembrandt. I decided to scrap it."

An array of accessories topped his workbench, presumably for the craft of forgery. There were solvents and resins, varnishes and turpentine, oils and brushes, canvases and frames, the container of Nescafé that Remy mentioned earlier. He had teabags, potatoes, bleach, flour, breadcrumbs.

"What's the hot chocolate for?"

"I drink it." He pointed to a teakettle. "I have a sweet tooth. Want a cup?"

"No thanks." I laughed. "If the forgery business dries up, you can always open a diner."

He didn't laugh.

"Rembrandts are the toughest to reproduce. His works were so varied," he said. "But there's more to it than that."

"Like what?"

"The Dutch climate of the fifteenth century rendered a unique craquelure, nearly impossible to duplicate." He smiled at me. "Unless you have a pal at M.I.T. who has a double doctorate in meteorology and chemistry, and who has access to a climate-controlled chamber, *then* it's not so impossible."

"How does a chamber fit into artwork?"

"The chamber serves a single purpose, to render craquelure. Here's how we figured it out. We placed a painted canvas, not a completed painting, just a painted canvas, into the chamber and applied different combinations of elements to it, and then rated the results. After rating the results, we adjusted the barometric pressure, the dew point, the temperature, and several other variables and tried again. Back in the studio, I tweaked the drying rates and oil ratios. We eventually perfected it. The key ingredient, wanna guess what it was?"

"Don't have a clue." He was dying to tell me. "What was it?"

"Saltwater. Instead of using tap water we used saltwater to manipulate the dew point. That was the X in the equation, Dermot. Controlling the relative humidity with saltwater proved ingenious."

"The yeast that leavened the loaf."

"Exactly. Next, we slowed the heating process, like the way your grandmother cooked a grilled cheese. Heat it slowly or else the bread burns before the cheese melts. My M.I.T. pal figured out the heating-cooling protocol, which also played into the dew point calculations."

"Not many people have pals like that."

"We experimented for three weeks to get the craquelure right." Remy walked to one of the easels. "We arrived at a sixty-hour protocol. Twelve hours in the chamber equaled one hundred years in the Netherlands climate. All Rembrandts were painted in the fifteenth century, so it came down to simple arithmetic. Twelve hours per each hundred years, for a total of five hundred years, equals sixty hours in the chamber. Twelve times five, get it?"

"I should have paid better attention in math."

"If the cracking isn't perfect, if the splintering surface doesn't match that rendered by the Dutch climate, a Rembrandt forgery can be easily detected. But if you get it right, if you duplicate the fracturing pattern of the region, you're gonna fool anyone. I guarantee it."

Remy Menard liked to guarantee things, the Joe Namath of forgers.

"So after weeks of experimenting, you duplicated the Dutch craquelure."

"We did indeed." He moved closer to the seascape painting. "You need the materials, too. Antiquing is important, but so are the materials. I got my hands on historical canvases, old rolls of woven linen. Linen is the best for stretching. I mixed my own pigments, using flake white. Amateur forgers use the wrong pigments, colors that weren't around when the originals were painted. Bad pigments, that's another way to get nabbed."

"Where'd you get the stuff?"

"The flake white is nothing more than white lead base. I got it from a friend who deals in such valuables. Flake white is essential to forgers, and it's essential that it's pure lead, unadulterated with zinc or titanium. Even better, get old grounds from the time period you're forging. That's what I procured, aged lead grounds, flake white from the fifteenth century."

"Mind-blowing," I said. Why was Remy telling me all this? I'd find out soon enough. "You got paints from the right time period."

"The proportion of oil to paint is crucial, so are the brushes. I got my hands on quality pig bristle brushes, perfect for Rembrandts." He considered another forged painting. "Wanna hear something funny? Forgery isn't hard once you get the technique down and get the right materials. Start with the underdrawing, then the underpainting, then the final layers, it's pretty simple."

"Sounds like a snap."

"I can teach you," he said. "I'd be happy to work with you and let you in on a couple of trade secrets. What do you say?"

"I'm on board. Point me to the crayons."

We laughed.

"Poppy oil, too, poppy oil for the final touches." Remy walked from the seascape to another painting, this one of a man sitting at a window next to a spiral staircase. "Another Rembrandt, *Philosopher in Meditation*. This masterpiece goes beyond genius. I'm talking about Rembrandt's original, not my copy. His use of light, his hand had to be guided by God. To call *Philosopher in Meditation* a work of genius elevates the meaning of genius."

"It's beautiful."

"My stuff passes all the tests. X-ray diffraction, ultraviolet fluorescence, infrared analysis, even Morellian analysis, my stuff beats 'em all."

"I'm impressed," I said.

"Sorry for the dissertation, I spend too much time alone. Didn't mean to go on and on, boring you with my passions, I just wanted to tell you about my work."

"I didn't find it boring at all," I said. "Where does Jeepster come into all this? What about the Oulipo Boys?"

"Ah, yes, the Oulipo Boys." He cracked his knuckles. "A few years back I painted some stuff for Jeepster, all Dutch, two Rembrandts and a Vermeer."

"Which Rembrandts?"

"Both were portraits, *Old Man in Prayer* and *Self-Portrait, Aged 23*. I did yeoman's work on *Old Man in Prayer*, good enough to fool any curator, but *Self-Portrait* was my best work ever, my par excellence. The original hangs in the Gardner Museum. I go there every couple of years to analyze it, and each time I see it I'm amazed. My reproduction of *Self-Portrait, Aged 23* matched the Gardner's to a tee."

"Which Vermeer did you paint?"

"*The Concert*," he said. "Regrettably, the original *Concert* was stolen in the Gardner heist, so I have nothing to compare to my work. To be honest about it, my Vermeer was lacking. It didn't possess the superior quality of my Rembrandts, especially *Self-Portrait, Aged 23*." Remy stepped to another easel. "This Vermeer here, *The Allegory of Painting*, is exceedingly good, perhaps excellent. The country of Austria owns the original. Göring wanted it, so did Hitler. Guess who won that battle?"

"I'll take a wild stab and say Adolf."

"Right," he said. "He snagged the painting in nineteen forty. After the war ended the Allies recovered it in a German salt mine and returned it to Austria. I think General Patton found it."

"I heard Hitler was a lousy painter."

"A lousy painter and a sick fuck, yet a remarkable collector," he said. "He robbed half the museums in Europe. Check out *The Rape of Europa*, a tremendous film about it."

"Why did Jeepster commission you to forge two Rembrandts and a Vermeer?" I said. "If commission is the right word."

"Commission works fine," Remy said. "He never told me his reasons, not directly. He alluded to a burgeoning underground market, the type of market you don't find in the Yellow Pages. He wanted to sell my works as paintings by students of Vermeer and Rembrandt. Rembrandt had an art school, where he trained the top young artists of Europe."

"I heard."

"Most of the students cut their teeth by imitating the masters. Once they perfected the imitation, they moved to their own concepts. These imitations proved to be enormously valuable, fetching hundreds of thousands of dollars. That's why Jeepster commissioned them, to sell them as works of Rembrandt's students."

"We're missing something, Remy. There must be another reason he commissioned them." I thought about the Rembrandts Remy painted. "He couldn't sell them as originals. The originals were hanging in museums, still are."

"Except for the Vermeer." He paused. "And *The Storm on the Sea of Galilee*, which I'm still working on. Both those were stolen from the Gardner Museum."

"Right, except for the Vermeer and the unfinished Rembrandt," I said. "Do you see what I'm driving at? All that work for two, maybe three hundred thousand dollars, and then dividing it up, I don't think so."

"I hate to even think this," Remy said. "It's so out of character for Jeepster."

"Think what?"

"Forged paintings are sometimes used to fund terrorism, kind of like an underground currency, a not-so-legal tender. The FBI and insurance investigators claim there's a connection between terrorism and forged art." He winced. "I'm not naïve. I knew I was an abettor in a scam. I just hope it wasn't terrorism."

I thought about Emma Hague and how she moved into Jeepster's apartment. I wondered if the link to terrorism had more to do with forged art than Somali immigrants. The idea of Jeepster and terrorists sickened me.

"No way," I said, perhaps out of denial. "No fuckin' way Jeepster helped those slimy bastards."

"You're probably right."

"I know I'm right," I said. "Back to the Oulipo Boys—"

"The Oulipo Boys are ramping up to make a move, and I'm pretty sure it involves the paintings I forged." Remy picked up a brush from the workbench and twirled it. "If anything comes of it, if there's any money to be had, I'd like to get paid for my work."

"That's only fair," I said. "How much?"

"A hundred thousand."

"A hundred grand?" I asked. Then I remembered that Father Mullineaux had paid me fifty thousand for *Old Man in Prayer*, no doubt a Remy Menard fake. I couldn't tell Father Mullineaux it was a recent forgery, I'd already disbursed half the cash. Besides, he loved it. It seemed to me I should give Remy a piece of the money when the time came. "If the deal goes through and the money comes in, I'll pay you the hundred."

"Appreciate it."

"I hope I come up with it." I remembered something Remy mentioned earlier in the conversation. "You said that Jeepster commissioned you a few years back. How many years ago was it?"

He put down the brush and rubbed his chin.

"About twenty, maybe a little more."

"Twenty years ago?" I wasn't even in kindergarten then. "You're a patient man, Remy."

"Not really. Jeepster was behind bars most of that time. When he wasn't doing time, he was on the lam. He holed up here for three months."

"He was always on the move."

"I don't want to sound petty. It's not just the money, I miss the camaraderie, too. Jeepster was a good friend." He picked up the brush again. "Dermot, you can, ah, visit again if you'd want. I don't mind the company."

"The feeling's mutual." I thought of Glooscap. "My uncle owns an auto-body shop in Andrew Square. An easy place to find, it abuts the Red Line tracks. He's a Vietnam veteran, too. His name is Glooscap. Bring the Bonneville to Glooscap's shop for the next oil change. You two will get along."

"I might just do that," he said. "Sometimes at night I go out to the garage and sit in the car and pretend I'm driving."

Sometimes at night I go to AA meetings and pretend I have contented sobriety.

CHAPTER 31

"Take a ride with me, Sparhawk," Captain Pruitt said. "It won't take long, and I don't have all day. Hop in the car."

Pruitt was waiting for me at my office when I arrived at work the next day. I never stepped inside the building.

"A ride to where?" I asked.

"Get in the car, I'll drive."

He never turned on the siren; he drove as if it were blaring. We sped down the expressway, past the *Herald*, past the *Globe*, and exited at Granite Avenue in Dorchester. Pruitt stayed on Granite Ave. over the iron drawbridge and turned left on Milton Street, then left again into Cedar Grove Cemetery. He sped by the head-stones and obelisks and memorials until we reached the reedy banks of the Neponset River, where scummy water lapped the shore. Three unmarked police cars were parked there, along with two cruisers and an ambulance.

"Follow me," Pruitt said.

I followed him to the river's edge. He told me to stay put while he talked to the other detectives. Then he called me over. I was growing impatient.

"Why am I here?"

"There's a corpse I want you to look at. A floater, he just washed ashore," he said. "You're our last hope for an ID. Dental charts are useless because his teeth were yanked out, probably with pliers."

"His teeth were yanked out? What about fingerprints?"

"They cut off his hands."

"I guess you're out of luck with fingerprints." I looked at the body. "Why drag me over here?"

"The guy's nose has more stitches than a softball, that's why. And he didn't get them at MGH, either. Looks like an arthritic seamstress sewed them." He took me by the elbow. "I'm betting he's the second Irish attacker."

"Now I get why I'm here."

"You chewed the guy's nose, remember? He's the one that got away. Humor me, Sparhawk, take a close look at him."

A medic unzipped the body bag just enough for me to see the dead man's face. Pruitt was right about the stitch job. It was a tangle of frayed threads. His skin had a bloodless texture. The face was bloated and milky, almost featureless, too decomposed to identify.

"I don't know. Maybe it's him, maybe not. I can't say for sure."

"Take your time, Sparhawk," Pruitt said.

I thought back to the day of the attack, when the two micks came at me with telescoping batons and beat my body numb. Sideburns and Saint Pat, flailing away like wild men. I almost forgot. Saint Pat had a tattoo on his forearm. I unzipped the bag another foot, turned over the arm, and there it was. A shamrock tattoo with St. Pat inked under it. I pointed to it.

"It's him," I said. "I don't know his name, but he's one of the guys who attacked me."

"Good job," Pruitt said. "Officer Hernandez will drive you back to Charlestown. Thanks, Sparhawk."

Hernandez nodded his head toward one of the cruisers and I got in.

I answered a heavy knock on the office door and came face-to-face with a man who was a collection of contradictions. He wore a yellow Nautica shirt, Kelly green trousers, a blue belt with little white whales, and tan Gucci loafers with tassels. His forearms, matted with hair and corded with muscles, extended to hands that had knuckles as big as walnut shells. Blue veins bulged in his neck.

Whisker stubble crusted his face like black barnacles. I didn't know whether to laugh at him or run from him. His clothes said prep school, his mug said reform school. I needed to find out which.

"You took a wrong turn, Buffy," I said. "The polo match is in Hamilton."

The man smirked, pinched his crooked nose with a thumb and finger, and shook his monolithic head.

"A wise prick." He eyed me. "A big prick, too."

"Got a name?"

"Buffy will do for now," he said. "We need to talk."

"About what?" I scanned the parking lot for a car to get a license plate number. No go. "Talk about what?"

"Let's walk around the neighborhood." He wasn't afraid of the projects. Was he a cop, an ex-cop? He was too young to be a retired cop, maybe a cop who got booted for excessive force. Or maybe he was just a tough bastard in preppy clothing. He bounded off the stoop, light on his feet. "Follow me."

"Why should I?" I remained on the stoop.

"Why not?" he said. "It's a nice day and we need to talk about things."

"I don't need to talk about anything."

"Come on, take a walk. Good things are in your future, you'll want to hear about them."

"What things?" I said.

"I like to walk when I talk. Come on, Sparhawk, take a walk. I'll tell you all about it." He knew my name. "You'll be glad you did."

"Okay," I said.

I let him take the lead, and he led me into the middle of the projects. The residents glanced at him and gave plenty of room. We walked down Walford Way. Naddi watched us from across the street and walked faster. Buffy began to talk.

"I understand you sold something to someone for a hefty sum of money."

No sense giving him too much too soon.

"I sold my father's Carl Yastrzemski rookie card for twenty-five dollars," I said.

"I'm not in a bullshitting mood."

"Neither am I," I said. "If you got something to say, say it. Don't jerk me around."

He laughed. Somehow the laugh made him more menacing. We turned left on Decatur Street and walked along the Tobin Bridge stanchions, crunching through broken beer bottles. I stopped when we reached Medford Street.

"What do you want?"

He scanned the area then turned to me.

"I represent an important person with a lot of money."

"Bully for you."

"He's a rich client who's willing to part with millions. Let's keep walking." We crossed Chelsea Street and entered the Navy Yard at Gate 5. Buffy was in no rush. He had all day. He took a pouch of Red Man chewing tobacco from his pocket, pinched a wad and chomped on it. "Where did you get the painting you sold the priest? Just so you know I'm not bullshitting around, I'm talking about *Old Man in Prayer*, the Rembrandt forgery."

Father Mullineaux promised me he'd keep my name out of his dealings. What happened? Why did he break his vow? This was bad. I thought about telling Buffy I didn't know what he was talking about. That seemed like a waste of time. He knew about the painting, that much was clear.

"What priest?" I said just to make sure. "What's the priest's name?"

"Father Mullineaux, Boston College." The way he said Boston didn't sound Boston. We walked deeper into the Navy Yard, walking along 1st Avenue. Buffy smiled again. I didn't like it when he smiled. "Father Mullineaux didn't give us your name. He promised to keep you out of it, that's what I heard. He never said a word."

"How did you find me?"

"Easy, we tailed a Judas goat. A person we were following led us to you, unknowingly no doubt." He spit brown fluid. "It's not as if the painting is a secret. Mullineaux plans to hang it in Saint Mary's lobby after the testing is done."

"So what? I sold a painting to Father Mullineaux," I said. "What of it?"

"Let's keep walking."

We turned onto Terry Ring Way and stopped at the Korean War Veteran's Memorial. I studied Buffy's features. His face was shaped like home plate: square on the sides, flat on the top, pointed at the chin.

"Are you the cabbie?"

"What?" He stared at me. "I don't drive a cab."

His voice didn't match the cabbie's. There was no Boston accent in it. I looked at him more closely. He had boilermaker forearms, but no prison tattoos. No blue ink means no prison time. If he didn't do prison time, he had nothing to do with the Oulipo Boys. We sat on a granite bench facing Dry Dock 2.

"I have two questions," he said. "Answer the questions correctly and you'll be paid a hefty sum of cash."

"I'm not too good at tests."

"Where did you get the Rembrandt reproduction?" He raised his right hand to signal he wanted to continue. "Hear me out on this, Sparhawk. You'll be glad you did. The party I represent will pay fifty thousand dollars for information about the reproduction."

"What's the second question?"

"Are there any other paintings?" he said. "My client will buy each additional painting for fifty thousand. That's fifty thousand apiece."

"Why does he want fake paintings?"

"The man I represent is a collector of rare things. He can't buy an original Rembrandt, because none are for sale. My client accepts that he'll never own a real Rembrandt. The closest he'll get to owning a Rembrandt is owning a student rendering. The painting you sold to Father Mullineaux was likely painted by a Rembrandt student. If *Old Man in Prayer* proves to be an authentic student rendering, that makes it both rare and valuable, which makes it something my client wants."

Remy's stuff was good enough to fool the experts.

"What's your client's name?"

"Nope, that's privileged."

Buffy's offer was tempting. My father told me that rich people overpay for trinkets they want. He'd cite the fools who paid twenty-four dollars for Manhattan Island. I had a chance to pocket a fast hundred grand, fifty for telling Buffy where I got *Old Man in Prayer* and fifty more for selling him *Self-Portrait, Aged 23*. A hundred thousand for disclosing a little harmless information and for handing over a fake painting, it seemed too easy.

I was about to accept his offer. I was about to tell him about Jeepster Hennessey's rented space at Mystic Piers Storage and the forged Rembrandt stowed inside, when an image of Jeepster's face flashed in my mind. I thought about the McSweeney key and Oswego. I owed Jeepster more than a sellout to a rich bastard.

"My answer is no," I said. "Tell your client I'm not interested."

"We're talking about fifty grand, Sparhawk. Fifty grand just to tell us where you got the painting," he said. "No matter where it came from, Father Mullineaux keeps it. We just want to know where you got it."

"Earlier you said something about millions. Now it's down to fifty grand. Is this a bait and switch?"

"Not at all," he said. "The potential for millions is real, depending on what you know."

I didn't like it.

"I have nothing more to say."

"Suppose we make it a hundred grand for the information and another hundred grand for all the paintings you can muster. That's a hundred thousand per painting."

He was making it harder to say no. With two hundred thousand, I could practically retire. I forgot about Remy. Remy Menard had six paintings in his studio loft, all Rembrandt reproductions.

If I got a hundred grand for his six, plus another hundred for *Self-Portrait, Aged 23*, and another hundred for telling Buffy about *Old Man in Prayer*, I'd collect eight hundred thousand.

With a windfall of eight hundred K, I could pay Remy Menard the money Jeepster owed him and split what's left between Mrs. Hennessey and me. I needed to talk to Remy Menard. Remy was the key.

"Give me a couple of days to think about it. I'll give you my answer then," I said. "Tell me, how many paintings can your man afford to buy?"

"As many as you can lay your hands on. If you come up with ten he'll pay you a million in cash, plus another hundred for telling us where you got Mullineaux's painting."

We walked back out to 3rd Avenue and stood in front of the 7-Eleven. An MGH shuttle bus pulled up and Buffy hopped aboard.

What the hell just happened? I dialed Father Mullineaux. We stayed on the phone for close to an hour.

CHAPTER 32

I don't like dealing in unknowns. I didn't know Buffy's real name, and I didn't know the name of the man he represented. These unknowns pestered me as I drove west on Route 20 for Weston, a ritzy Boston suburb and home to the Hub's power hitters. There are no housing projects in Weston, unless a cul-de-sac with four McMansions qualifies as subsidized lodging. I passed over Route 128 and parked on a shady lane near my destination.

Big manors built on big lots housed people with big money. Even the hydrants said purebreds only. Mutts can piss in the woods. Better yet, go to Waltham. I got out of my coughing Plymouth and climbed a path that led to the top of a craggy hill.

I stood on the rock formation and looked down at a sprawling estate, this one extra grand, with acres of apple trees and a swimming pool that could accommodate a pod of whales.

Military binoculars I'd borrowed from Glooscap hung around my neck. I adjusted the site lines, surveyed the property, and awaited my quarry. The day dragged and dragged as I waited and waited, hoping my hunch was correct.

The property belonged to a man named Halloran, who made his millions in engineering and construction. He'd built skyscrapers, bridges, and tunnels in most of America's major cities, especially in Boston. A Boston College alumnus, Halloran was the man who purchased *Old Man in Prayer* for Father Mullineaux.

When I had spoken with Father Mullineaux on the phone, he refused to tell me who bought the Rembrandt reproduction for the college, until I told him about Buffy's visit to Charlestown. Father Mullineaux gasped when he heard the story, saying he felt culpable in exposing my identity. We fenced for an hour before he relented and told me Halloran's name.

The good padre recounted the events that led to the purchase of the painting, and he was meticulous in his retelling. After he finished the story, Father Mullineaux and I concluded that only one man knew I was coming to pick up the payment for the painting that day, and that man was Halloran.

It wasn't the curator. The curator didn't know the time of the payment. It wasn't the Jesuits who lived at Saint Mary's Hall. As Mullineaux thought back, more came to him. He remembered that Halloran had pressed him for my name. When Mullineaux refused to tell him, Halloran feigned bashfulness, as if he realized he'd overstepped his station, badgering a priest. Father Mullineaux said that Halloran asked him what time he needed the money by. Mullineaux told him no later than 2:30, because I'd be collecting it at 3:00.

At that point in the conversation it became clear to both of us what had happened: Halloran hired Buffy to follow me from Saint Mary's Hall. Father Mullineaux said he felt foolish about his loose lips. I told him it wasn't his fault. He'd been dealing with a cunning person, a con man with a college ring. No way to spot the ruse, I said, not with a hustler like Halloran. I told Father Mullineaux he had no reason to suspect Halloran, because Halloran was purchasing an expensive painting for the college. Mullineaux grew furious at that point and gave me Halloran's address. And that's why I was standing on a rocky hill in Weston with Glooscap's military binoculars around my neck. I was hoping to corroborate what I suspected about Halloran.

Halloran finally appeared late in the afternoon. He had white hair, a trim build, and was dressed in tennis garb. A younger man accompanied him. They entered the red clay tennis court, which sat next to the swimming pool. Halloran served the ball to the younger man, perhaps his son. They played a few inept sets. And I thought golf on TV was boring.

Then he showed up.

Buffy came around the corner of the manor and stepped onto the tennis court. Halloran waved off his partner, who toweled his head and walked away. Halloran tucked the racket under his arm and walked to the net with Buffy. Buffy began to talk, he gestured with his hands. Every so often Halloran replied with a nod. Buffy continued talking. They both nodded. Then Halloran talked. He leaned against the net post, crossed his arms, and spoke as he stared at the red clay. Both men nodded again. Halloran slapped Buffy on the back. Buffy left the tennis court.

I raced down the backside of the rock formation and jumped into my car just as Buffy motored out from under Halloran's porte cochere in a tan Mercedes-Benz, a color that matched his Gucci loafers. I followed Buffy in my rust bucket. He drove south on Route 128 and ramped onto the Mass Pike eastbound. The traffic was light, so I tailed at a distance. He stayed on the Mass Pike into Boston and took the South Station exit. On Atlantic Avenue he pulled into the Boston Harbor Hotel and handed his keys to a valet. I parked at a cabstand and waited.

The valet returned to his station. With his thin hair graying and his sunken eyes watering, he had the air of a man who'd worked two jobs his whole life and was playing out the string until retirement. I approached him.

"Nice car, that tan Mercedes," I said. "How does it handle?"

"My Bentley handles better." He adjusted his billed cap. "You need help or something?"

"I do." I palmed him three twenties. "I need the name of the man driving the tan Mercedes."

"No kidding, his name." He slid the twenties into his hip pocket. "Where you from?"

"Charlestown."

"A Townie. My father came from Charlestown, lived near the prison by the potato sheds." He adjusted his cap again. "Gimme a minute."

He came back five minutes later.

"Karl Kloosmann," he said. "Karl, with a *K*, Kloosmann, with a *K*, two *O*s, and two *N*s."

"You could've written it down," I said, in a lame attempt at humor.

"I did." He handed me a sheet of hotel notepaper. "I didn't figure you'd remember."

Then he gave me a little extra for my sixty dollars. He said that Kloosmann came from Cleveland, Ohio, and he'd been staying at the hotel for a week. I thanked him for his help and handed him another twenty. Twenty-five grand goes a long way, long enough to give a good guy an extra twenty.

I drove home, went into my apartment, took a can of tobacco from the cabinet, and embarked on my nightly ritual. With my mother's tweezers I plucked a strand of tobacco from the can my father left behind. I placed the brown strand into the bowl of his meerschaum pipe. He claimed the pipe came from India. My mother wasn't so sure. I filled the rest of the bowl with my own tobacco to preserve my father's stash. I lit the pipe, puffed till it glowed orange, and smoked it cold.

CHAPTER 33

I sat in my recliner thinking. I flipped ideas and mapped out strategies. All I got was confused. How to play it? I had Kloosmann's name, I had Halloran's name. I could go straight to Halloran and ask him why he wanted forged paintings and why he didn't contact me directly, instead of sending his stooge.

Or I could go to the Boston Harbor Hotel and shanghai Buffy Kloosmann, and show him just how brilliant I am in figuring out his identity.

Or I could act dumb and not let on that I knew the connection between Halloran and Kloosmann, and between Father Mullineaux and Halloran. If I went that route, I'd become a counterpuncher, reading their moves and reacting to them. It was a pivotal decision in untangling this mess. Sometimes acting dumb is the smart move; sometimes it isn't.

I decided to talk to Buck Louis about it. Buck had become a sounding board for me, a clear thinker with clear ideas. I wanted to hear his thoughts, and I wanted to devise a plan with him. Plus, I needed to tell him something I'd been meaning to tell him for a while now. I walked down the flight of stairs and knocked on his door.

Buck rolled across the carpeting, unlatched the door, and swung it open.

"Dermot, come on in." He shut the door behind me with the flick of the wrist. "Just made a fresh pot of brew, how's about a cup?"

"Sounds good."

"Want to talk about the Oulipo puzzle?"

"Yes," I said, "I've been thinking about the Oulipo Man, the Eggman, and the painting I sold. I'm wondering if it's all one. The Oulipo Man, the Eggman, the paintings, the McSweeney key, Oswego, Jeepster's murder, I'm wondering if it's all connected."

"We already know that Oswego was Oulipo Man's chat room password," he said. "So we figured out Oswego."

"Yes, that's true." I sat on the couch with my coffee. "There's something I've been meaning to tell you. It has to do with Jeepster's storage room."

"Never too late, what is it?"

"Jeepster kept a shortwave radio in the room, kind of like a CB radio except bigger, with a mike and headset."

"A two-way radio, my uncle had one. He lived in Kentucky, in Appalachia. The guy survived on nothing. He got into the CB scene big-time after he saw *Smokey and the Bandit*, my uncle loved Burt Reynolds."

"The radio has a cable that goes through the ceiling," I said. "Maybe Jeepster put an antenna on the roof. Jeepster's storage room is on the top floor."

"I bet you're right. He probably punched a hole in the roof and hooked up an antenna," Buck said. "I say we take a look-see." Buck rolled to the kitchen, poured himself coffee, held up the pot, and I shook my head no. He wheeled back. "When do we go?"

"We'll check it out soon."

We went silent for a moment. The outskirts of the projects don't usually offer quiet.

"There's something else," I said. "I want your thoughts on this situation I'm in."

"Go on, I'm listening."

I told Buck about Buffy, now known to be Karl Kloosmann. Then I told him about Halloran. I said that Kloosman presented an intimidating front, but that he was strictly a go-between for Halloran. I told Buck about Halloran's offer, presented by Kloosman, to buy any and all the paintings I could muster, paintings equal to the quality of the one I sold to Father Mullineaux. I finished by telling Buck that neither Kloosman nor Halloran was aware I knew of their identities. They were in the dark.

"That's an advantage," Buck said. "You know their names, and that puts you on even footing. Better than even footing, because they don't know you know, so that gives you an edge. You're in a good position."

"What do I do with it?" I said.

"Yeah, what to do with it?"

We each waited for the other to say something, anything. It seemed like a long wait. Buck extended his hands, palms open, inviting me to talk. I accepted.

"I came up with three possible approaches to handle this. First approach, hit Halloran head-on. Ring his doorbell and get in his face. Spook him and see what shakes out. Second approach, way-lay Kloosmann at the Boston Harbor Hotel. Put him on his heels and see how he reacts. Catch Kloosmann off guard and he might panic, he might tell us something important. Third, don't let on. Lay in wait, so to speak." I finished the coffee. "What do you think?"

"God, I love this shit." Buck popped a wheelie. "If we wait too long we lose the upper hand. If we get too cute, they'll eventually figure out we're on to them."

"I see what you mean."

"I say we err on the aggressive side. Action, that's the key. Now is the time to act, now's the time to punch someone in the mouth."

"I agree, Buck. Which one do I punch in the mouth?"

"I like approach number one, hit Halloran hard. Halloran is the decision maker. Kloosmann is a lackey with no say." Buck wheeled forward. "Halloran calls the shots. Get in his face, back his ass against the wall, find out how tough he really is."

"That's how we'll play it, we'll go after Halloran."

"Good." Buck stopped squeezing the arms of the wheelchair. His shoulders dropped down from his ears. He seemed pleased that I took his recommendation. "I want to see the storage facility." He followed me to the door. "I want to get a gander at that radio."

"Tomorrow," I said. "I'll go to Halloran's house in the morning. I might be there for hours, or he might tell me to screw as soon as I get there. There's no way to know."

"I never thought of that, him telling you to screw." Buck wheeled back and forth a few inches. "No, he won't tell you to screw. He's gonna want to know what's up with the paintings."

"We can check the storage place when I get back from Halloran's," I said. "I'm going upstairs to watch the Red Sox, talk to you later."

The Sox were playing the Twins at Fenway, and the game was tied at one after five. My father loved baseball. I wondered what he'd think of Fenway's virtual TV ads. They looked real enough against the backstop, but they weren't real at all. Blink your eyes, the old ad was gone, replaced by a new one. People say it's no different than the ads when Ted Williams played, but somehow it seems different.

With runners on first and second the Twins executed a double steal. John Lester settled down and pitched his way out of the jam, stranding the runners in scoring position. In the bottom the inning, Kevin Youkilis crushed a hanging curve into the Monster seats in left. David Ortiz followed with a double to the centerfield triangle, a cannon shot that ricocheted off the 420 sign. A younger Ortiz would have legged out three.

Between innings a beer commercial showed a trio of trim men giggling with three toothsome women in a friendly bar. The barman had teeth and was clean shaven. Everybody smiled when they toasted a round. Nobody passed out or got shut off. Nobody shit his pants or took a beating in the men's room. I hit the mute button before I got angrier. That's when my cell phone rang.

My Irish cousin Timmy O'Hanlon of Homeland Security was on the other end. He said he wanted to drop by to see me. I told him to come ahead, and I went downstairs and waited on the front porch. The wind drifted from the Navy Yard, cooling Bunker Hill Street. Three Hispanic teens shuffled out of the projects, their baseball hats askew. An unmarked police car turned down Tufts Street, slowing as it passed them. Timmy O'Hanlon parked in front of my house and got out of his car. I stepped off the porch to greet him. We stood together on the sidewalk under a brightening sodium streetlamp.

"I checked into the situation we talked about at the courthouse the other day," he said.

"Naddi," I said.

"She's got papers. She's here legally, so is her daughter." Timmy pulled out a piece of paper and read from it. "Ayanna, that's the daughter's name. As for Naddi, we found no hint that she's involved in terrorist activity. She's clean, Dermot. If she was involved in anything we'd know about it."

"I wonder what's scaring her."

"Whatever she's afraid of, it has nothing to do with terrorism. There's no terrorist threat in Charlestown, Somali or otherwise." He read from the paper again. "I talked to a terrorism specialist, a man who infiltrated al-Shabab. He told me that nothing is happening in Charlestown with al-Shabab, not a damn thing."

"Do you think he's right?"

"He's right," Timmy said. "This guy is serious. His information is excellent."

I watched a car pass by and thought about the Red Sox game. Timmy continued.

"There's nothing happening in Charlestown."

"If there's no al-Shabab in Charlestown, what's Emma Hague doing here? And why is she living in the projects?" I thought back to my first meeting with Emma, when Captain Pruitt introduced us. "She talked a good game. She made a compelling argument about the threat of Somali terrorism in the projects."

"My information refutes her claim."

"When I think about it, the words Emma used were abstract. She said nothing concrete, no names, nothing about actual events. She speculated, what-if stuff, like what if a terrorist launched a handheld rocket at an LNG tanker, that type of thing. What's Emma Hague up to if she's not working on terrorism?"

"Don't know," Timmy said. "Can't help you there."

"And if there's no terrorist threat, then what is Naddi afraid of?" I said. "And what did she mean when she said un-American activities?"

"I don't know, Dermot."

None of it made sense. Emma Hague, Naddi and Ayanna, al-Shabab, Somali terrorism, no Somali terrorism, un-American activities, none of it made sense. I was putting together a jigsaw puzzle with the cardboard side of the pieces.

CHAPTER 34

The noon bells rang from a Protestant church as I parked in front of Halloran's Weston estate. My rust bucket Plymouth screamed like an eyesore against the backdrop of his landscaped flower beds and manicured lawns, a swine before pearls. I hoped he didn't have it towed. I knocked on the front door and a young man answered, the same young man who'd been playing tennis with Halloran. He was frail, the physical opposite of Kloosmann. I told him I wanted to speak to Mr. Halloran. He asked my name.

"Dermot Sparhawk," I said. "Tell Halloran I'm the man with the paintings, the man who sold Father Mullineaux the Rembrandt reproduction of *Old Man in Prayer*. Tell him I'm a friend of Karl Kloosmann. Kloosmann and I talked a couple of days ago."

"Karl told you about my father?" A blank gaze overtook his eyes. If he had a number two pencil he'd be chewing the eraser. "Please wait, I'll tell him you're here." He closed the door.

At least the kid didn't tell me to bring the deliveries around back. I glanced out to the street at my filthy car. It made no sense to clean it. A good rinsing might wash off the duct tape. But the inspection sticker was valid and so were the plates. The gas tank was full and the oil topped off. The tires showed only a hint of wear and the donut spare was inflated.

The front door opened, this time by Halloran himself. A lean man with erect posture, Halloran wore an olive tweed sports coat over a white shirt with a monogram on the cuff. He parted his thick white hair on the side and smelled of expensive cologne.

"I'm sorry to keep you waiting," he said. "Please, come inside. My name is Bill Halloran, Mister Sparhawk."

"Dermot," I said.

"A good Irish name, Dermot. Your mother must have been Irish, because Sparhawk is not an Irish surname, not even Mc-Sparhawk." Halloran wasn't offended that I didn't laugh. He just kept talking. "What kind of name is Sparhawk?"

"My father was a Micmac Indian from Canada."

"Ah yes, an Indian. I remember when you played football for B.C., a heck of a good linebacker, an all-American as I recall." He smiled as if he meant it. "I watched you play most Saturdays in the fall. Father Mullineaux and I would go to the stadium together. You were quite good."

"Thanks."

"Too bad about your knee, a horrible injury you suffered that day. I remember the play well, your own teammate rolled on your leg. You got carried off the field on a stretcher. Father Mullineaux told me later that the doctor botched the surgery. What a crying shame, a travesty."

"Yeah, a real crying shame."

We were standing inside his lofty foyer. The walls soared three stories high. Tall windows and long skylights encased the top, giving the room an atrium air. Marble floors, Oriental carpets, wide staircases, the place was meant for monarchs. I felt like a hired hand standing amid royalty, a modern day musketeer.

"My people hailed from County Cork," he said. "Both my mother and father immigrated to Boston from the Emerald Isle. From where did your mother hail?"

"Charlestown," I said. "I understand you're interested in buying old paintings."

The smile left his face. His bullshitting stopped. All the crap about hailing from Cork and immigrating from Ireland fell to the wayside. He led me into the sitting room next to the foyer. It was like walking from the concourse into the stadium. The entire New

England Patriots football team could fit in the room, coaching staff and taxi squad included.

"I'm quite curious," Halloran said. "How did you discover that I was interested in old paintings?"

"Karl Kloosmann told me."

"My son said something about a connection to Karl." Halloran buttoned his sports coat. "Karl told you I was in the market for paintings."

"Not directly. He never mentioned your name."

"How'd you find me?"

"Kloosmann gave me enough to track you down." I waited a second. Halloran remained silent. "Next time you talk to Kloosmann, tell him the Judas goat tracks both ways."

"Please, have a seat."

We both sat on chairs. Halloran picked up the phone on the end table and pressed a number and told the person on the other end to get ahold of Kloosmann and get him over to Weston. He didn't use the word pronto. His tone said it for him.

"It seems that Karl has been unforgivably careless. Nevertheless, it doesn't matter, not in the long run. You and I were destined to meet and now is as good a time as any." He stood and motioned me to do the same. "I want to show you something. Please accompany me, I'll lead the way."

We walked along an extended corridor that led to the rear of the house. If the New England Patriots got bored lounging in the sitting room, they could run forty-yard dashes in the corridor. We turned a corner. Halloran removed a large brass key from his pocket and unlocked a steel door. The door swung open like a bank vault. A concrete ramp led down to the basement. The ramp was as steep as a gangplank at low tide. I grabbed the banister to keep myself from speeding up. Halloran was used to it, walking down like an old salt.

When we got to the bottom I took in the room.

Paintings of all sizes hung on the walls. Old paintings, similar to the one I sold to Father Mullineaux, hung like plaques at a hall of fame. Ornate frames and muted lighting accentuated their beauty. Halloran approached one of the oils and extended his hand to it. I thought of Vanna White in *Wheel of Fortune.*

"Do you recognize this Dutch masterpiece?"

I studied it for a good ten seconds. The painting depicted a woman playing a piano, another woman standing in front of the piano singing, a man with long hair sitting between them. Though the painting was framed, the edges were jagged, as if someone had cut it with a crude tool. I had seen it before. Then it came to me, the place I saw it. A print of the same painting hung behind the bar at the Cazenovia Club on Utica Street, Aunt Bea's place.

"It's a Vermeer," I said. "I think it's called *The Concert* or the *The Concert Singer*, something like that."

"I'm impressed. It is a painting by Johannes Vermeer and it is called *The Concert*," he said. "Are you a collector of sorts, a person who appreciates famous works of art?"

"Neither," I said. "I recognized the painting from a barroom."

"A barroom? Must be a nice barroom." He stepped back from the Vermeer. "What if I told you *The Concert* is worth three hundred million in today's dollars? What would you say to that?"

"I'd say sell it."

"What if I told you I bought this painting for two hundred fifty thousand in nineteen ninety, thinking it was the authentic *Concert*, the one stolen in the Gardner heist?"

"I'd say you got yourself a good deal if the painting is authentic."

"The painting is a fake, a good fake, but a fake all the same."

"I can't tell a fake from an original."

"Evidently, I can't either." He continued to look at it. "Unlike the Rembrandt copy you sold to Father Mullineaux, which was probably painted by one of Rembrandt's protégés, this Vermeer reproduction is worthless. A Vermeer student didn't paint it." He ran his fingers along the serrated edges, stroking it to wish a frog into a prince. "I got taken, Sparhawk. Plain and simple, I got taken. I don't like getting taken, especially for two hundred fifty thousand. I intend to get my money back."

I stepped closer to the fake Vermeer, wondering if it was Remy Menard's work. Remy wasn't pleased with the job he did on the Vermeer.

"Your henchman Kloosmann said you wanted to buy more paintings, even if they were forgeries. He said you were offering a hundred thousand a painting. Is that true?"

"You have more to sell?"

"I know where I can get my hands on some." I thought about the Rembrandt replica in the storage facility, *Self-Portrait, Aged 23*. I thought about Remy Menard and the half dozen works in his Dorchester studio. "I'll have to confer with a colleague first."

"By all means, confer with him." Halloran walked around his underground museum, pacing like a man who had a lot on his mind. He must have owned fifty or sixty paintings. Halloran turned to me. "I'm growing increasingly curious about you, Sparhawk. I like people that make me curious."

"You gotta get out more," I said.

"I mentioned that I purchased *The Concert* assuming it was stolen from the Gardner Museum, yet you never asked me about the heist. You didn't even flinch."

"Why should I?"

"We're talking about the biggest art theft in history. The Gardner topped them all. No other theft comes close. Yet you didn't bat an eye when I implied I might be involved."

"I didn't bat an eye because I don't give a shit. The robbery means nothing to me. Besides, why should I waste my time and your breath?"

"What do you mean by waste my breath?"

"What if I asked about the heist? If I said, 'Bill, tell me about the Gardner Museum heist. Tell me how you engineered the biggest art theft in history, yet ended up with a forged Vermeer.'"

His jaw muscles tensed. I continued.

"It's a crying shame that you ended up with a forged Vermeer, a real travesty. You didn't mastermind the robbery, otherwise you'd have the original Vermeer, and I wouldn't be standing here. No Halloran, you didn't pull off the Gardner heist. You got duped by the men who did, or more likely, by men who didn't pull it off, but tricked you into believing they did."

"A know-it-all."

"Let's cut the shit," I said. "I'm here to sell forged paintings, and I'm pretty sure my colleague will sell his, too."

He tucked his hand inside his shirt like Napoleon.

"You're not in charge here, Sparhawk, I am." He pulled his hand out and pointed at me. "I'm the one who's calling the shots in this deal."

"Suit yourself. When you get serious about buying forged art, give me a call." I took a couple of steps up the ramp and stopped. "Call me directly this time. Don't send that goon Kloosmann again."

"Hold on a moment," he said. "Hold your goddamned horses for a goddamned moment. There's no need to become adversarial, Sparhawk. I already did you a good turn and you don't even know it."

"What are you talking about?"

"I'm talking about Liam McGrew. He's off your back now, isn't he? McGrew did me a favor. He's letting me deal with you," Halloran said. "You're lucky to be alive. McGrew wanted to kill you, and I talked him out of it. That's not all I did for you."

"Jeez, thanks, Halloran. Wherever would I be without you?"

"Suffering for your sins in purgatory, that's where." He led me up the ramp to the hallway. Halloran moved well for an older man. If his hair wasn't white, I'd think he was younger. "I'll contact you about buying the reproductions. You'll be dealing directly with me from here on, no more Karl Kloosmann."

"Give me a day or two to get organized before you call."

He agreed to give me a day or two, but he wasn't happy about it. Halloran was used to getting things immediately. Rich guys are like that, they think they can snap their fingers and get whatever they want. I enjoyed making him wait. It was a small bonus to go with the money I hoped to take from him. I told Halloran I needed the payment in cash. No problem, he said, cash was no problem. We stopped in the foyer.

"There's another thing," he said. "I'll pay twenty million for Vermeer's *Concert*, the original. That's twenty million, tax-free. I can set up an account for you in the Cayman Islands and no one will be the wiser."

"No thanks. The painting's worth three hundred million," I said. "An insurance company will pay me ten percent, thirty million."

"Do you have it?" He saw me smiling. "You don't have it, but I take your point. I'll pay thirty-five million for it. Anything else?"

"Does the name McSweeney mean anything to you?"

"I have no associates named McSweeney. Why?"

"How about Oswego?"

He didn't answer. He just closed the door behind me.

CHAPTER 35

All this talk about the Gardner Museum and Johannes Vermeer and forged paintings and an art robbery aroused my interest. I stopped at the Boston Public Library at Copley Square and took out a DVD titled *Stolen*, a documentary about the Gardner Museum heist. I also checked out two books: *The Gardner Heist* by Ulrich Boser, and *Priceless: How I Went Undercover to Rescue the World's Stolen Treasures* by Robert Wittman. According to the dust jacket, Wittman was an FBI agent who investigated the Gardner heist as part of the Bureau's Art Theft Team, headquartered in New York. I left the library with my stash and walked from Boylston Street to Milk Street, where I boarded the 93 bus for Charlestown.

I got off in front of Bunker Hill Street and stood on the sidewalk in a lazy frame of mind. The visit with Halloran had exhausted me. I trudged to the house. The flight of stairs to my apartment proved grueling, as if I were scaling the Monument lugging the granite blocks that built it. I made it to my apartment.

My escalating inertia prompted me to choose the DVD and to put aside the books for a more energetic moment. I queued up the disc, grabbed the remote control, and relaxed in the recliner, ready for an evening of mindless entertainment. And, of course, the doorbell rang. I ignored it. It rang again.

Special Agent Emma Hague was standing outside the door. My inertia dispersed. I escorted her into my apartment and asked if she'd like something to drink. She said no thanks. She wanted to discuss the Somali situation in the projects. I invited her to sit. Her silver hair bunched on her shoulders when she did.

"I talked with Naddi today," she said. "It's important to me that you know I talked to her. I tried to reach out to her earlier, but Naddi wouldn't talk. Trust doesn't come easily in the projects."

"I wondered why it took you so long," I said. "I should have figured that out on my own. What did she say?"

She wiggled in the chair.

"On second thought, I'll take that drink, a Coke, anything cold."

"Okay." I opened the fridge. "I have Coke, Hawaiian Punch, Gatorade, iced coffee, water."

"Hawaiian Punch sounds good," Emma said. "What flavor?"

"Berry Blue Typhoon."

"I'd like a glass."

I poured us each a glass of Hawaiian Punch and carried the glasses into the parlor. Emma swallowed a mouthful. I did the same. She unwound on the couch, letting her shoulders sink into the cushions. I sat on the recliner.

"Tell me about Naddi," I said. "It sounds like you made progress."

"Not the type of progress I was hoping to make. I learned some things from Naddi that I find disgusting." She put down the empty glass. "I can only give a rough sketch, Dermot, no details, no names. And then you'll understand why she feels threatened."

"Fine, Emma, no names. Just tell me what happened." *Had Naddi been harmed?* "Before you start, is Naddi all right?"

"Naddi is fine, so is Ayanna."

"Ayanna?" I said. "Ayanna was in danger?"

"She was, yes." Emma held up the empty glass. "Dermot, can I have a little more. I'm thirsty tonight."

I filled her glass to the brim with Berry Blue Typhoon and placed the bottle on the coffee table. She drank half a glassful, her throat working to swallow it.

"Continue, Emma."

"The un-American activities Naddi was talking about had nothing to do with terrorism. It had to do with, ah, cultural is-sues." She moved again on the couch. It was more of a squirm than a wiggle. "Back in Somalia the men practice a brutal tradition on women, barbaric, really. They practice it without the women's consent."

"Rape?" I said. "They use rape as a military tactic."

"It's worse than rape," she said. "Rape, you can get over with help."

I refilled my glass.

"Be more specific," I said. "What Somali tradition?"

"It's called FGC, female genital cutting, more accurately known as female genital mutilation, the removal of the exterior genitalia." She didn't blanch, she didn't cringe, she talked in a clinical manner. "FGC is a problem in Great Britain, because of the prevalence of African immersion there. Women are getting carved up across the pond."

"The sick fucks," I said.

"FGC is an ancient tradition that dates back thousands of years, predating both Islam and Christianity. Today it's mostly a Muslim practice."

"Assholes."

"Hold on, Dermot, Coptic Christians and Falasha Jews perform it, too. Needless to say, the mutilation degrades women."

"I don't get it," I said. "What's the benefit in butchering women?"

"There's no benefit for the women, but it's a man's world in Africa and the Middle East. The men believe FGC deters promiscuity and thus promotes virginity. They also believe it improves male sexual pleasure during intercourse, something to do with the increased friction." She drank more punch and licked her lips. "More than anything else, FGC is a way for men to control women. The societal pressures are enormous. Men who marry uncircumcised women are shunned, even stigmatized."

"I get the idea," I said. "What about Naddi and Ayanna? What's FGC got to do with those two?"

"FGC is performed when a girl is between four and eight years old. Ayanna is five, a prime candidate." She looked at the empty glass, looked at the bottle of Hawaiian Punch, and let both of them sit on the coffee table. "A Somali man, who is considered a wizened elder by his fellow émigrés, lives in the projects near Naddi and Ayanna. He made it clear to Naddi that he planned to maim Ayanna."

"What's the bastard's name?"

"I can't tell you his name."

"This is my neighborhood, Emma. Let me handle it. I'll nail his scrotum to a tree stump." I leaned toward her. "He'll never harm another girl again."

"You're too late, Dermot. He's been deported to Somalia." She curled back on the couch and reached for the ceiling, stretching her torso long, pushing her breasts against her blouse. "Naddi and Ayanna are safe. He presents no threat to them any longer."

"Thank God."

She picked up the *Stolen* DVD, flipped it over, and read the back of the case. She glanced at the two library books and opened the one written by the FBI agent who investigated the Gardner heist. She read the dust jacket.

"What's your interest in the Gardner Museum robbery?" she said.

"No interest, just mildly curious," I said. "A friend of mine told me about the *Stolen* documentary, he said it was worth watching. While I was at the library, I borrowed the books, too."

"Two books and a DVD because you're mildly curious?" She dropped the book on the table. "I'd hate to see what happens when you get extremely curious."

"Stay here. Watch the film."

Without hesitating, she said yes. We sat together on the couch facing the TV. She nestled into me. If she nestled any closer, my ego might pop. I clicked on the DVD player and hit play. Five minutes into the movie she leaned her breasts into my arm, and her silver hair brushed the side of my face. I lifted my arm and she fell into my ribs. We stayed that way and watched the movie.

The magnitude of the Gardner theft proved immense. The loot

was valued at more than five hundred million. The thieves stole three Rembrandts, including his only seascape, *The Storm on the Sea of Galilee*. They also stole Vermeer's *Concert*, a forgery of which Halloran owned. They filched works by Degas, Manet, and Flinck. I'd never heard of Govaert Flink. For good measure, they swiped a gilded eagle finial that once topped a Napoleonic flagpole, perhaps in a gesture of thumbing their noses at the police, the film speculated.

Yet they left behind Titian's *Rape of Europa*, one of the museum's most valuable masterpieces, an oversight that led investigators to speculate that amateurs pulled off the job. The paintings they stole had been cut from their frames, further confirming what investigators suspected, that the culprits were amateurs.

The thieves, amateur or otherwise, were now in a good position. The statute of limitations had long since passed, and a five-million-dollar reward sat on the table if the art was returned in good condition. To sweeten the tempting pot: immunity from prosecution.

The documentary told the story of two robbers masquerading as Boston policemen, who perpetrated the heist in the wee hours of March 18, 1990, basically on Saint Patrick's Day night. The thieves probably assumed the police would be busy arresting reveling drunks, the film reasoned. Not a bad assumption on Saint Paddy's Day in the Hub. It also came as no surprise when the film's protagonist, Harold Smith, cited an Irish connection to the crime, the Irish mob in Boston and the IRA overseas. I thought of Liam Mc-Grew.

The film proved excellent and Emma's company most excellent. Sitting next to Emma Hague, I'd have thought *Tango & Cash* was excellent. Beautiful women affect me that way, they distort my judgment. Emma moved closer if that was possible. I slid my hand under her shirt and along her ribcage. Her ribs were as taut as banjo strings, she was so lean. My hands navigated north, to meatier terrain. We kissed. My hands went all over her. We kissed again. I led her into my bedroom.

CHAPTER 36

Emma was gone when I awoke. There was no note, no sign she was here, she had vanished. I showered, shaved, and dressed. I took the White Owl box from my top drawer and opened it. The military .45 looked back at me. I took it out, ejected the magazine, thumbed the top bullet, and popped the clip back in again. I was getting comfortable handling the weapon, because of the trips to the gun club with Harraseeket Kid. I proved to be a pretty good shot, too. Kid told me my long arms helped with the aim.

I pulled back the slide and chambered a round. Halloran was tough and dangerous. Any man capable of scaring off Liam Mc-Grew had to be tough and dangerous. I unloaded the gun and put it back in the cigar box. I'd clean it tonight.

Still feeling great after my night with Emma Hague, I walked downstairs and knocked on Buck Louis's door. Buck let me in.

"Dermot," he said, as he wheeled back a few feet, "you get a haircut or something?"

"No haircut, Buck."

"Then you musta got laid. Yes sir, that's it. Silverado hauled your ashes. I saw her under the porch light last night, looking at herself in the reflection of the window, playing with her hair and shit." Buck rolled out to the kitchen. "Fresh-made java, my man. Drink a cup?"

"Sure."

We sat in the parlor drinking coffee. Buck parked in front of me.

"How'd it go with Halloran yesterday?"

"Halloran's a beauty," I said. "What is it with rich people? Are they all soft as shit?"

"Probably," Buck said. "Tell me what happened with Halloran, and I'll give you my take on him."

I told Buck about my visit.

"Interesting he knows about Liam McGrew," Buck said. "Also interesting he owns a fake Vermeer. The thing that makes it even more interesting is the sucker bought the fake for a quarter million. Makes sense why he wants to know about you. He wants to know because of that painting you sold the priest, which also happens to be a fake."

"Lots of interesting things with Halloran, aren't there?"

"Yeah, you're right about that." Buck grabbed my cup and rolled to the kitchen, refilled it and brought it back. "Are we still planning on checking out the shortwave radio today?"

"Sure, why not."

"Then let's do it, 'cause I ain't got all day."

Getting Buck into my car was now an easy task. We worked out a system. He grabbed my neck while I lifted him from under his knees and placed him in the front seat. I then folded his wheelchair and stored it in the trunk. Simple.

Buck snapped his seat belt. We were on our way to Mystic Piers Storage.

"Is this jalopy gonna make it the half mile down there?"

"It's three quarters of a mile. I think it'll make it."

"Like my mama used to say, old folks shouldn't buy green bananas," he said. "I wouldn't fill the tank if I was you."

We drove down Chelsea Street toward Mystic Piers and drove right by it, turning onto Terminal Street.

"I want to make sure no one's following us."

I looped Charlestown twice before I drove back to Mystic Piers and parked in front of the storage facility. I helped Buck into his wheelchair and we went inside. I waved to the man at the front desk, who never looked up from his newspaper. We continued past him to the elevator and rode it to the sixth floor.

"An old Otis," Buck said, "nice and roomy, nothing cramped."

We got off on six. I unlocked the storage room door with the

McEwan key. Remy Menard's Rembrandt reproduction of *Self-Portrait, Aged 23* welcomed us into the room. Remy told me that *Self-Portrait, Aged 23* was his best Rembrandt work. Remy's claim was not groundless. For years he had studied the original at the Gardner Museum. He studied its paint strokes, its use of shadow and light, its craquelure. He internalized the original before he made his assertion: that his reproduction was a perfect match. Buck wheeled up to the painting.

"I know nothing about forged art, but I'll be goddamned if this is a fake."

"You should see his other paintings," I said.

"Check out the old cracks. Are you sure it's a fake?"

"The painting's a fake, Buck. The real one hangs in the Gardner Museum."

"Amazing, the talent people have."

Buck rolled up to the radio, and like a musician testing equipment before a gig, he clicked dials, turned knobs, squelched speakers, tested the mike. After completing the sound check, he bobbed his head with a nod that said the gizmo was ready to go. Buck knew what he was doing. What else was new?

He emitted a vague message over the airwaves, using Oulipo Man as his handle. Nobody responded. He grumbled about things that went beyond my shortwave acumen. He didn't know which band Jeepster used, didn't know the broadcasting range, didn't know Jeepster's actual handle—Oulipo Man was a guess. As the minutes ticked by, our hopes for new discovery dwindled.

We learned nothing.

The results from the shortwave proved disappointing. We had been spoiled, Buck and I. We had gotten used to instant success. We got lucky finding the Oulipo Boys chat room, luckier contacting The Go Between and Main E Ack, and luckiest of all meeting The Eggman, Remy Menard. We learned Jeepster had hired Remy to paint forgeries of the Dutch masters. The shortwave radio yielded nothing by comparison. Buck turned off the set.

"Let's take it with us," he said.

"Why?"

"I'll set it up next to my computer and fool with it some more, see what I can find out. I'll have Harraseeket Kid nail an antenna on the roof." He rolled back from the radio. "Break it down and take it with us. Disconnect the cable to the roof. Stack the equipment on my lap, and we'll wheel it out of here."

I disconnected the cable and we took the radio with us.

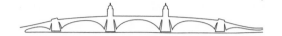

CHAPTER 37

Each Wednesday at eleven o'clock, just before the noontime AA meeting, Father Dominic celebrates the Alcoholics Mass at Saint Jude Thaddeus. Alcoholics and addicts call it the Hump Day Mass, marking the midpoint of the week. The pews fill up with people in recovery, people who bounced in and out, and people who never got sober. Needless to say, the ushers don't pass the basket. During the Prayers of the Faithful, Father Dominic prayed for recovering alcoholics and addicts, and for those who still suffered.

After Holy Communion, I was kneeling in the last pew next to my sponsor, Mickey Pappas. We blessed ourselves and stood. I noticed Skinny Atlas walking down the center aisle. I stuck out my hand to shake. He took it.

"Do we know each other?" he said.

"My name is Dermot Sparhawk. We met at Aunt Bea's Cazenovia Club a while back."

"I must've been in a blackout. It's nice to meet you, Dermot. I take it you're sober in the program."

"One day at a time, I am."

"Does it get any easier?"

"Some days are easier than others," I said. "And some days are a rock fight, being honest about it. Give it time, it gets better."

Skinny left the church, his head pitched down. Mickey elbowed me in the side and pointed with his chin up the aisle.

"Check her out," he said. "She's coming our way."

A young woman with thick auburn hair and a freckled face walked toward us. Airy and confident with a prep-school posture, she could have balanced a Big Book on her head. She had to be a high-bottom drunk, someone who drank but got in no real trouble. Hangovers, not handcuffs, got her to look at AA. She extended her hand to me.

"Hi, Dermot, I'd like to introduce myself. My name is Bonnie Og," she said. "My father is Angus Og. He was a friend of your father and Jeepster Hennessey. They served in Vietnam together."

Dad delivers again.

"Dermot Sparhawk, but you already knew that," I said. Mickey drifted out of the church. "It's a pleasure to meet you. What brings you to the Alcoholics Mass?"

"I came here to see you," she said. "I don't drink, not after watching Angus battle his demons."

"The disease can destroy families," I said. "My father talked about Angus Og. I don't think I ever met him."

We stepped out of the church and onto the sidewalks of Hayes Square. The sunshine delineated the reds and browns in her hair, adding dimensions that votive candles can't render. She appeared to be a couple of years older than me, twenty-six or so.

"I grew up in Roslindale," she said.

"I have friends over there," I said. "What street?"

"Washington Street, near the Pleasant Café."

"Nice place, the Pleasant."

"My brothers and I were reared on their pizzas." She smiled. "Their spaghetti and meatballs, too."

We walked up Bunker Hill Street in no particular hurry and turned left on Lexington. When we reached Monument Square, we sat on a bench. A park ranger glanced at Bonnie, confirming he was a man of good taste.

"I have a message from my father," she said. "He needs to talk to you."

"Sure, what's his phone number?"

"Angus Og doesn't believe in telephones, he doesn't trust them." She crossed her legs, hiking her skirt. The park ranger noticed, so did I. "My father insists on talking to people in person."

"No problem." I worked hard not to ogle her thighs. "Where does he live?"

"He lives in Antigonish."

"Up in Nova Scotia?" I said. "My father's tribe came from there. What's your father doing in Antigonish?"

"Can we go somewhere for coffee or something, so we can talk about it?"

"Sure."

We walked from Monument Square over the Charlestown Bridge to a coffeehouse in the North End, where we ordered espresso and pastries. We didn't say much until we finished eating. Bonnie talked.

"A few years ago my father showed signs of severe emotional problems. The problems got worse. He'd stare out the kitchen window and scream: 'They're coming to get me, Bonnie. They're coming to take me away.' He'd talk about Micmac Indians with tomahawks and feathers. He thought he saw a Micmac chief wearing war paint outside his window." She pushed her cup and dish to the center of the round table. "We hospitalized him. He'd been in detoxes before. This was different, this was a hospitalization. He was hospitalized twice, the second time in Canada. His family came from Nova Scotia."

"My father came from Antigonish," I said. "It's one of the reasons he became friends with Angus in the marines."

"I know, my father told me," she said. "Angus's medication seems to be working. He's doing much better."

"I'm glad."

"I think there's another reason he's doing better."

"The Canadian air?"

"He can't drink on his medication. Angus's problem is single malt Scotch, not Micmacs with tomahawks. Because of the meds he was forced to stop drinking the Auchentoshen, his Glasgow elixir. In my father's case, his Glasgow eraser—he suffered blackouts after emptying a liter. Know what I think? I think if the doctors gave my father a placebo and ordered him not to drink, he'd be just fine."

We walked out to Hanover Street, past the fire station, and sat on a bench under a shade tree in Paul Revere Park.

"My father's crazy in many ways, yet he has lucid moments. Most of the time he goes on and on about the wildest adventures." Bonnie waited for an older couple to pass by. "One morning he talked about initiating peace talks with Ho Chi Minh in Hanoi."

"Why are you telling me this?"

"In one lucid moment he said he needed to talk to you, and he sent me to find you. Angus said you owed him money. I know it sounds crazy," Bonnie said. "He told me he needed to talk to you about the money."

"How do you know he was lucid?"

"My father vacillates between fantasy and reality, a swapping of the imitation for the genuine. It's not a conscious choice. One moment he's in Vietnam, the next he's in the Scottish highlands, the next he's in Boston with his street pals. To confuse matters more, he mixes between them. I listen for his accent. When he talks with a Scottish burr, he's completely gone. When he talks with a Boston dialect, there might be truth in his words."

"You want me to go to Antigonish to talk to your father. That's a twelve hour drive, Bonnie." As pretty as she was, I still snorted. "I don't think so."

The benches in Paul Revere Park filled up with neighborhood workers, most of them eating brown-bag lunches. A crew of phone company men sat on a bench across the cobblestone plaza, their sunglasses barely hiding their glances at Bonnie.

"Angus said he knows," she said.

"Knows what?"

"He knows about the Rembrandt," she said. "Does that make sense?"

CHAPTER 38

Bonnie and I left Charlestown at five a.m. the next day for the Canadian Maritimes en route to Antigonish. The highways were clear and I put the gas pedal to the floor, getting the Plymouth up to a trembling fifty-five. A garbage disposal has more horsepower. Bonnie was a sport about it. She never complained once about the bucking, pinging, and gagging.

We cruised through coastal New Hampshire up into Maine, stopped in Bar Harbor for lunch, drove through most of New Brunswick, and pulled into Moncton for dinner. The Plymouth operated at peak performance, its burning ratio was perfect. Each time I filled the tank with gas, I topped off the oil with a quart— my car's version of a shot and beer.

We arrived in Antigonish at seven p.m., Atlantic Standard Time, got out of the car, and stretched. Bonnie unlocked the door of her father's house, and we went inside. Angus Og got up from his wingback chair in front of the fireplace and greeted us. He hugged Bonnie and began to sing.

"My Bonnie lies over the ocean, my Bonnie lies over the sea, so bring back my Bonnie to me." He kissed her cheek. "Aye lassie, you're the image of your mother."

Og shoved the pipe back in his mouth. He had short white hair and a long-toothed smile. Splintering blood vessels lined his face into geometric shapes, a mosaic of maroon polygons. He stood lanky and tall and shook my hand with a tight squeeze.

"So you're Chief Sparhawk's boy. Look at cha! A fine moose of a lad you are, bigger than Chief, too." He put a lit match to the pipe. "I thank ye for driving all this way to see me. And I thank ye for driving my daughter Bonnie."

"My pleasure, Mister Og," I said.

"Aye lad, call me Angus." He sat by the fireplace again. "Join me at the hearth for a wee gathering of the clan."

I sat next to him and put my feet on a footrest. It was hard to believe that Og was a contemporary of my father's. He seemed from another place and time, a character from a Robert Burns poem. Og grew up in Roslindale.

"I served in Vietnam with your kin. Fine Micmacs, your dad and Glooscap. I served with Jeepster Hennessey, too. We toiled together in the Battle of Hill 881, beating back Charlie at every turn. Charlie, what a foe he was. 'Twas May of '67, we lost a thousand men in that blood skirmish. Aye, a heavy toll it 'twas."

"My father told me Hill 881 was hell," I said. "Glooscap doesn't talk about it much, neither did Jeepster."

"Nay, not a good thing to discuss." Angus Og nodded as if he understood. He chomped on the pipe and gritted his long teeth. "After we beat back the red bastards, we chased a group of them north, clear up the Ho Chi Minh Trail."

"Up the Ho Chi Minh Trail?"

"We took heavy fire along the way, me, your father, Glooscap, Jeepster. We chased them into Laos, lost 'em up there in the thistle." He shook his head. "We should have stormed Hanoi. We should've freed John McCain and his fellow POWs at the Hanoi Hilton. Alas, the brass derailed our heroic quest. A chopper pilot tracked us down, a fine lad the pilot. He said our commanding officer ordered us to rejoin the regiment and flew us back to Saigon."

My father never told me about chasing Vietcong up the Ho Chi Minh Trail.

"Did you get in trouble for leaving the, ah, regiment?"

"Trouble? Hell no, lad! They deemed to honor us with medals." Og leaned forward in his chair. "The company commander recommended us for the Congressional Medal of Honor.

Couldn't get it through Congress, though. The asswipes in Washington vetoed the nomination. They said we ventured into Laos and Cambodia, which was off limits for the U.S. military."

"Must've pissed you off, not getting the Medal of Honor."

"Know what I say to that?" Og drew on his pipe and exhaled a plume of smoke. "I say Tiddy-Aye-Aye for the One-Eyed Reilly. Ever hear that fine Irish song? Think about it, lad. Four marines from Boston disrupted the entire supply line on the Ho Chi Minh Trail. I don't need a medal to prove I'm a man, no sir."

I wasn't sure how to respond to Og's story, so I stared at the fire instead. Og tapped out his pipe, banging it on a big glass ashtray, and refilled the bowl with fresh tobacco from a plaid leather pouch. He tamped the wad with his forefinger and he lit the bowl with a long wooden match and he blew a cloud of smoke toward the ceiling. His actions rolled out in slow motion. I thought I was watching a dream. Bonnie stuck her head in the room and said goodnight to us. She smiled at me before she headed off to bed. I turned to Og.

"Bonnie said you have money coming to you," I said. "She said you wanted to talk to me about the money."

"Yes, yes, you're quite right. I wanted to talk to you about that situation. Not in front of Bonnie, 'tis a private matter." He puffed the pipe. "A matter to do with Jeepster, Chief, and me."

"You'll have to explain."

"Aye, lad, I plan to explain everything." Another lungful, another exhale. "We pulled a big job and Jeepster promised to pay me a hundred thousand for my part in it."

A hundred thousand dollars, the same amount Jeepster promised the forger, Remy Menard.

"If Jeepster owed you the money, why send for me?"

"Because you were Jeepster's godson—I attended your Christening—and Jeepster died at your feet from what I'm told. Chief partook in the job, too."

"My father?"

"Yes sir, he was in on it, too," he said. "I figure it this way. If

I'm gonna see any of that hundred grand, I'm most likely to see it from you."

He kept saying the job. *What job?*

"Did you hit a bank?" It must have been a bank if Jeepster promised him a hundred thousand. "Or an armored car?"

"It wasn't a bank, young Sparhawk, it was the Gardner Museum. We hit the Gardner Museum," he said. "We pulled off the biggest art theft of the century."

After I stopped laughing, I told him to get serious.

"You don't believe me?" He puffed. "No, I suppose not. What I say is true. God in heaven, it's true."

"Sure, if you say so," I said. Og needed stronger medication. Or maybe he needed to unplug the single malt. "Angus, I need to get some sleep. It was a long drive."

"No sir, you aren't going to bed, not until you hear my story. You drove all the way up from Boston, and I'm grateful you did, but now I must ask you to sit and listen. Listen to my story. You owe me that much."

The Scottish burr was gone, replaced by the Boston streets. He sounded like a guy from this century.

"Go on, let's hear it."

Og set himself in the chair.

"I'll never forget the date," he said. "Saint Patrick's Day, 1990, we had it all planned out, right to the last detail. I rented a van, one of those cargo vans, and we picked up the stuff."

"What stuff?" I played along. "The paintings?"

"The plywood crates, we loaded the crates into the van in Dorchester. They were built of thick wood, none of that particle board crap. We needed crates to smuggle the paintings out of the museum once we removed 'em from the frames. Think about it. You can't walk out of the Gardner Museum with a Rembrandt under your arm, not on Saint Patrick's Day, not when every college student in the city is drinking in the streets." He rubbed his palms together. "Plus, we needed the crates to get into the museum. Trojan crates, if you follow me."

"Like the Trojan horse?" I said. "How does a plywood crate get you into the Gardner?"

"We pretended to be delivery men, delivering a shipment to the museum. That's how we got inside, by pretending we were delivering the crates. A brilliant idea, Jeepster came up with it." Og smiled at the genius of it. "Once we got the crates inside, we figured everything would fall into place, and it did. We planned it out like this: we'd put the paintings inside the crates and carry the crates out to the van."

"What about the guards?" I said. "What about the alarms, the cameras?"

"The guards? Let me think. I remember now, we had a guy on the inside, a night watchman. I think Jeepster bribed him or something. Anyway, the watchman was no problem. We took care of him easy enough."

"The Gardner Museum had two guards on duty the night of the robbery."

"Don't believe everything you read in the newspapers. Let me tell you exactly how it played out and you'll see how it fits together." He ignored the pipe and lit a cigarette. "And don't interrupt me so much."

I wondered what he'd been smoking in that pipe.

"I'm listening."

"We were over there by Northeastern drinking a few pints in Punter's Pub. You know, trying to calm our nerves. It takes balls to rob a museum, big hairy balls, and we had 'em. You don't chase a slew of gooks up the Ho Chi Minh Trail unless you got a pair of planets swinging between you legs. And I ain't talkin' Pluto. I'm talkin' two fuckin' Jupiters."

Was I watching Canada's version of *Saturday Night Live* or *Monty Python*?

"Let's get back to the Gardner Museum, Angus."

"We had a few drinks at Punter's, Guinness and Bushmills in honor of Saint Paddy's Day. We made our move when it got dark, six-thirty or so. It was clockwork, man, precise clockwork. I drove the van to the delivery area of the museum. Jeepster and Chief got out and unloaded the crates."

"What time did you get the crates?"

"We were proactive on the crates. I got the van around noon-time and we picked up the crates around three o'clock," he said. "We picked them up in Dorchester."

"Where in Dorchester?"

"Fucked if I remember, it was somewhere in Dorchester."

"So the crates were in the van before you went to Punter's Pub."

"That's right. I drove from Punter's to the museum with the crates. After Jeepster and Chief unloaded the crates I drove off, so as not to arouse suspicion. I parked near Boston Latin, next to a pay phone over there. This was before cell phones."

"And then?"

"And then I waited."

"Did you actually see my father and Jeepster go into the museum?"

"I didn't see them go into the museum, no." Og closed his eyes and then opened them as if he figured something out. "They had to go inside to steal the paintings, right?"

"What happened next?"

"The pay phone was my signal. When the phone rang twice, I was to drive back to the museum, back to the loading dock. And sure enough the phone rang twice and I drove back." His face flushed in the telling. "They loaded the crates into the van and we got the hell out of there, and I mean lickety-split."

"What time did you leave?" I said, and then rephrased it. "What time did you leave the Gardner Museum?"

"It must've been nine o'clock, give or take." He paused for a beat. "Jeepster and Chief were inside for a couple of hours, more or less."

Og's story didn't match the corroborated account of the Gardner Museum heist, not even close, and yet he sounded as if he were telling the truth. Perhaps Og believed he was telling the truth, perhaps he believed his own yarn. His version of the robbery couldn't be true. The timetable didn't fit the crime.

"Where did you go from there?" I said.

"Huh?"

"Where did you take the paintings?"

"Oh. First we drove to Charlestown. Jeepster had a storage unit over there in Charlestown, so we went there first. Jeepster and Chief stowed a couple of the crates there. I think it was under the bridge, yeah, under the bridge." Og nodded. "Then we drove to the South End, not far from Harry the Greek's. Is Harry the Greek still in business?"

"He's closed."

"Great store, Harry the Greek, one of the best as far as I'm concerned. I bought my underwear there," he said. "We unloaded the other crate at a warehouse somewhere behind Harry the Greek's."

"What happened next?"

"What do you think happened next? We celebrated. Boy, we tied one on. We drove to a Chinese restaurant down in Quincy. The place was more of a pick-up joint than a restaurant. We sat at the bar and ordered drinks. We started cutting up, throwing the little umbrellas and winging cherries at people, having a fuckin' ball. We drank scorpion bowls and Heinekens, got hammered as hell."

"They didn't shut you off?"

"Of course not, not the way we were spending money. Then Jeepster acted up. I guess he liked one of the bartenders, a pretty Italian girl from Quincy Point, and he hit on her, laying on the charm. She was dating one of the cooks. I think he mighta been the head cook, or maybe the chef. Anyway, the guy was Chinese." He dragged on the cigarette. "Jeepster yelled to her, 'Are you still pining for that Chinaman at the fry station?' All hell broke out, real pandemonium. The Quincy cops arrested us. They threw us in jail, me, Chief, and Jeepster."

"You guys got arrested?"

"What a way to end the night. We rob the Gardner Museum and get pinched for a barroom fight. Go figure."

The police report of the Gardner heist refuted everything Og said. The theft happened at one thirty in the morning on the eighteenth, not seven in the evening on the seventeenth. The *Stolen* DVD rebutted Og, too, so did the books I read. Angus Og had a fertile mind, a mind tilled in black Highland farmland. It yielded rich images, but the images were mixed clippings of historic events—a shredded Sunday newspaper strewn across the floor and reassembled randomly.

The next morning Bonnie cooked us a country breakfast. Bacon and eggs, French toast, home fries, sausage, and toast. The three of us ate at a small maple table in a kitchen nook and drank plenty of orange juice and coffee. Outside, the Nova Scotia sky hung gray with clouds, good weather for driving. Og cleared his throat.

"Have ye been to Fenway Park lately, lad?"

The Scotch burr had returned. I was now talking to an old Highlander who did battle at Glencoe, a foot soldier of William Wallace. I wondered if Og served as an advisor when they filmed *Braveheart*.

"I've walked by Fenway," I said. "I can't afford to go in."

"Aye, you must have seen the Ted Williams statue," he said. "It's just outside the ballpark."

"I've seen it. It's on the sidewalk behind the right-field stands. A big bronze thing, it's a beauty."

"I saw Ted hit his last home run in person, I was there at the game."

"No kidding."

"His last at bat and Teddy Ballgame hit number five twenty-one, parked it over the visitor's bullpen. A line shot, the ball was still rising when it hit the back wall of the pen. Woulda traveled six hundred feet if it didn't hit the back wall."

"Must have been something to see."

"It was late September, nineteen sixty, I was eleven years old.

The Sox played the Baltimore Orioles that day. My teacher took us to the game, Sister Mary Agnes was her name. She probably thought it had to do with Baltimore catechism." He ate a couple of strips of crisp bacon. "Aye, 'twas a thin crowd, we sat in the third-base grandstand."

"Nowadays they call them box seats and charge accordingly."

"Sister Mary Agnes pointed to a distinguished-looking gent sitting near to the field, and she said to me, 'Angus, that's John Updike, the writer for *The New Yorker* magazine. Ask him what he's doing up here at Fenway Park.' Sister Mary Agnes was an avid reader, always reading magazines." Og ate more bacon. "You know how it is, you can't say no to a nun. So I ventured down to the boxes and introduced myself to John Updike, who happened to be a right nice fellow. He told me to sit down next to him, to join him for a few innings."

"You met John Updike at Fenway Park?"

"Aye, lad I did, September twenty-eighth nineteen sixty." Og topped off his coffee. "I asked Updike what he was doing at Fenway Park, and he told me he was writing a piece for *The New Yorker* on Ted Williams's last at bat. He already had the title for the story: *Hub Fans Bid Kid Adieu*. A great title, I told him. He nodded. Updike appreciated my approval."

"My father read that story to me when I was a boy."

"I said to him, 'John, I know more about Ted Williams than any man alive.' Updike put down his pen and listened. I told him that Williams batted three eighty-eight in nineteen fifty-seven at the age of thirty-nine, and that three eighty-eight was the highest batting average in baseball since Williams himself hit four-o-six in forty-one, and that four-o-six was the highest since Rogers Hornsby in nineteen twenty-four. I stunned Updike with my knowledge. He put all that stuff in the article. He wanted more and told me to keep talking. I told him that Teddy won the Triple Crown twice, one a major league Triple Crown, and both times he lost the MVP because the Boston sportswriters hated him and didn't put his name anywhere on their ballots, not even tenth place. This disgusted Updike. I gave Updike all the poop, stuff nobody but me knew. He used all of it in the article."

"Did he include your name in the byline?"

"I got a picture of me and Updike around here somewhere. Sister Mary Agnes took it. I can't remember where I put it. What's so damn funny, lad?" Og didn't wait for an answer. "Years later I met the Splendid Splinter in Florida and taught him how to fly-fish. As battletested marines we hit it off immediately, just a couple of regular guys wetting a line together, two guys who put on their waders one leg at a time. Aye, we caught a basketful of fish, too. Bass, as I recall." Og checked to make sure I was listening. "I asked him, 'Teddy, how did you do it? Between the Williams Shift and no-good pitches to hit, how did you thump the apple the way you did?' Teddy said he was blessed with two God-given gifts: the gift of exceptional eyesight and the gift of quick wrists. The pitch came in like a beach ball and went out like a golf ball, that's what he told me."

We talked more baseball, first about the Red Sox and then about the Boston Braves. Og told me he saw Warren Spahn hurl a shutout at Braves Field, just before the Braves moved to Milwaukee. In Vietnam, Og listened to the 1967 World Series between the Red Sox and Cardinals on Armed Forces Radio. Yastrzemski batted .400. Lonborg pitched a one-hit shutout. He met Roger Staubach, the Naval Academy Heisman Trophy winner and future Dallas Cowboys star, in a Saigon pub. They tossed the pigskin around after they drank a few beers. Staubach was a right nice fellow. Then he claimed to have irrefutable evidence that Golda Meir was a cross dresser.

"Did I tell you about the time I ran away to join the circus?" he said. "I lived with a family of dwarfs. Nice people, dwarfs."

I tried to leave, he wouldn't have it.

"In nineteen thirty-eight Johnny Vander Meer threw two no hitters in a row for the Reds, then finished the season in the minors. Did you know that?"

I finished the pot of coffee. Og continued his harangue, trumpeting his triumphs and detailing his travails. I told him I had to get back to Boston. He grudgingly piped down, but not before he told me about his clandestine talks with President Nixon and Henry Kissinger in 1972, just before they visited the Peoples Republic of China. Nixon and Kissinger grilled Og for hours regarding his dealings with Ho Chi Minh. They picked his brain for insights. They probed his psyche for intuitions. Og delivered on all fronts. The men from Washington alighted on China well prepared, thanks in large part to Angus Og.

We walked outside.

"Aye, I like your car, lad." He tapped a rust spot with his knuckles. "A frugal man, you'd fit in nicely with my clan."

Bonnie packed me a lunch. She said she'd be staying with her father in Antigonish for a while. She wasn't sure for how long. She followed me to the car and kissed me goodbye. The kiss seemed affectionate, more than a sisterly peck. I wanted to make sure I was reading it right and kissed her back. She didn't pull away.

I drove twelve hours to Boston. It felt like a drive to the corner store.

CHAPTER 39

I missed the start of the noontime AA meeting at Saint Jude Thaddeus, caught the last three speakers, and joined the group in the Lord's Prayer at the end. My sponsor, Mickey Pappas, stopped me on my way out of the hall. He was about to say something when a woman wearing a sheer peach shirt walked by us. The top outlined her figure better than body paint, accentuating every curve.

"Her shirt's so tight, and the flesh color," he whispered. "At first I thought she had no nipples."

She got into an expensive car and drove away.

"I shoulda got her license plate," Mickey said to himself. He turned back to me. "Are you doing okay? I haven't seen you in a couple of days."

"I'm doing fine, Mick."

"How'd you make out with that redhead at the Alcoholics Mass?" Mickey waited. "Cripes, even Father Dominic noticed her. I thought he was gonna spill the altar wine."

"We got along pretty good." I wondered how much to tell Mickey. "We spent a little time together and then I drove her to her father's house."

"Drove her to her father's house? That sounds promising." He slapped me on the back. "As long as you didn't drink."

"I didn't drink."

Why did I hold out on Mickey? Why didn't I tell him about the trip to Antigonish with Bonnie Og? Is the sin of omission still a venial sin when it involves your sponsor? Or does it ramp up to mortal? Not everything is your sponsor's business, is it? Life doesn't become an open book because I'm sober, does it? It felt funny to keep Mickey in the dark. We shook hands and parted.

I walked to the office and caught up on a backlog of work. I submitted a two-ton food order to the food bank then answered a mountain of e-mails. Having finished the compulsory, I began the elective.

I called Harraseeket Kid at the garage in Andrew Square and asked him to research a question for me. He said yes and told me he'd be home mid-afternoon. For the next couple of hours I ran Google searches and printed the results. I wanted to hash out the results with Harraseeket Kid and Buck Louis. There must have been a dozen pages of screen shots. I locked up the office and left for home.

Buck was out, Kid was in. I went to the basement to talk with him. Kid had added a new amenity since my last visit, an additional dehumidifier with a hose that drained into the sump pump. The place smelled fresh and the air felt dry. Kid waved me in. He was smoking a cigar as he relaxed in a cordovan leather recliner. I sat on the matching couch next to him.

"Corinthian leather furniture," he said, "handmade in Corinth, Spain."

"Must've cost you."

"I bartered it on an insurance claim." He twirled the lit cigar tip in the ashtray stand next to his chair. "A guy cracked up his shiny Mercedes. The guy with the shiny Mercedes has a shady past. He paid for the repairs with furniture."

"Cushy."

"I checked into to that thing you asked about." Kid crushed out the cigar. "That research question about Vietnam, I talked to Glooscap. He said that Chief, Jeepster, Og, and him never went up the Ho Chi Minh Trail. They never chased Charlie up the trail, never went into Laos or Cambodia."

"Doesn't surprise me."

"I specifically asked him about the Battle of Hill 881, like you told me. Glooscap said they returned to the base immediately after the battle, beat to shit. Glooscap told me that they weren't chasing anybody anywhere, let alone up the Ho Chi Minh Trail."

"What about Og's Congressional Medal of Honor story?"

"Glooscap laughed when I asked about it," Kid said. "I hadn't seen him laugh that hard since your father was around, God be good to him. The Congressional Medal of Honor, Glooscap got teary when I told him Og's tale."

"I figured as much." I reclined on the couch and stared at the rafters and told Kid about my trip to Antigonish. "Og's mind is mush," I said. "He talked about meeting President Nixon and Henry Kissinger and Ho Chi Minh. Then he told this story about meeting John Updike at Fenway Park."

"John who?" He shook his head. "Never mind. So you drove Og's daughter up to Antigonish and Og filled your head with nutty exaggerations. His daughter, is she any good?"

"She's gorgeous, a redhead with a big smile."

"Red all over?"

"Bonnie's not that kind of girl."

"Relax man, I was just asking, especially since she's a redhead." He punched my shoulder. "I didn't know you liked her."

We laughed.

"Og told me he fished with Ted Williams in Florida and talked to him about hitting. The more he went on, the more embellished the stories got."

"Let me ask you a question. Why are you bothering with Og's nonsense? Glooscap said Og is a whack job. He's been shipped to Bridgewater five or six times, down to the drunk tank and the mental ward. Og is gonzo, Dermot. The man's brain is kaput."

"Did Glooscap say anything else?"

"Gloosap said that Og was reliable, a good man to have on a job or next to you in a foxhole. He also said that Og's flights of fancy are baseless."

"I Googled a few things Og bragged about." I wondered if Kid had an extra cigar. "The info he gave me about John Updike and Ted Williams checked out."

"What are you talking about?" Kid said. "And who's John Updike?"

"Updike wrote a famous magazine article on Ted Williams. Og said he talked to Updike and gave him the statistics that appeared in the article," I said, feeling my face turn red. "Obviously, Updike didn't need Og to get those stats."

"You're starting to catch on, Dermot boy. Og probably read Updike's article and parroted the stats back to you, that's all," Kid said. "Og is delusional."

Bonnie Og said Angus was delusional before he got on the right medication, and now Kid said he was delusional.

"You're probably right," I said. "Besides, one of his claims didn't check out. Og claimed he saw Warren Spahn pitch a shutout at Braves Field. The Braves left Boston after the nineteen fifty-two season. Og would have been three in fifty-two."

"See what I mean? The guy is bonkers," Kid said. "Now that we've established Og's bonkersness, it's time to answer a bigger question. What's wrong with you?"

"What do you mean?"

"Why did you *want* to believe Og? Why are you dying to buy his bullshit?" Kid brought the recliner forward. "You grew up in the projects. You sniff out bullshit better than anyone I know. Why can't you see through Og's crap? His mind is punched out on pharmaceuticals and Scotch. He smoked enough hasheesh in his day to leave him stoned forever."

"Yeah, I know."

"Forget about Angus Og," Kid said. "You're wasting your time."

For some reason I couldn't let Og go.

"But what if he's right?" I said. "Suppose Og is right about some of the things he said."

"What if he is right? So what. Who gives a shit about fly-fishing with Ted Williams in the Everglades?"

"I don't care about Ted Williams or John Updike or Warren Spahn. Og said other things." I thought for a second. "Let's bring Buck into the conversation. Between the three of us, we'll figure it out."

"Buck's a smart bastard," Kid said.

CHAPTER 40

Buck was futzing with Jeepster's radio when we came into his parlor. He pointed to the couch and chair and told us to have a seat, as he continued to fiddle with the shortwave buttons. Sheens of sweat dampened his brown forehead. He sighed, shook his wet head, and rolled into the parlor.

"Those old vacuum tubes throw serious heat. If I wasn't black, I'd a got sunburned."

"Cool down, Buck," I said.

"I'm getting nowhere with the shortwave. It's fun to fool around with, but I haven't learned a thing about the Oulipo Boys," he said. "I thought I'd be tapping into their headquarters or something. Another thing, I tried to schedule a chat room meeting with the Oulipo Boys. They aren't responding. It's like they dropped out of sight."

"Who are the Oulipo Boys?" Kid said.

"I'll fill you in later." I clicked off the radio. "Forget about the Oulipo Boys for now. I want to pick both your brains about another matter. As Kid already knows, I met with a man named Angus Og in Canada."

"You were up in Canada? I wondered where you went," Buck said. "I didn't hear anything for a couple of days, so I figured maybe you got lucky, maybe got your ashes hauled again by Silverado."

"Who's Silverado?" Kid rubbed his red cheeks with both hands. "And what the hell is Oulipo?"

"I'll tell you later, Kid," I said. "Let's get back to Angus Og. I already told Kid part of the conversation I had with Og. I wanted both of you to hear the rest." I bulled my neck and cracked it. "Angus Og is off kilter, always has been. He went haywire after Vietnam: booze, drugs, violence, PTSD. He's been institutionalized more than once, hospitals in the U.S. and in Canada. He was medicated when I spoke to him. He was sober, too."

"Off the bottle or not, Og is fuckin' nuts," Kid said. "He can't pass through airport security he's got so much shrapnel in his head."

"Agreed, he's nuts and he's unreliable, but he said a few interesting things. He said he knew about the Rembrand," I said. "That's the reason I went up to Antigonish, Og said he knew about the Rembrandt."

Sled dog trotted out of the back hall wagging his tail and rammed his brow into my leg. I scratched behind his ear. He flopped on the floor and pointed all fours in the air.

"I think I see the problem." Buck rolled his wheelchair back and forth on the rug. "On the one hand, everything Og says is suspect, on the other, parts of it might be true."

"Come on, you two. Og exaggerates like a bastard, makes himself out to be the king of Antigonish," Kid said. "He lathers it on like a barber, he's the ultimate bullshit artist."

I rubbed Sled dog's belly, his almond-shaped eyes closed. The evening sky remained bright. The long days of summer were still with us, the horizon would stay blue until eight thirty. I thought about Bonnie Og's dark red hair in the sunlight after the Alcoholic's Mass, her freckles, her smile, her body.

"Before we get started, I have an idea," Buck said.

"Oh, boy," Kid said.

"Let's treat everything Og said as true. No matter how crazy it sounds, let's pretend it's true. It makes no any sense to discuss Og if we already decided he's full of shit." Buck ran his thumbs along the rubber tires. "We'll play what-if. Instead of shooting down Og's claims, we say 'what if it's true?' Judge Og in a positive light instead of a negative one. Act as if everything Og said was gospel. See if his story passes the sniff test. You got the floor, Dermot. Tell Og's tale, soup to nuts."

"Nuts is the right word," Kid said.

"Here goes." I repeated Og's account of the Gardner Museum robbery from beginning to end. To my surprise, neither Kid nor Buck interrupted. They listened to the entire story without laughing. "That's Og's story."

We agreed to take a five minute bathroom break before we resumed. We returned to our seats.

"You heard Og's story," I said. "What do you think?"

"The first part," Kid said, "where Og said they picked up the crates to haul out the stolen paintings—"

"And to get inside the museum," Buck said. "Og called them Trojan crates, like the Trojan horse. That's how the Greeks got into Troy, the Trojan horse."

"Are you a history major?" Kid said. "The crates are hard for me to swallow."

"According to Og they needed the crates," I said. "That's how they got into the Gardner Museum. Think of the Gardner as another walled fortress, like Troy. The crates served a twofold function. First, to get Jeepster's crew into the museum. Second, to get the loot out of the museum. Remember, Og never went into the Gardner. He waited outside in the van."

"Let's go with Buck's what-if approach," Kid said. "What if that's exactly what happened? What if Jeepster and Chief pretended to be delivery men and got into the museum? Og then parked around the corner and waited for their call, so only two of them needed to get inside. Two delivery men with crates, that's not suspicious."

"No museum accepts unscheduled deliveries at seven p.m.," Buck said. "No way the guards let them in with a spur-of-the-moment delivery."

Kid: "Og said they had a man on the inside. The inside man might have been a guard."

Buck: "There were two guards on duty. No way Jeepster gets past both two guards."

"I agree with Buck," I said. "Two guards make it impossible."

Kid: "We can at least agree that Jeepster and his crew were drinking at Punter's Pub that afternoon. After all, it was Saint Patrick's Day."

Buck: "I'll give you that one. I bet someone dropped a tab of acid in Og's Scotch."

"Punter's Pub isn't important one way or the other," I said. "What bothers me about Og's story is the time. Every news article puts the time of the robbery at one thirty a.m. That's the graveyard shift. The two guards working the graveyard were bound and gagged by two crooks disguised as Boston cops, and it happened at one thirty in the morning. The time of the Gardner heist has never been disputed. Og's story doesn't fit, seven p.m. just doesn't fit."

Buck: "You're not doing a very good job playing what-if, Dermot."

Kid: "I know we're supposed to pretend everything Og said was true, but I can't do it, even pretending."

Buck: "Jeepster, Og, and Chief were behind bars when the real robbery took place."

"They were in a Quincy jail," I said. "I verified it."

Buck: "It's funny in a way. Og brags that he robbed the museum, but his arrest in Quincy makes it impossible. His own arrest is his own unwanted alibi. The Quincy bust shoots down his Gardner Museum fantasy. You can't rob a museum when you're in jail."

Kid: "Dermot, I know what you're like and I know how you think. Deep inside, you want to believe that Chief, Jeepster, and Og pulled off the Gardner. You're a romantic bastard. You want to believe your father pulled off the heist of the century."

Buck: "Look at the facts, Dermot. They were in jail when the Gardner got held up. Jeepster, Og, and Chief were sitting in a pokey at the time of the heist. The time of the robbery is on record. Their arrests are on record. Hundreds of articles have been written about the robbery. Let's be generous and say Og is confused."

Kid: "Even the nonsense that Og said about the Ho Chi Minh Trail is crap. Glooscap was in the same unit, he confirmed it was crap. And the baloney about Ted Williams and John Updike, more crap."

"He was only a kid back then."

Kid: "Og's on another planet, he's out there on the moon."

"He seemed so sure," I said. "I guess you're right. I guess I wanted to believe him. Kid said it best, I am a romantic. You two must be right."

Buck: "Then we're agreed. Angus Og's tale isn't just improbable, it's impossible. Pure fantasy from a confused man."

"I think we need to do more work on Og's Gardner story," I said. "He knew about the Rembrandt."

It bothered me to dismiss Og as a confused man lost in fantasy. The facts of the Gardner heist—two decades worth of facts detailed in books, police reports, investigative accounts, and a documentary—invalidated Og's timeline of the crime. Og was locked in a Quincy jail when the heist took place. Jeepster, my father, and Og could not have done it. But something about Og's story rang true to me.

CHAPTER 41

Amigo Joao and I were busy at work in the food pantry. Joao sorted breakfast cereals, while I sliced open cases of canned beans with a box cutter. We were mindlessly doing our mundane tasks when Captain Pruitt walked in.

"Amigo Joao," Pruitt said.

"Captain, all is well, yes?"

Joao's brother is on the police force. Pruitt knows and likes Amigo Joao.

"All is well, Joao." Pruitt pointed at me. "Let's take a walk." He turned back to Amigo Joao. "Hold down the fort while I talk to Sparhawk."

"Sí, Captain, go with Dermot. Talk, talk, talk." Amigo Joao smiled at me. "Adios, boss."

Pruitt and I left the food pantry and walked down Tufts Street toward the river. It was ten in the morning and the heat of the day had yet to come. We stopped at the intersection of Walford Way.

"We arrested Hennessey's killer."

"What?" My mind raced. Was it George Meeks or Jackie Tracy or Liam McGrew? Or all three conspiring? "Who was it?"

"Manny Carlo, a hotshot card player from Little Cuba in Miami." Pruitt said. "Your information about the poker game was good."

"What?" I assumed Jimmy Devin's story was rubbish. "Come on, Captain, the information was sketchy at best. There's no way I helped much, no way possible. I never heard of Manny Carlo."

Pruitt chuckled as he spoke.

"I didn't say you helped much, I said your information was

good. The hearsay you passed my way kept us looking in a certain direction. Was your info vital? No. Was it valid? Yes. More than that, it was timely."

"Manny Carlo," I said. "When's the trial?"

"There's not going to be a trial."

"No trial?" I said.

"Carlo copped a plea." Pruitt popped a stick of Beemans gum into his mouth. "Beemans, good for the digestion, it's got pepsin powder. Want a piece?"

"No thanks, I'm a Pepto-Bismol man."

"The pink stuff." Pruitt chewed and swallowed the juice. "Carlo pleaded guilty to involuntary manslaughter. His lawyer, a Miami big shot, pushed for self-defense. Our evidence was marginal, and with Hennessey's criminal past, self-defense would be an easy sell to a jury. We were damn lucky to get involuntary manslaughter, Sparhawk. At least Carlo will do time."

"Yeah, I guess so." Something Pruitt said bothered me. "If self-defense was an easy sell to a jury, why didn't Carlo's lawyer pursue a trial? Why did he settle for a plea bargain, especially one with jail time?"

"Carlo had other charges hanging over his head, one of them federal." Pruitt tossed the chewed gum into a water drain. "It's the way the system works. Carlo got a package deal. We got a conviction."

"How much time?"

"Ten years, he'll probably serve six."

"Six years for killing Jeepster Hennessey?"

"Hey, at least he got time."

"What did Carlo say about it?" I said "What was his defense?"

"In Carlo's allocution, he said Hennessey bet counterfeit money in the poker game. Carlo didn't realize it was counterfeit until later, at which point he stalked Hennessey and confronted him. Hennessey pulled a knife on Carlo, they fought, Carlo won." Pruitt put a fresh stick of Beemans in his mouth. "This kind of stuff happens every day, Sparhawk, especially in the projects."

"Did you believe him?"

"What difference does it make if I believed him?" he said. "We put a scumbag behind bars for six to ten. That's a good day's work."

"But did you believe him?"

"I believe he killed Hennessey, yes." Pruitt chewed. "Whether he killed him in self-defense or not, I don't know. I know this much, Manny Carlo admitted to sticking a knife in Jeepster Hennessey's back. Nobody admits to killing a man unless he killed him."

"That's true."

Pruitt walked away.

I still hadn't seen George Meeks since my visit to FCI Otisville in New York. I wanted to ask him about the prison book club. Why had George lied to me about his membership in the club? Most ex-cons would boast of such an affiliation. I drove to Tibbetstown Way in the Mishawum projects, where George lived. He wasn't home. From Mishawum I circled back to the Bunker Hill projects to visit Emma Hague in Starr King Court. She wasn't home, either.

I walked out to Decatur Street alongside the Tobin Bridge. A group of Hispanic men were sitting in lawn chairs beneath the bridge, enjoying the shadows cast by the double-decked hulk. They were also enjoying some midday libation. I went over to say hi. An older gent wearing a Panama hat and three day's growth offered me a can of beer from his Igloo cooler. I told him no thanks. He cracked open a can and took a swig.

"Are you looking for the woman with the silver hair?"

"Yes," I said. "She's not home."

"Everyone knows she's no project woman." He drank more beer. "She's not around much lately. I think maybe she's gone."

"Do me a favor." I handed Panama hat a twenty. "Next time you see her lights on, call me." I wrote down my number. "Twenty more if you call me."

I sat in the car in front of my house with the motor off, doing my part for the green movement. The air conditioner didn't work anyway. Mickey Pappas pulled up beside me and powered down the passenger-side window.

"You up for a meeting?" He glimpsed the rearview mirror and ran his fingers thought his reddish-gray hair. "There's an open meeting over in the South End, starts in twenty minutes. Whatda ya say?"

"Sure, I'll go." I thought about the can of beer the Hispanic man offered me under the bridge. The simple click of the cooler got me salivating. "I'll definitely go."

I got into his car and he pulled away. Mickey was wearing a Cleveland Browns windbreaker and matching cap. We took the Mass Ave exit off the Expressway, and after a few right turns, we ended up on Columbus Avenue, where Mickey found a metered space and parked.

"Pump a few quarters in that thing," he said. "The meeting's over on Shawmut Ave. It's easier to park here and walk."

We walked down West Newton Street to Shawmut Avenue by Blackstone Square and went into a school building. We sat in the front row, sipping strong coffee and listening to the secretary's report. Tradition Three states the only requirement for AA membership is a desire to stop drinking. If there were a Tradition Three B it would state: the only requirement for staying awake during the secretary's report is drinking lots of strong coffee.

At the break I refilled my cup. Mickey stayed up front, talking to a long-timer. As I headed back to my seat for the raffle drawing, I saw a familiar face in the back. It was Skinny Atlas from Aunt Bea's Cazenovia Club. His stupor gaze had been replaced by an alert expression.

"Skinny," I said, walking up to him.

He drank his coffee and studied my face.

"Do I know you?" he said.

"We met at the Cazenovia Club."

"No wonder I don't remember. Wait a second, we met at the Alcoholics Mass." He extended a steady hand. "Obviously, you know I'm Skinny. What's your name again? What's your group?"

"My name is Dermot. I go to the noontime meeting at Saint Jude Thaddeus in Charlestown, been in Charlestown my whole life."

"Your whole young life," he said. "I remember when the el train ran through Charlestown, long before your time. The old elevated Orange Line ran from Forest Hills to Sullivan Square, right down the middle of Washington Street to Main Street in Charlestown. I loved the rattling noise. I'm a Boston lifer myself, been in the South End since before urban renewal ruined the neighborhood."

"Really?" Something didn't jibe. "I thought you were from New York."

"Nope, the South End," he said. "Why did you think I was from New York?"

"The day we met at the Cazenovia Club you said you grew up on the New York streets. You said you lived in Troy or Rochester or something like that."

"Oh, boy." Skinny laughed. "I must have had a snootful that day, must've confused the hell out of you. I grew up in the South End, a section called the New York Streets. They demolished the streets in the fifties, razed them during urban renewal to make room for the Mass Pike extension."

"That explains it."

"What I said about Troy and Rochester was half right. We lived on Troy Street before we moved in with my aunt on Rochester Street. The New York Streets are mostly gone now, except for Albany and Utica streets. That's why I drank at the Caz Club, because it was on Utica Street. I was longing for my old neighborhood." Skinny stopped. "Listen to the denial. I drank because I'm an alcoholic, not because I'm nostalgic."

"True enough," I said. "Longing for your old neighborhood seems natural. I hear it in Charlestown all the time, Townies longing for how it used to be."

"I loved the neighborhood. The people, the stores, the place was great. We played in the Dover Street Yards, pretending to be train engineers and conductors. When my father went on a toot, he'd sleep it off at the Hotel Roosevelt, a fleabag of a place. My mother bought my first pair of sneakers at Harry the Greek's."

"Must have been great."

"I memorized the New York Streets, won't ever forget 'em," he said. "Troy, Rochester, Seneca, Genesee, Oneida, Oswego."

"Oswego?"

"The New York Streets, God I miss them. They were short lanes that ran between Albany Street and Harrison Avenue, over by the *Herald*. The streets are gone now, nothing left but old memories."

"Did you say Oswego Street?"

"Yes, why?"

CHAPTER 42

I was sitting next to Buck Louis in front of his computer as he wiggled the mouse back and forth. He was searching the Internet for information on the New York Streets and seemed to be making progress. Sled dog rubbed his snout against my leg and panted.

"What I got on this tab is a map of current-day Boston, the Albany Street area." He clicked the other tab. "And what I got here is the Albany Street area from the early fifties, before the bulldozers came in."

"I'm with you so far." I patted Sled dog's head. "Keep talking, I'll tell you when to slow down."

"I'm going to overlay the two maps and snap a digital chalk line, showing the location of Oswego Street today if it hadn't been demolished." He adjusted the sizes of the two maps, manipulating one, then the other. "I need three landmarks that were around in the fifties and are still around today."

"You need three landmarks to line up the two maps?"

"That's right," he said. "I found two so far, the Cathedral of the Holy Cross on Washington Street and South Station."

"How about City Hospital?"

"Too many changes down there, plus it's too close to the cathedral. I want 'em spread out to increase the accuracy."

"How far east do the maps go?"

"Halfway into Southie, roughly Dorchester Street."

"Try Telegraph Hill."

"Yeah, that's good. Telegraph Hill is on both maps," Buck said. "And it's far enough away from the other two points to be useful. Now I have to scale the maps, match 'em up apples to apples, which won't be too hard with three reference points. Once we scale them and align them, we'll zero in on Oswego Street."

Buck printed the two maps, they didn't match in scale. He re-sized them on the monitor and printed again. Sled dog paced the room. I wanted to join him. After about ten stabs Buck nailed it. He tried to print the current-day map on tracing paper. The tracing paper crimped in the printer. He taped the tracing paper to a regular sheet and printed again, and this time it went through. Buck laid the tracing paper with the current map atop the old map. He lined up the reference points.

"Here it is, the location of Oswego Street," Buck said. "Oswego Street is practically on top of what is Traveler Street today."

"Nice job, Buck."

Sled dog wagged his malamute tail.

A Haitian taxi driver dropped me off on Albany Street near the Pine Street Inn. A group of men, who probably lived at the inn, were enjoying a smoke in the parking lot. One of them nodded when I passed by, none of them asked for money. On Harrison Ave. I turned right, not sure what to look for. I turned right again on Traveler Street and slowed my pace, shuffling amid boarded-up warehouses and defunct factory buildings, signposts that not all of Boston had been redeveloped. I came out to Albany Street again. My efforts proved fruitless, a fool of a man on a fool of an errand.

Maybe Oswego Street had nothing to do with Jeepster's Oswego utterance. My gut told me it did. In AA the long-timers say there are no coincidences. They say that things that appear to be coincidences are blessings from God acting in anonymity. That type of thinking might be over the top. I was banking it wasn't.

Angus Og said that one of the warehouses used to stash the stolen art was near Harry the Greek's store. Skinny Atlas told me Harry the Greek's was near Oswego Street, one of his beloved New York Streets. Jeepster Hennessey handed me a key and said the word Oswego. Coincidences? There had to be something in these overlapping references to Oswego and Harry the Greek.

I ended up on East Berkeley Street, formally Dover Street, and walked to Washington Street, location of the long-closed Harry the Greek's Clothier. I retraced my steps and turned north on Harrison Avenue and began walking that way for a second time. I stopped at a dilapidated warehouse. The warehouse had lengthy slabs of granite stacked atop each other, forming steps that rose to a loading dock door. A happy-go-lucky juicer came up to me and asked for a buck, which I handed him.

"That's how they built loading docks back in the day," he said. "See how it worked? They staggered the granite steps to accommodate carts of different heights. Nowadays they use hydraulic dock plates."

"Thanks for the info." I handed him a five and held the roll of bills in my hand. "Do you remember Oswego Street?"

"I guess so." He looked at the money. "Sure, it was a street that used to be here, what's to remember? It was just a street."

"What can you tell me about it?" I handed him another five. "What do you remember about Oswego Street?"

"Nothing at all."

"You must remember something." Another five. "Try a little harder."

He looked at the bills in his hand.

"You notice things." He pointed to the granite loading dock. "When you walk with your head down, you notice things like that dock. Follow me."

He led me up Harrison Avenue toward Herald Square. He slowed, rubbed his nose, shook his head, and walked again. The older parts of the city mesmerize me. I love the areas where the pavement wears thin, where the cobblestones flex to the surface like artifacts of history, the vertebrae of the city. I walked along Harrison Avenue with my head down, just like my thirsty friend, gazing at sewer grates and manhole covers, noticing other granite docks, now aware of their utility.

He stopped at the corner of Traveler Street and pointed down.

"Found it," he said. "Do you see?"

Carved into the cornerstone of a ramshackle warehouse were the words Oswego Street.

"Back in the old days they cut street names in the cornerstones at intersections," he said. "Do you see it?"

"I see it." I gave him five more. "Thanks."

The entranceway on Harrison Avenue was shuttered, no way to get in. I found an alley on the side of the building and walked out back, where a chain-link fence cordoned the small courtyard. Crumbling concrete steps led up to a rotting door, which was shaded by a weathered awning. A small brass plate read H&O SELF-STORAGE, with a South Boston telephone number. The phone number had no area code, and the exchange read ANdrew-8 instead of 268.

I climbed the steps and reached into my pocket when I got to the top. The McSweeney key fit the lock and opened the door. I jerked it. The hinges growled like an unfed lion. I stepped inside and saw nobody in the foyer. I yelled hello and all I got in return were echoes. To my right I saw an elevator, the kind whose doors opened horizontally, similar to the one at Mystic Piers Storage. I turned over the McSweeney key and saw the number 406 etched on the back. The freight elevator took me to the fourth floor.

The hallway was dark. The only light came from an opaque window at the south end of the building. The window at the other end was boarded up. If it had been cloudy, I'd be feeling my way down the corridor. Each footfall creaked. Each foot I lifted crinkled with the sound of cracking linoleum.

I found room 406 and inserted the key. The lock unlatched; it must have been a series key. I shouldered the door open and clicked on the lights. I saw a dehumidifier and a humidifier, similar to the combo at Mystic Piers Storage, with the same kind of switching mechanism. A sturdy easel draped in a white cloth stood in the middle of the storage room.

I removed the cloth. Underneath was a framed painting. My heart rate picked up. My eyes stopped darting, and I studied the canvas. Overlapping oil strokes rendered an undulating quality, giving the work a tidal texture. Splintering craquelure crested its topography. Wrestling swaths of shadow and light dramatized the surface into strobes.

The painting depicted a woman playing a piano, another woman singing, a man in a seat, only his back revealed. Black-and-white tiles checkered the flooring. I recognized the painting, *The Concert* by Vermeer, maybe authentic. I studied the Dutch tour de force, a fifteenth-century time capsule. Halloran owned a reproduction of *The Concert*, likely forged by Remy Menard. If Halloran bought Remy's reproduction, this might be the original.

In the corner of the room behind the climate-control machinery stood a crate, perhaps one of the crates Angus Og mentioned. I considered crating the Vermeer and taking it with me then decided against it. The painting was safer here, climate-wise and otherwise. Perched above the crate on a metal shelf was a small sculpture of an eagle on a platform. Its wings spread, its head cocked, the numeral one embossed on its base. I remembered something in one of the books, or maybe from the *Stolen* documentary. The gilded Napoleonic finial, the golden eagle that once crowned Napoleon's First Regiment flagstaff, was one of the treasures pilfered from the Gardner Museum.

The Vermeer, the Napoleonic finial, I hit the mother lode.

I picked up the finial and found an index card under it. The card read: GAY CHOIRBOY. Gay choirboy? I refilled the empty humidifier reservoir, filling it from a slop sink at the dark end of the hallway, grabbed the finial, locked the storage room, and left the warehouse.

CHAPTER 43

Harraseeket Kid was waiting on the front steps of my house. Something was wrong. He came down the stairs as my cab drew closer. I got out and stood with him on the sidewalk.

"What's happening?"

"It's Mrs. Hennessey," Kid said. "She's in the hospital and she ain't coming home. She's dying, Dermot, cancer. George Meeks told me."

"Are you sure?"

"That's what Meeks said."

"I just saw her the other day. She said nothing about cancer."

"Meeks came here looking for you," Kid said. "He gave me the message to tell you."

"Which hospital?"

"Brigham and Women's," Kid said. "She's been there a week according to Meeks."

I wondered if Captain Pruitt told Mrs. Hennessey about the arrest and conviction of Jeepster's killer, Manny Carlo. Probably not. He had just told me about it, and she'd been in the hospital a week. It might make Mrs. Hennessey feel better to know that Jeepster's killing wasn't premeditated, that he wasn't hunted down and killed in the street like a dog. He died over a misunderstanding in a poker game.

"I have to see her," I said. "I gotta tell her about Jeepster's death."

"I'll give you a ride. I'm taking Sled dog to Jamaica Pond for a walk," he said. "I'll drop you at the hospital on the way over and pick you up on the way back."

Kid dropped me off at the hospital. I made my way to Mrs. Hennessey's room, where I found her in bed. She was hooked up with tubes and wires from head to toe, connected to more strings than a centipede puppet. When she moved to greet me, everything rattled. I took her hand and gave it a squeeze. She squeezed back.

"The morphine drip kills the pain," she said. "I know it's killing me, too, and that's okay. I've had a good life." She squeezed harder. "I have something to say to you. Listen to me, Dermot. Don't interrupt."

"I'm listening."

"I've had liver cancer for six months now. I don't have much time and I don't have much strength, so let me say what I have to say before I can't say it." She swallowed. "The twenty-five thousand you gave me is paying for my funeral. I got myself a nice casket up at Clancy's. When they lay me out in lavender, I'll be at peace. I bought a plot at Forest Hills, a headstone, too. The twenty-five thousand paid for all of it."

"The money came from Jeepster—"

"You were very careful not to say how you got the fifty thousand we divvied up. Too careful for my liking, and it got me thinking. The item you sold for fifty K, it was a painting, wasn't it?" She raised her skeletal hand. "It was a painting. Yes or no?"

"Yes."

"I knew it."

A middle-aged attendant with frosted hair came into the hospital room. She read the monitors, took a pulse, nodded to herself, jotted notes, gave a cursory smile, and left.

"Fifty thousand dollars, that's a lot of money," she said. "That's once-in-a-lifetime money."

"Sure is."

"Fifty thousand doesn't fall off the back of a truck."

"Nope."

"I know things, Dermot."

"Know what things?"

"I know that Jeepster pulled off the Gardner Museum heist."

She said this with no urgency, a matter-of-fact remark about the heist of the century. People show more emotion ordering eggs at a diner. "My husband was in on it with Jeepster." She rubbed her bruised forearm where a needle went in. "No offense, Dermot, your father had a hand in it, too. And there was another guy from their Vietnam days."

"Go on, Mrs. Hennessey, keep talking."

"The day after the heist the four of them came into my apartment, giddy as sailors on shore leave. They drank liquor at the kitchen table, slapped each other on the back, whispered, and laughed." She smiled at the memory. "My husband never laughed in his life, never sat down with Jeepster, either, and here he was, sitting down with Jeepster and laughing his face red." She stopped and breathed. "Four of them, Jeepster, Chief, my husband, and a man I didn't know." She squirmed. "It's been more than twenty years since that day."

"A long time ago."

"I guess what I'm saying is: What difference does it make now? What difference does it make if I say a few things out of school? It can't hurt anybody."

"You didn't say anything out of school."

"I'm about to," she said. "It doesn't really matter anyway. My husband is dead and I'm dying, so I feel okay saying it. My husband hadn't looked at me in years—romantically, I mean. That night, after his pals left, he stared at me all goo-goo eyed, the way he did on our wedding night. I knew right then they robbed the museum. God forgive me, I was proud of them." She took my hand. "You've been a wonderful friend to me over the years, Dermot. I love you like a son. You have to leave now, I need my rest."

She closed her eyes. I kissed Mrs. Hennessey goodbye as a single teardrop ran down my cheek, and then I smiled. I never did tell her about the capture of Jeepster's killer.

Harraseeket Kid picked me up outside the hospital on his way back from Jamaica Pond. I barely got in the truck when Sled dog plopped his massive head on my lap and let out a sigh. I rubbed his broad snout. Kid told me that Sled dog took a shine to a collie and tried to nose her into the woods. The collie seemed interested, but the collie's owner wasn't. She refused to budge on the matter despite Kid's pleas, Sled dog's advances, and her own dog's eagerness for action.

"I asked her if she'd like to meet for a drink or two this weekend. She said she was bisexual, busy this weekend," Kid said. "I said how about we meet every other weekend. I got a laugh out of her. I wonder about her bisexuality."

"Why?"

"The way she stared at Sled-dog, I'm wondering if she's tri."

Kid dropped me off a block from the house in Hayes Square, just in time for the AA meeting at Saint Jude Thaddeus. I didn't see Mickey Pappas or Skinny Atlas, so I sat on the side, my back to the wall, grateful to be sober.

A physiological shift occurred when I stopped drinking, a reallocation of bodily resources. The most overworked organ switched from my liver to my brain. Now I can't stop thinking. I do various things to distract myself, to derail the dizzying iterations. I solve crossword puzzles, do rafter pull-ups, swing Indian clubs, and in the privacy of my bedroom, say rosaries. They all help.

Whenever I get bored at AA meetings I doodle, and that's what I was doing today: doodling. Armed with scrap paper and a number two pencil, I drew lines and circles and triangles, an AA geometry whiz. My mind drifted to the Oswego warehouse. I had talked with Buck Louis about my Oswego Street findings and gave him the index card with the cryptic message.

Buck didn't find the message cryptic at all. He matched "gay choirboys" against a list of Oulipo restrictions and concluded that Jeepster was pointing us to homovocalism, an Oulipo lipogram where you extract the vowels from one word or phrase and form another word or phrase with the same vowels. Buck figured out Jeepster's clue. Gay led to homo; choirboy led to vocalism, homovocalism. Buck and I dabbled with homovocalisms a while back and came up with nothing.

It was nice to have something to doodle about. I wrote the word The Eggman on the scrap paper and isolated the vowels: *E E A*, and like magic I saw it: *E E A* Remy Menard. The Eggman is Remy Menard. I knew that.

I sat up straighter.

I tried McSweeney: *E E E*. Again the word assembled itself: *E E E* Vermeer. McSweeney is code for Vermeer. McEwan: *E A*. I did nothing and the word materialized: Rembrandt. McEwan is Rembrandt.

The Eggman-Remy Menard connection was clear enough, and the McSweeney-Vermeer link seemed plausible, but the McEwan-Rembrandt connection was tougher to understand. Unlike Vermeer's *Concert*, neither of the Rembrandt forgeries I found at Mystic Piers Storage was stolen. Neither *Old Man in Prayer*, the reproduction I sold to Father Mullineaux, nor *Self-Portrait, Aged 23*, the original of which hangs in the Gardner Museum, were stolen during the Gardner heist or any other heist. *Old Man in Prayer* was never in the Gardner Museum, it hangs in the MFA.

Now what?

After we said the Lord's Prayer, I helped clean up the hall and then walked home to get my car. When I got there, the postman, a strapping Townie with a blond flattop and a jaw of sheer ledge, handed me the mail. I sat inside my car and riffled through the envelopes. I came across a handwritten envelope postmarked Nova Scotia, Canada, with no return address. Maybe Bonnie Og. My heart rate picked up speed.

I tore open the envelope and found a letter inside. The letter wasn't from Bonnie, it was from Angus. Folded in the letter was a black-and-white photograph. The picture showed three people smiling: a young boy, a young man, and a nun. The photo had been taken at close range, making it difficult to discern the background.

The note said it was a picture of Angus Og as a young boy, accompanied by Sister Mary Agnes and John Updike at Fenway Park. John Updike? I studied the photo more closely and recognized Updike's distinct Yankee facial features, the long face, the long nose, the long teeth and chin. The young man was John Updike.

Og's Updike story was true.

CHAPTER 44

My ailing Plymouth gagged on Morrissey Boulevard as I drove past the *Boston Globe*, the Savin Hill Yacht Club, and the Dorchester gas tank. From Morrissey I picked up Victory Road on the armory end near the old Linda Mae's restaurant, and stayed on Victory to Train Street, and on Train to North Munroe Terrace. I pulled into Remy Menard's driveway, nosing up to his black Bonneville ragtop, vintage 1970, with its chrome grill poking out of the undersized garage.

The day was hot and the tide was low. Humid air advanced from Dorchester Bay, mugging Pope's Hill with a pall of salty steam. No doubt Atlantis smelled like this.

I had contacted The Eggman, Remy Menard, through the Oulipo Boys chat room, protecting our privacy via a sidebar communiqué. Remy agreed to meet me today and even seemed eager to do so, confirmed by the fact that he was standing at the back door when I reached the top step.

"Come in out of the heat," he said. "I have central air, gotta have it for my art collection. Can't afford too much humidity, else it all goes to hell."

"Thanks for meeting me today."

"Let's go upstairs to my studio." He twirled his gray handlebar moustache and smiled. "I'll show you my latest stuff."

We went up to the third floor of his Philadelphia two-family where he housed his studio. The room was just as I remembered it, massive windows and beveled skylights sandwiched between ceiling rafters. The beveling acted as a prism, diffracting the sunlight into rainbows of colors.

"To perfect a Rembrandt forgery, you have to perfect the contrast of light and shadow," he said, "in art-world parlance, the chiaroscuro."

Remy had completed his reproduction of Rembrandt's *The Storm on the Sea of Galilee*, which rested on a plank easel. He walked up to it.

"What do you think of it?" He touched the edge. "My version of *The Storm on the Sea of Galilee*."

"It's spectacular," I said.

"I built the frame and easel myself. I love to dabble in the basics of carpentry. I build all my frames and easels."

"They're rock solid." I grabbed the top of the easel and shook it. "You could moor a ship on this baby."

I stopped mid-shake. Remy's carpentry talk sent shivers down my arms. I wasn't sure why. An idea percolated in my mind, watery drops of an idea that produced no flavor, not yet. Something was there, and it was something important.

"The paintings you forged for Jeepster, the Rembrandt and Vermeer—"

"You mean Rembrandts and Vermeer. I gave him three paintings, two Rembrandts and one Vermeer. *Self-Portrait, Aged 23* and *Old Man in Prayer*, those were the Rembrandts. *The Concert* was a Vermeer. Only thirty-six Vermeer oils exist in the world."

"I didn't know that," I said. "*Self-Portrait, Aged 23* and *The Concert*, when did you deliver them to Jeepster?"

"I didn't deliver them, Jeepster picked them up," Remy said. "Jeepster said he needed the paintings by the Ides of March. I completed them beforehand, of course. I don't like to rush. But the deadline was the Ides of March."

"March fifteenth," I said. "And the year was nineteen ninety."

"Correct, March fifteenth, nineteen ninety."

"And Jeepster picked them up on March fifteenth," I said. "He took the paintings from you on the Ides of March."

"No, he picked them up on Saint Patrick's Day."

"Saint Patrick's Day?" I said. "What time?"

"I'm not sure of the exact time." He craned his neck to the sky-lights. "It was midday, two or three in the afternoon, not much later than that."

Remy Menard's timetable supported Angus Og's. Og said they picked up the crates in Dorchester in the afternoon.

"Jeepster Hennessey came here to Dorchester," I said. "And you gave him two forged paintings, *Self-Portrait, Aged 23* and *The Concert*" The percolating stopped, the coffee was done: Remy's carpentry skills. "And you built two crates to ship the forgeries."

"How did you know about the crates?"

"It just came to me." My mind worked to complete the puzzle. I almost had it. "Remy, I'll get the hundred grand you've been wait-ing for. Give me a few more days and you'll have your money."

I walked to the top of the stairs, and Remy Menard spoke.

"Before you leave, there's something I want to tell you. A hun-dred thousand is a lot of money and I can sure use it. Do you know what I really want? Do you know what would make my life com-plete? *Self-Portrait, Aged 23*. If you found my version of *Self-Portrait, Aged 23*, I'd be the happiest man in Dorchester. It was the best forgery I ever painted."

"I think I can get it for you, Remy," I said. "Give me a few more days, and you'll have your money and your painting."

My cousin Timmy O'Hanlon of Homeland Security called me back. He said he found the information I'd asked for. I had a hunch about something, and there was only one man who could confirm or disprove the hunch. Timmy located him.

"I used all my FBI connections to find the name," he said. "I called in every marker, and now I'm on the hook for return favors. I hate debts. Federal IOUs are the worst."

"Appreciate it, Timmy."

"I'm not trying to sound like a hero, it's just—information comes at a price. Information isn't cheap."

"You're a good man."

"The man's name is Henry Farleigh. He lives in Brattleboro,

Vermont." Timmy paused a few seconds. "Sorry for the pouting. It was actually fun hunting Farleigh down. It's good to know I have that kind of juice."

"Thanks, Timmy."

Timmy gave me the address and hung up.

I exited I-91 in Brattleboro after driving three hours from Charlestown and found Henry Farleigh's house on a dead-end street that ran alongside abandoned railroad tracks. The weedy lawn around his home hadn't been mowed in weeks. The car out front had an expired inspection sticker. The trash barrel wasn't lidded. I walked up the front steps and opened the mailbox and saw an overdue notice from a cable company.

I rang the doorbell and waited. A few minutes later a slight man in his early forties answered. He sported an unkempt beard, a stringy moustache, and longish gray hair. He'd mastered the rumpled style, which had gone out of style in the 1960s. Farleigh presented a paradox, a man who couldn't decide whether to be a biker or a college professor.

"Yes?" He unlatched the screen door and opened it. That never happens in the city. "What do you want?"

"My name is Dermot Sparhawk," I said. "I'm from Charlestown."

"Yes? And?"

"I'd like to ask you about the Gardner Museum robbery," I said. "I'm told you worked security there."

"Are you with the FBI?"

"I'm a citizen."

"A citizen?" he said. "What does that mean?"

"It means I answer to nobody."

"That sounds like a threat." He rubbed his runny nose. "Are you threatening me?"

"Not really, I'm just here to talk," I said. "That's my goal, at least, to talk to you and be on my way."

"That doesn't sound very reassuring," he said. "You have no

authority here. I don't have to talk to you if I don't want to, you know. You can't make me."

His words had no oomph. A Townie would have told me to fuck myself, the way Mr. McGillicuddy did in Southie.

"This will only take a second," I said. "My godfather was recently killed. I think he had something to do with the Gardner heist."

"That heist happened twenty years ago. I only worked there a few months," he said. "I talked to the FBI back then, told them everything."

"I know you did," I said. "My cousin's an FBI agent. He gave me your name and said it was okay that I follow up on some things."

"There's nothing to tell." He pulled the screen door. "I'm finished talking."

"I'll make it worth your while." I didn't give him a chance to reply. "You worked the second shift the night of the robbery, correct?"

"Sure, the second shift. But the heist didn't happen till two in the morning. That's the overnight. My shift ended at eleven, okay? I punched the clock at eleven, you can check. I'd been outta there for what, three hours? The robbery happened three hours after I left."

"Take it easy, Henry. Or do you prefer Hank."

"Hank? No one calls me Hank."

"All I want is a little information," I said. "I understand that information isn't cheap, that it comes at a price, and I'm willing to pay that price."

"What do you mean?"

"There's money in it for you," I said. "Talk to me and I'll pay you. You can't get in any trouble. Even if you robbed the place, the statute of limitations is up."

"Don't say that. I didn't rob the place." He eased up on the door. "The money, how much are we talking?"

"I can muster a grand."

"You'll pay me a grand?"

I had him. Now to make him an offer he can't refuse.

"Let's make it four grand, Henry." I pulled out a wad of hundreds and thumbed the pile. "Jeez, it's more than I realized. Let's round it up to five."

"Five thousand? Are you pulling a fast one? I hope not, 'cause I can use the scratch." He opened the door and led me inside, the act of a desperate man. Henry Farleigh had information to sell, his body language screamed it. We walked to the kitchen. "No checks, it's gotta be cash."

Why do you think I fanned the bills under your nose, Hank?

"Sure, cash." I slowly counted out fifty $100 bills and laid them on the table in front of him. The stack sat on the Formica like thirty pieces of silver. "Five thousand dollars in cash, it's yours. You have something important to say, Farleigh. Say it."

"Will you still give me the money if what I say ain't worth that much?" He sniffled. "See, I'm behind on a few bills."

"The money's yours," I said. "Now let's hear it."

CHAPTER 45

I was sitting in Buck Louis's parlor, trying to figure out how to tell Buck and Kid about my brainchild without getting laughed out of Charlestown. They must have sensed my uneasiness. Buck fidgeted with the wheelchair, popping wheelies. Harraseeket Kid straddled a kitchen chair, his chest against the Naugahyde back, his arms folded across the top. Kid spoke first.

"You have the floor, Dermot."

"I'd like to play what-if again," I said.

"The last time we played, we didn't learn a thing," Buck said.

"I'd like to play again. This will be the last time, promise," I said. "I have a theory, and I want you guys to shoot holes in it. I think I know what happened the night of the Gardner Museum heist."

"You'd be the first," Kid said. "And you sure as hell got our attention."

"My first what-if," I said. "What if Jeepster's father was one of the watchman on the night of the heist?"

"He wasn't," Kid said. "I read the book you gave me. Two guards were on duty that night, both of 'em were bound and gagged, neither was Jeepster's father."

"What if Jeepster's father worked the earlier shift?" I said. "Suppose he worked the second shift, the three-to-eleven."

"What if he did? The robbery took place at one thirty in the morning," Buck said. "The heist didn't happen between three and eleven, Dermot, it happened at one thirty in the morning."

"What if there were two robberies that night?" I said.

"Two robberies in the same night?" Kid said.

"Go on Dermot, we're listening."

"Suppose Jeepster caught wind of the known heist before it happened?" I said. "My theory is based on a number of assumptions. One of them is that Jeepster Hennessey learned about the heist before it happened."

"Okay," Kid said. "Let's pretend he heard about the heist."

"After Jeepster heard about plans for the heist, he hired a forger to paint two reproductions, one of Vermeer's *Concert*, the other of Rembrandt's *Self-Portrait, Aged 23*."

"The thieves didn't steal Rembrandt's *Self-Portrait, Aged 23*," Buck said. "I watched the documentary. They stole Rembrandt's *The Storm on the Sea of Galilee*. I'll grant you they also swiped *The Concert*, but they didn't take *Self-Portrait*."

"I know they didn't," I said. "What if Jeepster assumed they'd steal *Self-Portrait*? Suppose Jeepster heard that the second crew planned to steal a Rembrandt."

"Okay." Buck tapped the wheelchair. "They planned to steal a Rembrandt."

"What if Jeepster guessed that the Rembrandt they'd steal was *Self-Portrait, Aged 23*? Suppose he guessed wrong, and they stole *Storm on the Sea of Galilee* instead. See what I'm getting at? What if the second crew stole the wrong Rembrandt?"

"You better start making sense pretty soon," Kid said. "I'm getting confused with all this what-if shit."

"Ah." Buck's head jerked up. "I think I see what you're getting at. I don't see all of it, just some of it. Maybe you're on to something."

"I pieced together two stories," I said. "One from the forger, the other from Angus Og."

"Angus Og? We already dismissed him as a drug-addled lunatic," Kid said. "Get serious, Dermot, Og is nuts."

"Og *is* nuts, but supposing he was in on the Gardner job?" I said. "If Og was in on the heist, his account of events might prove useful, especially when it's matched against the forger's account of the events."

"You're drifting into bullshit," Buck said.

"I contrasted the forger's story against Og's. I compared their points of agreement," I said. "I'll say it again. What if there were two robberies in the same night?"

"Question," Kid said. "How did Jeepster find out about the heist?"

"The Irish connection. Jeepster had close ties with the Irish, so did his father. The Irish connection explains Liam McGrew's interest, too," I said. "That's probably how Jeepster learned about the heist and what they intended to steal, he overheard something. Then he commissioned a forger to paint a Vermeer and a Rembrandt, because he knew the thieves planned to steal a Vermeer and Rembrandt."

"Here's where you lose me," Buck said. "Why the forgeries? Why did Jeepster want forgeries?"

"He used them as decoys," I said. "Jeepster and my father got inside the Gardner on Saint Patrick's Day at seven o'clock in the evening. They replaced Vermeer's *Concert* and Rembrandt's *Self-Portrait, Aged 23* with fakes. Then they stole the originals. When the second crew struck at one thirty in the morning, they stole a forgery of *The Concert*, the same forgery that Jeepster commissioned."

"This is wild," Buck said.

"How do you know this?" Kid said.

"It's just a theory."

"Keep with the theory," Buck said.

"Chief was in on it?" Kid said.

"I think he was."

"I'm gonna poke a megahole in your guesswork, Dermot," Buck said. "You said Jeepster replaced *The Concert* and *Self-Portrait, Aged 23*. But *Self-Portrait, Aged 23* was never stolen. The so-called second crew didn't take *Self-Portrait*. That fact alone destroys your theory."

"Unless what?"

"What do you mean, unless what?" Buck said.

"Unless the *Self-Portrait* reproduction is still hanging in the museum," I said. "What if the museum didn't bother to inspect the paintings that weren't stolen? What if they focused on the missing paintings only?"

"Jesus," Kid said. "That could happen."

"Not so fast," Buck said. "Are you saying that a forged Rembrandt is hanging in the Gardner Museum? A fake's been hanging there since 1990 and they don't know? No way possible." He rolled forward, his black knuckles squeezing to pink. "How did they get the forged art into the Gardner? It's not like they could walk through the front door with forgeries under their arms. And how did they get the originals out? And how did they do all this before the second crew got in?"

"Crates," I said.

"What the hell does that mean?" Kid said.

"Think back to Angus Og and the forger. Both of them mentioned crates. Og referred to Trojan crates, comparing them to the Trojan horse. Og's metaphor was more apt than he realized, but he was only half right. Og believed the crates were empty, a means to get inside the museum as deliverymen. What Og didn't know was the forgeries were inside the crates."

"How do *you* know the forgeries were inside the crates?" Buck said.

"The forger told me. He built the crates to ship the fakes."

"The forger was in on the heist, too?" Kid said.

"The forger knew nothing about the connection to the Gardner Museum," I said. "Jeepster and his crew swapped the reproductions for the originals. A literal swap, they framed the fakes and crated the originals, and took the originals out of the museum in the crates."

"What about the night watchmen?" Buck said. "Even if they hit the place earlier, there were two watchmen. Last time we played what-if, we agreed it was impossible to get past two guards. What's different this time?"

"Only one of the watchmen was on duty when they hit," I said.

"The other one was in Kenmore Square, playing a Saint Patrick's Day rock-and-roll rumble at the Rathskeller."

"The Rat's closed," Kid asked.

"Not back then it wasn't. One of the watchman played the rumble's opening act," I said.

"How do you know that?" Kid asked.

"I tracked him down in Vermont and talked to him," I said. "His name is Henry Farleigh. Farleigh told me the story."

"Why did he tell you?" Kid asked. "After twenty years of hush-hush, he decides to spill it? Why?"

"I paid him five grand."

"So what?" Buck said. "Even if Farleigh was jamming at the Rat, the other guard was still on duty at the museum."

"Yeah, Dermot, the museum was still guarded."

"I know it was guarded," I said. "Jeepster's father was the guard. Before you ask again 'how do you know' I'll tell you. Mrs. Hennessey told me on her dying bed. She didn't come right out and say it. She didn't have to, I knew what she meant."

We stopped for a break.

CHAPTER 46

Buck rolled to the center of the parlor.

"I don't get it. Why did they rob the museum the same night as the other guys?"

"It makes no sense, Dermot," Kid said. "Jeepster boxed himself in. Why did he put himself under that kinda time pressure?"

"He used the second crew's heist as a cover for his own," I said. "He set up the perfect alibi. Every cop in Boston knew the Gardner got robbed at one thirty in the morning on March eighteenth." I shivered at the brilliance of Jeepster's scheme. "Jeepster planned everything—the robbery, the alibi—he covered every detail."

"Tell us more about the alibi," Buck said.

"After the robbery, Jeepster, Og, and my father went to a Chinese restaurant in Quincy for a few drinks. They purposely started trouble in the bar, the cops came in, and the three of them got locked up."

"Why is that important?" Kid said.

"They were sitting in a Quincy jail when the second crew hit the Gardner," I said. "They were in court the next morning when the cops swarmed the museum. Jeepster concocted the perfect alibi."

Kid and Buck looked at each other.

"How did you come up with the double-robbery idea?" Buck said.

"I asked a lot of people a lot of questions, that's how I came up with it. And I'm still not sure it's right."

"How do we find out if it's right?" Buck said.

"Yeah Dermot, what do we do now?"

"I'm going to walk straight into the Gardner Museum and ask for the head curator, a guy named Luigi Lovetti. I'm going to tell Lovetti I have Vermeer's *Concert* and Rembrandt's *Self-Portrait, Aged 23*. That's how I'll find out if I'm right."

Jeepster had given me the McSweeney key, he had said the word Oswego, and I figured out the secret, or most of it. Now it was time to finish the job.

I'd be dealing with the police, the FBI's Art Theft Squad, the Gardner team, insurance investigators, possibly the press, and probably others. Law enforcement had promised anonymity and amnesty in addition to the reward. I didn't believe them. I might also be dealing with the crew that pulled off the known heist, especially if they had a Gardner insider on the team. The insider would violate my anonymity even if law enforcement didn't. And I might end up dealing with the angry buyers of replacement forgeries, con men like Halloran and henchmen like Karl Kloosmann. And there was Liam McGrew and the IRA.

Maybe I should forget the whole thing, hang *The Concert* in the parlor and enjoy it.

CHAPTER 47

I drove my life-support Plymouth along Park Drive through the West Fens, hugging the contour of the Muddy River, and pulled into Simmons College. A Townie working the security booth waved me in and pointed me to the rear lot. I killed the ignition, which gladly died, and I walked The Fenway to the Isabella Stewart Gardner Museum.

Long-matured shade trees canopied the three-lane parkway, providing an emerald tunnel for the merging vehicles. Across the parkway the community gardens of the Back Bay Fens swayed in the breeze, or maybe from the pull of the passing traffic. I walked up Palace Road toward the museum.

I paid the admission and squeezed through a metal detector. No alarms sounded. I roamed the Italianate villa, viewing the master works. When I reached the Dutch Room, I stood in front of Rembrandt's *Self-Portrait, Aged 23*, or if my theory was correct, Remy Menard's *Self-Portrait, Aged 23*. A security guard with broad shoulders stood in the corner and watched the goings-on. I approached him.

"I'd like to talk to the curator, Luigi Lovetti," I said. "I want to talk to him about two of the museum's stolen paintings."

"What do you mean by talk?"

"I have information that can lead to their recovery."

The security guard was well trained. He didn't laugh at me. He didn't leap at the chance to get cracking on my claim, either.

"Of course, sir." His face didn't change expression. "Which paintings?"

"I have the missing Vermeer and one of the Rembrandts."

"One moment, sir," he said.

He spoke into his mouthpiece. A minute later, two more security people entered the Dutch Room, a black man and a Hispanic woman. Both wore the requisite uniforms. I was still dealing with staff. The Hispanic woman scowled at the young guard as she walked past him.

"Please follow us, sir," she said. "We'll go to a private room where we can talk."

We walked up a flight of stairs to a windowless office that had three chairs and a desk in the corner. We remained standing. The black man cleared his throat.

"Tell us your name, please."

"No offense, I'm here to talk to Luigi Lovetti."

"He's a busy man," he said.

"I have two of the Gardner's nineteen stolen paintings. I have the Vermeer and one of the Rembrandts. I'm here to return the paintings and collect my reward."

"There were only eighteen items stolen," the Hispanic woman said, "not nineteen".

"That's what you think."

"Tell us your name, sir," the black man said.

"Not yet."

"This is a serious claim," she said. "We'll need to contact the Boston police and the FBI." She sighed. "We can't disturb Mr. Lovetti every time a crank—every time a person says he has the stolen paintings. Do you understand?"

"Do I look like a crank to you?" I stepped closer to them. "I'm asking you to use your judgment. It took a lot to come here today, and if I walk out that door, I'm not coming back. This is a one-time opportunity. Take a risk. Tell Luigi Lovetti what I said. Otherwise, I'll walk out of here and never return."

"I won't violate protocol to suit you," she said.

I couldn't blame her for snubbing me. I'd have snubbed me, too. I felt relief when she told me to screw, a freedom from responsibility. Now I didn't have to explain how I came by the paintings. Now I didn't have to duck the shadier elements of the art underworld. My life could return to normal, whatever that was. I reached for the doorknob.

"Wait," the black guard said. "Hold on."

"Are you crazy, Lamont?" she said. "He doesn't have any stolen art. He's just a big lug, a jock on a dare."

"I believe him," he said. "And besides, Mr. Lovetti should sort this out, not us."

"Leave me out of it." She went to the door. "It's your neck, Lamont." She left.

"Sit down a minute, I should be right back." He stuck out his hand. "My name's Lamont Hayes. I'm not asking your name, because I understand the situation."

"Thanks."

"I have one question before I go," Lamont said. "Are you shooting it straight or are you pulling my pecker?"

"I'm shooting it straight."

"That's what my gut tells me."

Lamont left the office. Half an hour passed before he returned with Luigi Lovetti. I recognized Lovetti from the documentary.

"Should I leave now, Mr. Lovetti?" Lamont said.

"Excuse me." I spoke before Lovetti answered. "I insist that Lamont stays. That's a condition of this meeting—Lamont is at the table. We wouldn't be having this talk if not for him, and you wouldn't be on the verge of recovering two Dutch oils."

Luigi Lovetti must have endured more bullshit from more conmen than any person in Boston. The hoaxes he'd heard over the years had probably washed away any hope of ever finding the lost art.

"Lamont can stay if it makes you feel more comfortable." He had an unforced accent, aristocratic in tone. His suit was pressed and his shirt was starched, yet his movements were fluid. He wore his thick black hair combed straight back off the forehead. "What is your name, please?"

"My name is Dermot Sparhawk and I'm from Charlestown.

My godfather was Jeepster Hennessey." I wasn't sure where to begin, so I started at the end. "I have Vermeer's *Concert* and Rembrandt's *Self-Portrait, Aged 23*."

"Another charlatan," Luigi said. "Lamont, please escort Mr. Sparhawk to the egress. The Rembrandt he referred to was never stolen from our museum. It hangs in the Dutch Room as we speak."

"Hold your horses. I want to show you something." From under my shirt I removed the golden eagle I'd found in the Oswego Street storage room. It must have been carved of wood or stone, because I got it through the metal detector. "The Napoleonic finial, the finial stolen during the heist."

Lamont smiled. Luigi Lovetti reached out his hand.

"May I see it?" Luigi hurried to put on his glasses. He studied the finial from different angles, rubbing the open wings, thumbing the numeral one, examining the flagpole hole. "I don't know, I'm not sure. Is this for real, Mr. Sparhawk? No, no, it can't be real."

"I think it's real," I said. "I collected evidence from a number of different sources. Too many things tie together to be explained away by coincidence. I'm confident it's the stolen Napoleonic finial."

"Where did you get this?" Luigi said, with his eyes fixed on the golden bird. "Please, Mr. Sparhawk, tell me."

"If we arrive at a deal, I'll tell you everything I know."

"What exactly did you mean about *Self-Portrait, Aged 23*?" he said. "At least tell me what you meant about that."

"It's a fake."

"What?"

"The Gardner's *Self-Portrait, Aged 23* is a fake." I let it sink into Luigi's head before I continued. "A fake *Self-Portrait* is hanging in the Dutch Room. It's been hanging in there since Saint Patrick's Day, 1990."

"This is insanity." He studied the finial as he spoke. "It's not feasible. No way on earth our *Self-Portrait, Aged 23* is a fake, it's simply not possible, Mr. Sparhawk." He stopped. "Tell me the truth, where did you get the finial?"

"The details of my findings are complex, but there's a difference between complex and not feasible. A man such as yourself must know this." I walked to the door. "If you want to hear my story, call me. I'll leave my number with Lamont. Keep the finial. Hell, it's yours anyway. Test it. See if it's authentic."

"We will. Believe me, Mr. Sparhawk, we will."

"If it is authentic, chances are the paintings I recovered are authentic, too."

"It's not possible," Luigi said again.

"Call Special Agent Emma Hague," I said on a whim. "She's the FBI point person on the Gardner heist. She can vouch for me."

"You know Ms. Hague?" Luigi said. "She isn't the point person, although she is a member of the FBI's Art Theft Team. Of course, you already knew that. The fact that you know Miss Hague sheds new light on the matter."

"I'm not playing you, Luigi," I said. "If I'm wrong about the items I recovered, it's because I made a mistake, not because I'm running a con."

"It's impossible."

"I think he's telling the truth," Lamont said.

"We've been duped before. Not to belabor the point, Mr. Sparhawk, but you have no idea how many stories we hear like this each year." He damn near hugged the finial. "You know Miss Hague and produced the finial, both bode well for your claim. I thank you for bringing me the finial. We'll test for its authenticity. If it proves genuine, I'll be in touch."

We shook hands like cautious politicians, and I walked out of the museum convinced I had it right. I started the Plymouth, which retched like a chain smoker sucking his first Lucky Strike of the day, then coughed its way to a flat gurgling sound.

CHAPTER 48

That evening the Red Sox were playing the A's in Oakland, which meant a ten o'clock start time. Matsuzaka was slated for the Sox, and Sheets was pitching for the A's. The Old Town Team had hit a tailspin, losing three of their last four at Fenway Park to the surging Texas Rangers. A tough way to come out of the all-star break. Getaway day couldn't come fast enough for the Boston nine.

The team was set to embark on a ten-game West Coast swing, a road trip that would likely determine their playoff chances this season. The Yankees led the Sox by six games in the division, and the D-Rays had them by four in the wild card. With nearly half their starting position players on the disabled list, a hobbled pitching staff, and a closer who'd lost his mojo, Boston's prospects appeared bleak.

I kicked back in the recliner and clicked on the television, ready to watch the pregame show. That's when the doorbell rang. I suspected it might ring tonight. I went down to the foyer and found three people standing on the stoop: Luigi Lovetti, Lamont Hayes, and Special Agent Emma Hague. I opened the door and let them in. They followed me up to my apartment.

"The Napoleonic finial proved to be authentic," Luigi Lovetti said. "How did you come by it, Mr. Sparhawk?"

"Before I tell you anything, I want to discuss the deal."

"What deal?" Luigi said. Emma and Lamont had taken seats. "We're talking about priceless works of art."

"It might be priceless to you, but it holds a distinct value for me," I said. "I'm in possession of two stolen paintings, Vermeer's

Concert and Rembrandt's *Self-Portrait, Aged 23*. I don't have *The Storm on the Sea of Galilee* or the other missing pieces. For the safe return of those two paintings, I want six million. I'll throw in the finial as a bonus, no charge."

"Why the inflated amount?" Emma said.

"Stud fees," I said. She blushed. Lamont and Luigi seemed confused. I continued. "I incurred a million dollars in expenses, money I promised to four people if I won the Gardner reward. They get a quarter million apiece. Without their help, I'd have never recovered the paintings."

"Why not pay them out of your own share, that is, if we pay you," Luigi said. "We still haven't authenticated the paintings."

"The paintings are authentic," I said. "If you want the two Dutch masterpieces, you'll pay my price."

"The Gardner Museum always keeps its promises," Lamont said. "Right, Mister Lovetti?"

Luigi didn't answer. Emma did.

"I can get a search warrant in a nanosecond, Dermot." Emma's silver hair was coiled atop her head. She had played me for a fool, yet I still found her attractive, but now in a sluttish way. Most guys prefer that anyway. Emma's face flushed, as if reading my thoughts. "The FBI will turn this place inside out to find what we're looking for. We'll search your office, your computer. We'll do whatever it takes to recover the Gardner loot. And we will recover it," she said. "I did you a favor, Dermot."

"The type of favor every guy dreams of."

"We considered swarming this place," she said, ignoring my crack. "We almost stormed in with the troops. Instead, we decided to work with you."

"You're a peach, Emma."

"What on earth is transpiring between you two," Luigi said.

Lamont smiled.

"You guys are blowing it," I said. "You're nitpicking your way out of a Vermeer and a Rembrandt. Tell Emma to get a search warrant, see if it does any good." I tossed the McSweeney and McEwan keys on the coffee table. "Take 'em, the keys to the paintings. Go ahead, the keys are yours, but you won't find the doors they unlock." I tapped the side of my head. "It's all up here."

"What are you saying, Mr. Sparhawk?" Luigi said, "Are you saying you won't give us the paintings?"

"I want to give you the paintings. I have no use for them," I said. "Are you ready to get serious, or are you going to keep with the games?"

"Dermot." Emma's voice changed to FBI mode. She was now calling the shots. "We could offer you a million dollars, or even half a million. Who refuses half a million dollars? Not a man who lives across the street from a housing project. Men who live across from housing projects don't say no to half a million dollars."

"Emma's fucking it up, Luigi. She's blowing this deal." I played the Halloran card. "Suppose I told you a man offered me thirty-five million just for Vermeer's *Concert*."

"Why didn't you sell it to him?" Luigi said.

"I didn't like him. I'd rather see the masterpieces back where they belong, in the Dutch Room of the Gardner Museum."

"Don't believe him," Emma said. "If someone offered Dermot thirty-five million for the paintings, he'd sell them for thirty-five million."

"Can I have a glass of water?" Lamont said. "I'm thirsty."

Lamont's request cued a break, no doubt his intention. We all went out to the kitchen. I put on the kettle for tea and coffee, filled a pitcher with ice cubes and water, and once the kettle whistled, I told the group to help themselves, which they did.

Lamont filled a glass with iced water, Luigi Lovetti steeped a teabag, and Emma Hague and I mixed instant coffee. We remained in the kitchen, leaning against countertops and sipping drinks. The tension faded. Kitchens affect people that way, kitchens generate comfort.

"The five million reward is for the return of *all* the stolen items." Luigi said. His tone took on a conversational air. "The re-muneration has certain stipulations. For one, the paintings must be in suitable condition, that's a requisite for the reward's dis-bursement. Frankly, Mr. Sparhawk, I don't see how that is plausi-ble. The robbers cut the paintings out of their frames, most likely ruining them in the process."

"My robbers didn't cut any paintings out of their frames. My robbers acted as professionals. They knew what they were doing. Both my paintings are unharmed. They're as flawless as the day they were swiped." I waited. Nobody said anything. "I'll share my findings with you if you want to hear them. When you hear the story, you'll understand why my paintings are in perfect condi-tion."

"What do you mean by *my* robbers, *my* paintings?" Lamont asked.

"You got it all wrong, Dermot," Emma said. "The forensics of the crime refutes your claims. The paintings were torn from their frames."

"Mr. Sparhawk," Luigi said. "I'm afraid I must agree with Spe-cial Agent Hague on this. You are sadly mistaken, and I emphasize the word sadly. Believe me, sir, I wish you to be right. On that dreadful morning after the robbery, we collected paint chips off the floor. The chips came from the stolen artwork. We know this for a fact because we tested them. The thieves cut the artwork from the frames, destroying them in some measure."

"No argument from me," I said. "*Your* thieves cut them out of their frames, *mine* didn't."

"Mr. Sparhawk, please drop the amphibology!" Luigi flushed.

"Only if you drop the vernacular," I said.

He took a moment to breathe.

"You are a most complex man, my dear sir." Luigi continued. "My biggest fear is this, that even if we get the masterpieces back, they'll be ruined, irreparably marred by the clumsy thugs who cut them loose, never again to render their original beauty. In point of fact, Mr. Sparhawk, I know the paintings are at least marginally damaged. They'd have to be, based on the frayed canvas strips and scattered chips left behind."

Luigi Lovetti gazed into my eyes, begging me to account for the paint chips and canvas strips, pleading for me to explain the debris left behind, praying for me to allay his fears. He wanted to be wrong about the pilfered art. For the first time in his privileged life, Luigi wanted to be wrong about something.

"I can only speak for two paintings, the two paintings I have in my possession, and those two paintings are mint. I'll say it again, the paintings are in the same condition they were in when my thieves carefully removed them from their frames, boxed them in plywood crates, and took them out of the museum. Since the night of the robbery, they've been stored in humidity-controlled rooms, the same rooms the keys on the coffee table unlock."

"What do you mean by *my* robbers?" Lamont asked again.

"Tell us about it, Dermot."

"Yes, Mister Sparhawk, please do."

I laid it out for them. I even mentioned the names of the dead. No one was at risk, the statute of limitations had run out. I told Emma, Luigi, and Lamont everything. I told them my double-robbery theory. I told them about the replacement forgeries, which were then stolen by the second team of thieves. I told them about the arrests in Quincy, giving my guys alibis for the time of the known robbery.

"A fantastic story and seemingly possible," Luigi said. "I've never heard of such a convoluted scheme if it's true. But how to prove it?"

"There's nothing to prove," I said. "My theory is nothing more than a theory, a wacky hunch that can't be verified, not at this point anyway. The parties involved are either dead or crazy." I paused for a couple of beats. "I can think of one thing you can prove."

"What's that?" Lamont asked.

"You can prove the paintings I have are Dutch masterpieces."

I rinsed out my coffee cup and put it in the drain rack. "And there's another thing to consider."

"What, pray tell, is that?" Luigi said.

"Yeah, Dermot, what is it?" Emma said. "I can hardly wait."

"Your legacy," I said. "Can't you see it? This is the chance of a lifetime, a chance to be heroes, celebrated legends of law enforcement. Elliott Ness and Melvin Purvis rolled into one."

"You're being dramatic, Dermot," she said.

"Picture it. The FBI, in partnership with the Gardner Museum, opens the locked door that holds the lost Vermeer. The three of you, with a film crew at your side, uncover a stolen Gardner treasure. That has to be worth six million."

Lovetti and Hague glanced at each other. Lamont checked his watch.

"Tempting," Luigi said.

"I'll sign a confidentiality agreement, which is no big sacrifice on my part, because I want to protect my anonymity. You three take the credit. And consider this, Luigi. You can remount *Self-Portrait, Aged 23* and no one will be the wiser. No one will ever know that a fake Rembrandt has been hanging in the Dutch Room of the renowned Isabella Stewart Gardner Museum for the past twenty years. No one will know the Gardner staff had no clue it was a fake," I said. Luigi's chocolate eyes darted. "Maybe I should ask for more money. Oh, I have one more demand."

"What's that?" Emma asked.

"I want the forged Rembrandt, the reproduction of *Self-Portrait, Aged 23*."

"We can't do that," she said. "Why do you want it?"

"Personal reasons," I said. "There's no deal if I don't get the forged Rembrandt."

Nobody spoke. We leaned on the kitchen counters, silent in thought, waiting for someone to break the stillness. The projects across the street soughed with urban quiet. Remote sounds of traffic whirred from the Tobin Bridge. A muffled siren grew louder.

Sled dog unloosed a howl from Buck's below. The action in the bricks would soon pick up: junkies prowling, lonely hearts searching, drunks scrounging. A 93 bus whooshed open its pneumonic doors and closed them with a thump after letting off passengers. It churned up Bunker Hill Street for Sullivan Square.

"Mister Sparhawk," Luigi said, "you should have been a salesman."

"I prefer con man," I said. "A con man with integrity. The Napoleonic finial must have given me some credibility. Am I right? If the finial was a fake, you three wouldn't be here tonight."

"Con man and integrity, both fit you well. We're all con men in the world of art, Mister Sparhawk, and we hope to have a little integrity, too." Luigi laid down his empty teacup. "I believe we can come to terms on this matter. Do you agree, Miss Hague?"

"Are you surrendering the forged Rembrandt to Sparhawk?"

"The surrendering of the Rembrandt faux appears to be non-negotiable. If we don't turn over the fake, the deal goes kaput. Is that correct, Mister Sparhawk?"

"That's correct," I said.

"Here's what we'll do," Luigi said. "If our *Self-Portrait, Aged 23* is in fact a fake, and Mister Sparhawk has the original, then yes, I will surrender the forgery to him." Luigi moved closer to me, close enough to sniff my scent. He drank in my face with his liquid eyes, swished it around in his mind, savored it for a while, and considered whether to swallow what I had to sell. He stepped back from me for a broader assessment. "We're making the deal."

"I don't like it," Emma said.

"Don't force me to go over your head, Miss Hague," Luigi said. "This is far too important."

Emma shrugged, Lamont smiled, Luigi nodded, and the three of them left my apartment. I pocketed the two keys on the coffee table and clicked on the ballgame.

CHAPTER 49

Emma Hague called me at home the next evening. The FBI's Art Theft Squad met with the Gardner Museum, and the two agreed to do business with me. She told me that two experts along with Luigi Lovetti examined the *Self-Portrait* that hung in the Gardner and couldn't determine with certainty its authenticity. The museum made a conditional offer to me. The condition: the paintings have to be authentic. If the paintings prove authentic, I'd get six million, my anonymity, and a pardon from any wrongdoing that pertains to the Gardner heist. In addition I'd get Remy Menard's reproduction of *Self-Portrait, Aged 23*.

In exchange, the Gardner would get Vermeer's *Concert*, Rembrandt's *Self-Portrait, Aged 23*, the Napoleonic finial, and my promise of silence. I'd forego any credit for uncovering the stolen art. The FBI and Gardner would grab the glory, and that was fine with me. The last thing I need was for my project neighbors to know I had millions in the bank. If word leaked out about the money, every junky in the bricks would paint a bull's-eye on my back and take aim. And if that happened, I'd have to leave Charlestown, and I didn't want to leave.

Emma Hague told me she'd pick me up at my house in fifteen minutes. I told her I'd be waiting out front. I didn't want Emma inside my apartment again. The plan sounded simple: I was to lead Emma and a line of SUVs, soldiered by FBI agents and Gardner personnel, to the location of the Vermeer painting. After we secured the Vermeer, we would get the Rembrandt in Charlestown. I went down to the street and waited.

A convoy of vehicles humped down Bunker Hill Street, subtle

as an elevated train. The motorcade moved in unison, as if each gas-guzzler were hitched to the one in front of it. The procession snaked down the asphalt slope like a sheet-metal caterpillar and stopped in front of my house.

I got into Emma's Explorer and she pulled away from the curb. We didn't greet each other, we just drove. I told her to take the Zakim Bridge and she ramped onto it.

"Can you answer me a question?" I asked.

"If I can."

"Your Somali terrorism fib was a smokescreen, a way to get into the neighborhood so you could investigate Jeepster's connection to the Gardner heist." The traffic on the Zakim was good, all the lanes were moving. "I understand your ploy, Emma. Deception is part of your job. You were doing your job."

"Dermot, that night in your apartment had nothing to do with—"

"Forget that night," I said. "My question is this: how did you know that Jeepster Hennessey was involved in the Gardner heist?"

She checked the rearview mirror, presumably for the caravan in tow, and drove ahead.

"The connection to Hennessey was Liam McGrew. We suspected that McGrew and his IRA cohorts were involved in the Gardner robbery. Then he showed up in Boston. He hadn't been to Boston in years." She stayed in the center lane and dipped into the O'Neill Tunnel. "Because McGrew is IRA, he's on the FBI terrorist watch list, which means we can bug his phone and trace his computer without a search warrant. The Patriot Act gives us sweeping leeway when it comes to monitoring suspected terrorists. McGrew called Hennessey six times in two days. At that point we got interested in Hennessey. Then Hennessey got killed, and that's when the FBI decided that I would move into the projects. Liam McGrew pointed us to Jeepster Hennessey."

"Thanks for telling me."

I told her to take Exit 20 to Albany Street. We stopped at a red light, and the irregularly spaced line of V-8s compressed like a Slinky on a landing. We stayed on Albany Street a few blocks, turned right on East Berkeley and right again on Harrison Avenue.

"Slow down." I pointed to the alley at the corner of Traveler Street. "There, pull over there."

She no sooner shifted into park when the SUV entourage raced around us and blocked the street. I handed Emma Hague the Mc-Sweeney key.

"Do the honors," I said. "Follow me."

With Emma at my side, I led the Dacron-clad troops down the alley to the rear of the building. I pointed to the backdoor. Emma snapped on a flashlight, unlocked the deadbolt, and stepped inside. I guided her to the freight elevator and opened the horizontal door. Eight of us fit inside, including Lamont Hayes, the only person of the group I trusted.

"Fourth floor," I said. "Room four-o-six, the last door on the left."

They piled off the Otis and moved in formation to the storage room. Emma inserted the McSweeney key. The latch clicked. Two of the team members readied their cameras, one for filming, the other for photos. White flashes lit the doorway like bolts of lightning, an FBI Fourth of July party. I waited in the hallway. Emma came out after a few minutes.

"We boxed the Vermeer, if it really is a Vermeer. The Art Theft Team will transport it to the Gardner." She holstered the flashlight. "We have three curators waiting there, along with a lab crew." She made a face. "And that priest you insisted on."

"Father Mullineaux from Boston College," I said. I didn't say that one of the curators was Mullineaux's man, the man who examined *Old Man in Prayer* and determined it to be the work of a Rembrandt protégé. He was wrong, of course. Remy Menard painted it. Remy fooled them all. "It'll be a big thrill for the padre."

"I'm sure it will," she said. "Now take me to the Rembrandt."

"Drive to Charlestown," I said.

Emma led the team out of the South End and back to Charlestown. Ten minutes later we drove under the Tobin Bridge into the parking lot of Mystic Piers Storage. I handed Emma the McEwan key.

"Sixth floor," I said. "I'll wait out here."

The crew went inside. I got out of Emma's SUV and walked home.

CHAPTER 50

The next morning I found Luigi Lovetti standing on my front steps when I went down to answer the bell, still in my bathrobe. His smile told me the paintings passed muster. He had a crate at his side. I let him in and we went up to my apartment. I carried the crate for him and laid it on the kitchen table. Luigi tapped it with his finger.

"The forged *Self-Portrait, Aged 23*, as we agreed," he said, and then he handed me a thin legal-size envelope. "A check for six million, it was worth every cent of it."

I asked Luigi if he wanted something to eat or drink. He said yes, that sounded good. Inside the breadbox I found a package of Effie's oatcakes, placed a few of them on a plate, and put the plate on the table.

"Milk?" I said.

"Yes, a cold glass of milk." He ate oatcakes and drank milk. "Tell me, Mister Sparhawk, how did you know that our *Self-Portrait, Aged 23* was a forgery?" He patted his mouth with a napkin. "It's been hanging in the Dutch Room for more than twenty years, and in all that time nobody has questioned its veracity."

"I didn't know for sure until just now when you handed me the reproduction and the check," I said. "But I would have been surprised if I was wrong."

"Clearly, you were most sure of yourself," he said. "How did you figure it out? How did you unpuzzle this tortuous matter?"

"It's a long story."

"I'd very much like to hear it," he said. "I fully understand that it's not part of the settlement, but please tell me how you recovered

the lost art. Will you reveal the juicy details, the back-alley dealings, the clandestine meetings?"

Luigi struck me as a good guy.

"I'd be glad to tell you, Luigi, but it will take a while," I said.
"What are you doing for supper on Saturday?"

"This Saturday? I have no plans. Why?"

"I'd like you to be my guest," I said. "Come by at six, and I'll
serve you the best franks and beans you ever ate."

"Franks and beans, it sounds delightful."

"I'll tell you the whole story, all the juicy details. I'll introduce
you to Buck Louis and Harraseeket Kid, my investigative team.
Once they smell the franks grilling, they'll want to join us for supper. Buck and Kid will flesh out the vague with the specific. We
might have to eat downstairs in Buck's apartment. He's in a wheelchair."

"I can hardly wait," he said. "Brown bread, too?"

"Sure, brown bread too, sliced and buttered, warmed in the
oven."

"Fantastic, absolutely fantastic."

I told him I'd see him on Saturday. He stopped in the door. I
asked if everything was okay. He stepped back toward me.

"Not to be presumptive, and please forgive me if I am." He
swallowed. "I was wondering if we might meet occasionally, if we
might, perhaps, convene for coffee or tea intermittently."

I smiled at him.

"Luigi, I think this is the beginning of a beautiful friendship."

"Ah, Humphrey Bogart in *Casablanca*, how fitting. You're Rick
and I'm Louie, absolutely perfect."

"See you Saturday."

CHAPTER 51

I opened my father's cigar box and took out the military-issue .45, the gun he took off a dead second lieutenant at the Battle of Hill 881. I inserted the magazine and pulled back the slide to load a round into the chamber. I tucked the gun in my waistband under a dangling shirttail and headed to the Navy Yard for a meeting.

The man I was meeting agreed to wait for me at Pier 10, a derelict berth of rotting pilings with a small platform area topside. One wrong step and it's into the drink. But the tide was low tonight, and with the jagged rocks jutting below and the snapped-off timbers tickling the water's surface, an impaling seemed more likely than a drowning.

Pier 10 is isolated at the north end of the Navy Yard, far from traffic and pedestrians, with plenty of privacy for a heart-to-heart. George Meeks was standing on the pier when I arrived.

"What's this about?" George lit a corona and blew a smoke ring into the harbor breeze. "Why are we meeting out here?"

"First, the introductions," I said.

"What're you talkin' about, introductions?"

"George Meeks" I pointed at him, "meet The Go Between."

The *E O E E E* from The Go Between gave me George Meeks. Pretty easy once I had the homovocalism key.

"I'm the Oulipo Man, George, your pal from the Oulipo Boys chat room," I said.

"You ain't making sense."

"You dropped out of sight from the chat room. I'm guessing Bill Halloran told you to back off, just like he told Liam McGrew to back off."

"You don't know that. And who's Halloran?" George asked.

"It's over, George. The paintings have been returned to the Gardner Museum where they belong." I pulled out the .45 and aimed it at him. "You played me."

"Are you gonna shoot me?"

"Shut up." I lowered the gun for a moment. "I came here tonight to kneecap you. When I finally figured out your role in this thing, I said to myself, I'm gonna blast both George's kneecaps. A forty-five slug in the knee has to hurt, it's gotta cause serious damage." I squeezed the gun in my hand. "I said to myself, I'll kneecap George and put him a wheelchair for a while, and then he'll know how it feels to be Buck. You remember Buck, the cripple you beat up."

"You can't prove none a that."

"I proved it to myself and that's all I need." The dusk sky darkened, giving me better cover. "The Irish hitters in the parking lot, you hired those clowns. I nearly got killed."

"It wasn't suppose ta go that way."

"You dressed up as the cab driver," I said. "Where'd you get the nifty hat, watching Charlie Chan movies?"

"I don't drive a cab."

"Knock it off, George, I know what happened," I said. "Jeepster's dead because of you."

"Whatda ya mean, 'cause of me? Jeepster's dead 'cause he fucked with the wrong poker player. A guy named Carlo, outta Miami, the guy's in jail 'cause he killed Jeepster. He went away for killing Jeepster. Carlo pleaded out, Dermot. I had nothing to do with any of that." He paused. "I'll admit to the cabdriver thing and the Irish thing, and I'll even grant you The Go Between, but I had nothing to do with getting Jeepster killed. I needed him alive for the paintings. Carlo killed him."

The seagulls and terns stopped cawing from under the Tobin Bridge. The city lights gave outline to the bridges and skyscrapers across the inner harbor. Restless waves slapped the rocks below, slapping them like saliva anticipating a meaty feast. My finger rubbed the trigger. The .45 felt natural in my hand, an appendage of my palm.

"Manny Carlo plunged the knife into Jeepster's back," I said. "But you provided the motive."

"What are you talking about? I don't even know Carlo."

"Jeepster got hooked on gambling," I said. "He bet, bet, bet. Red Sox, Patriots, Celtics, he bet them all—his new addiction. Jeepster lost a fortune on the Bruins in the playoffs."

"Who didn't?"

"Shut your yap, George. I'm talking," I said. "Jeepster heard about a high-stakes poker game. He needed fifty grand to get into it, so he went to his old pal George Meeks and asked for a loan." I poked George in the chest. "Jeepster offered quality collateral."

"I don't know what you're talking about."

"In exchange for fifty thousand, he promised you a piece of the Gardner reward, or more likely, a piece of Halloran's payment if Jeepster gave him the paintings instead. Jeepster had the Gardner loot and you had the cash, a perfect scenario for old-fashioned street bartering. The vig was steep. He agreed to pay you a hundred grand, plus repayment of the loan, a Shylock's profit."

"So what?" George said. "I made him a loan, what's the problem?"

"The problem is you lent him counterfeit money, and he's dead because of it." I raised the gun. "You lent him schlock bills and got him killed. You got my godfather killed."

"Dermot." George extended his hands. "It wasn't supposed to happen that way. I figured the bad money'd get mixed in with the good stuff and nobody'd know the difference."

"You figured wrong, George."

"It was an accident, an honest-to-God-mistake. I wasn't tryna get Jeepster hurt," he said. "Jeepster knew what I was like. He probably figured the money was counterfeit anyway. Yeah, he'd've assumed the worst. He knew the money was phony."

"Keep telling yourself that and someday you'll believe it." I had attended Mass earlier in the day. I received Holy Communion. Blowing two holes in George's kneecaps after attending Mass seemed wrong. I tucked the gun in my belt. "Stay away from me. I don't want to see you again."

"Come on, Dermot. Gimme a break, will ya? You're the only guy I can talk to in Charlestown. Don't shut me out."

"Stay clear of me."

From the Navy Yard I drove to Weston to meet Bill Halloran. I had called to say I was on the way. He answered the door when I arrived.

"It's getting late, Sparhawk," he said, "What's this about?"

"Vermeer's *Concert*."

"Really? Do you have it? My thirty-five million offer still stands." He opened the door wider. "I can get the money together in three days, providing the Vermeer's authentic."

We were standing inside his foyer, the door ajar. I elbowed it shut.

"*The Concert* is back where it belongs, in the Gardner Museum," I said. "The painting will be hanging in the Dutch Room by the end of the week."

"I don't believe you," he said. "I've heard nothing on the news, nothing on the streets. No sir, I don't believe you."

"Give it a few days. The story will hit the news in a few days."

"If that's the case then why are you here?" he said. "Let me guess. You're here to gloat, to rub my face in it."

"I'm here to make you an offer."

"An offer?" He laughed. "*You* making *me* an offer? This I have to see. An offer for what?"

"An offer to buy the forged Vermeer in your cellar," I said. "I'm giving you a chance to recoup the quarter million you paid for it."

"Why?" he said. "It makes no sense. Why buy a known forgery for that much?"

"Personal reasons," I said. I wanted a memento of Jeepster and my father's feat. I wanted to hang the fake in my parlor. "I know how you got conned, Halloran. Believe it or not, the guys who sold you the Vermeer didn't realize it was fake."

"Say that again?"

"The art thieves thought they were selling you the original Vermeer stolen from the Gardner Museum. They were wrong, of course."

"Damn right they were wrong."

"I'm here to make good on their mistake," I said. "I'm here to refund your money."

"That's noble of you, but I don't buy it, no sir. What's the catch?" He walked to a window. "You're up to something, I can tell. There's something you're not telling me."

"There's a lot I'm not telling," I said. "But the things I told you are true."

I joined him at the window. His landscaped acreage gleamed in the glow of floodlights, brighter than Fenway Park at night. With all his money and all his shrubbery and all his art, he was still the embodiment of boredom: humorless, joyless, charmless.

"Okay, I get it," he said. "I got double-crossed and ended up with a forged painting. The thieves probably frayed the edges to make it look like the original. I'm not stupid. I figured that out already." He turned to me. "Wait a minute. You know what happened. Will you tell me? I'll make it worth your while."

"It doesn't matter now. *The Concert*'s been returned to the museum. I'm here for one reason and it's not to gloat," I said. "If you want to sell your Vermeer reproduction, and it *is* a reproduction, I'll buy it."

"I smell something fishy."

"Nothing's fishy, Halloran."

"How much did the Gardner pay you? The reward money, how much was it?" he said. "You must be the man who returned the Vermeer to the museum."

I didn't answer.

"They paid you five million, tops. Yet I offered you thirty-five million." Apparently he didn't like the discrepancy. "On second thought, I don't believe the Vermeer's been returned to the museum. No man leaves thirty million on the table."

"Do you want to sell your reproduction or not?"

"I don't think so. You're up to something, Sparhawk, up to no good. I can sense it. You're trying to rake me over the coals just like those other guys," he said. "I'm not taking the bait this time. I'm keeping the Vermeer."

"The fake Vermeer," I said. "So long, Halloran."

CHAPTER 52

My wheezing Plymouth choked to a halt in Remy Menard's driveway high atop Pope's Hill in Dorchester. The hot weather had passed and along with it the God-awful humidity. I popped open the trunk and removed the plywood crate, walked to the back door, and gave it a rap. The lace curtain inched from the side of the window, just enough for a city glance, and draped back into place. Remy unlatched the door and stared down at the crate.

"Even after twenty years, I recognize it. I built that crate."

He hadn't shaven in days. His handlebar moustache flopped unwaxed, fanning his mouth like whale baleen. I stepped inside and rested the crate on the worn linoleum floor. The place was a mess. Empty beer bottles crowded the countertop, a throng of dead soldiers yet to be buried. Cartons of Chinese take-out overflowed in the trash barrel. Dirty plates with cigarette butts crushed in the grime filled the sink. I didn't see any roaches.

I handed him an envelope.

"A quarter million, the money Jeepster owed you, adjusted for inflation." I slid the crate toward him. "Your reproduction of *Self-Portrait, Aged 23* is inside."

Remy dropped the envelope on the kitchen table and went to the crate. He pried it open with a butter knife and removed the cover.

"My greatest work, my magnus opus," he said. "Where did you find it?"

"The Gardner Museum."

"Excuse me?"

"It's been hanging in the Gardner Museum for the past twenty years."

"Don't poke fun at me, Dermot."

I stood next to him and admired the painting.

"Jeepster swapped your reproduction for Rembrandt's original," I said. "Then he stole the original. Do you understand what I'm saying? Jeepster mounted your forgery in the frame that held the original *Self-Portrait* in the Gardner Museum's Dutch Room then stole the original. Your reproduction has been hanging in the Gardner since the heist. Nobody knew the difference, Remy. Not the public, not the museum, nobody. I tracked down Rembrandt's *Self-Portrait, Aged 23*, the one Jeepster stole, and traded it back to the Gardner for yours."

Remy didn't know whether to believe me. His head did an owl spin, turning to me then back to the painting. If I were standing behind him instead of beside him, he'd have wrenched his neck. He leaned closer to the oil, his nose nearly touching it.

"This isn't mine, it's the original," he said. "I've gone to the Gardner ten or twelve times since the robbery. I went there explicitly to examine *Self-Portrait, Aged 23*. This is the painting I examined on my visits there. I am positive of that. Wait a second, you said—I'm confused."

"You're not confused," I said. "This *is* the painting you examined at the museum. It is also your painting, your reproduction."

"You said that, but it didn't sink in." He twirled his limp moustache. "Are you saying my painting has been hanging in the Gardner Museum for the last twenty years? Yes, that's what you're saying, that's what you said." His eyes blinked. "And everybody thought it was a Rembrandt?"

"That's right, Remy. Everybody thought it was a Rembrandt," I said. "And now you have your treasure back and two hundred fifty thousand to go with it."

"My God, everybody thought it was a Rembrandt—the curators, the going public, everybody." He picked up the painting and held it in front of his eyes. He smelled it. "You have no idea, Dermot, no idea at all."

He laid the oil on the table, closed his eyes, and swept his fingertips across the craquelure terrain, an artist's Braille.

"Thank you."

"You're welcome."

CHAPTER 53

Glooscap sat in the office of his Andrew Square auto-body shop. He was dressed in denim, head to toe, and had plenty of blue bling pinned to his shirt, the silver and turquoise stuff the Navajos make in the Southwest.

With unhurried care he held a lit match to his pipe, puffed on it until the bowl glowed bright, then shook the match cold. Columns of smoke jetted from his large nostrils. A cloud of spent tobacco gathered above his head, a smoke signal that said he was ready to talk.

"You have been busy," he said this in his customary manner, enunciating each syllable, never using a contraction. "You have been very busy."

"It's over now, Glooscap. The whole Jeepster Hennessey ordeal is over." I propped my feet on his desk and rocked back in the chair. "Were you in on the Gardner Museum?"

"The robbery?"

"Yes, the robbery. Were you involved with my father and Jeepster?" I waited, he didn't answer. "You three were Siamese triplets."

"Yes, we were close."

"I ask again: Were you part of it, Glooscap? The first of the two robberies that night, were you in on it?"

He smiled. A series of curved lines carved his face into pairs of embedded parentheses. He grabbed his string tie, tugged it, and with the other hand raised the pipe to his mouth.

"Most intelligent, you learned of the two robberies." He puffed and exhaled a lungful. "No, I was not part of the actual heist."

"Please elaborate," I said. "I think you know more than you're saying."

"Okay, Dermot." He rested the pipe on the desk. "Your father asked me to be the driver the night of the robbery. I declined. After I declined, they offered the job to Angus Og instead. I heard about your trip to Antigonish."

"How did you hear about that?"

"Do not fret, Dermot. Harraseeket Kid told me." He exhaled some residual smoke. "There was a difference between Og and me. Og knew none of the robbery details, he simply drove the van, where I was privy to the whole scheme. Or perhaps I should say most of the scheme. Jeepster withheld a few details from us, from me, anyway. He devised an ingenious plot and pulled it off."

"Why did you decline?"

"Because of Harraseeket Kid, I could not risk jail time. Kid was an infant and I did not want to take the chance." He picked up the pipe and put it down again. "I do not mean to imply that your father thought less of you by engaging in the heist. He loved you dearly, but your father needed action. He needed adrenaline coursing through his Micmac veins. And as you know all too well, when there was no action to be had, he uncapped a liter of whiskey. The scheme of Jeepster Hennessey gave your father the rush he needed, a risk-addict's rush."

"How did Jeepster hear about the robbery, the second robbery? The crime has never been solved. No one ever talked to the authorities or turned state's evidence. The loot's never been recovered." I rocked forward. "The robbery was military in execution. Certainly the thieves guarded against leaks. How did Jeepster find out?"

"His father overheard some things. Jeepster's father worked at the Gardner Museum and he heard murmurings, nothing specific, just bits and pieces. The second team of thieves had an inside man. Mr. Hennessey passed along the information to Jeepster. Jeepster started digging and figured out the rest."

"Why the forgery of Rembrandt's *Old Man in Prayer*? The

original hangs in the MFA, not the Gardner. What did Jeepster want with *Old Man in Prayer*?"

"The Gardner heist went so well they planned to do it again at the Museum of Fine Arts." He turned the ashtray half a rotation. "Then Jeepster went to jail and they never got around to it. I gather that you found the reproduction of *Old Man in Prayer*."

"I sold it to a Jesuit priest at Boston College," I said. "I also found a Rembrandt original."

"You found a Rembrandt original?" He stood. His smile deepened. "*Self-Portrait, Aged 23*, it had to be. I know it was not *The Storm on the Sea of Galilee*. We never intended to steal that one. We had no reproduction for it."

"Correct, *Self-Portrait, Aged 23*."

"For years and years I wondered what happened to that painting. Our plan called for swapping the forgery for the original, but I never heard anything about it in the news. I assumed that Jeepster and Chief did not have time to make the swap. Based on what you said, they made the swap and the swap was never detected."

"That's right," I said.

"Fantastic. What you uncovered is utterly fantastic."

"I found the Vermeer and the Napoleonic finial, too. I turned both of them in," I said. "The FBI and Gardner Museum are scripting their heroic narrative for the press as we speak. It will all come out in a week or so. *The Storm on the Sea of Galilee* is still out there somewhere, Glooscap. Jeepster's team never touched it."

"The second team took it." He tapped the tobacco out of the pipe. "And the reward money? Did you get any reward money?"

"I got the reward money."

"God, I am proud of you."

On the way out of the auto-body shop I talked to Harraseeket Kid, who was replacing an Avalon's rear door. He must have been doing clean work today. His coveralls were unstained. I handed him an envelope.

"What's this?"

"A quarter million," I said, "for your help."

"I didn't do anything." He opened the envelope. "You don't even charge me rent."

"You keep the house shipshape, you got Sled dog for Buck," I said. "Don't worry Kid, I got plenty."

"A man can always use a packet of money." He folded the envelope and stuffed it in his coveralls pocket. "Come here, I want to show you something. I have this car, a silver Cadillac DTS with eight thousand miles. It's a repo. I got it for a steal, and I got it legit."

We went out to the lot and Kid pointed it out.

"She's like a beauty, Kid."

"Here's the deal, Dermot. I take the envelope, you take the Caddy."

"Just take the money."

"It has to be that way." He dangled the keys in the air. "It's time to dump the Plymouth. Leave it here and I'll scrap it. And just to make you feel better, I'll keep the pennies I get for it. Your new car, take the keys."

Dump the Plymouth? I'll have to sell my shares in Bondo.

"Thanks," I said. "I think you're right, it's time for a change."

I got in my new car and drove to Charlestown.

CHAPTER 54

I stood in Hayes Square in front of Saint Jude Thaddeus church, the patron saint of hopeless cases and of things despaired. I said a prayer of gratitude for a day without a drink. I thanked God for lifting the whiskey obsession and for putting positive people in my life. Although I'm a slow learner, I'm starting to understand this dreadful disease. My porous brain has absorbed just enough knowledge to keep me sober today. I now know that the problem isn't the barroom, but the patron: me. It isn't the house of pain, but the souse of pain: me. Whiskey in a jar is harmless if it stays in the jar. Sobriety rests squarely on me today, yet I don't have to do it alone. I can't do it alone.

Night had fallen over the brick city. TV-blue tinted the tenement windows, all thrown open to ventilate the stifling heat. A wino walked out of the package store, flat bag in hand. Junkies prowled the streets. They skulked past the police station and vanished into the maze of the projects, a drug addict's lair. They'd hunker down in flash houses for amphetamine boosters to keep them awake for the hard stuff later on.

Night calls for crack and heroin would soon begin, as predictable as the dawn caws of Atlantic seagulls. Rooftop exchanges and street-corner deals, it's a nightly custom in this subsidized quarter. I used to get discouraged about it. Today I know I'm powerless over it. But being powerless does not absolve me from responsibility.

Amigo Joao walked up to me. He walks up and down Bunker Hill Street to stay in shape. Without stopping, he said, "Bad out there, Boss, bad, bad, bad."

"I know, Amigo."

"See you tomorrow. Tomorrow's a new day. Tomorrow's good."

My slate was nearly clean. I'd paid Buck Louis a quarter million dollars, paid him in cash, so as not to foul up his benefits. He told me he'd get a safety deposit box and save the money for a rainy day. Remy Menard, Harraseeket Kid, Buck Louis, my debts were almost met. One more payment and I'd be even. I was two hundred and fifty grand away from ground zero.

I got into my silver Cadillac. With the gas tank full, passport in the glove box, envelope in my pocket, I started the engine and braced for a twelve-hour drive to Antigonish, Nova Scotia. I owed Angus Og money. I could have mailed him a check, but if I mailed him a check, I wouldn't get to see Bonnie Og.

I hope she likes my new car.